SIMON PULSE

New York | London | Toronto | Sydney

This book is a work of fiction. Any references to historical events, real people, or real locales are used fictitiously. Other names, characters, places, and incidents are the product of the author's imagination, and any resemblance to actual events or locales or persons, living or dead, is entirely coincidental.

Produced by Alloy Entertainment
151 West 26th Street, New York, NY 10001

SIMON PULSE
An imprint of Simon & Schuster Children's Publishing Division
1230 Avenue of the Americas, New York, NY 10020

Designed by Amy Trombat
The text of this book was set in Scala.
Manufactured in the United States of America
First Simon Pulse hardcover edition June 2006
First Simon Pulse paperback edition May 2007
2 4 6 8 10 9 7 5 3 1
The Library of Congress has cataloged the hardcover edition as follows:
Serros, Michele M.
Honey blonde chica : a novel / Michele Serros.
p. cm.
Summary: Evie Gomez, while trying to form her own identity, must decide if she wants to be a fun-loving, high-heeled, blonde-streaked Sangro, or a laid-back surfer chick Flojo, which are two very different worlds.
ISBN-13: 978-1-4169-1591-1 (hc)
ISBN-10: 1-4169-1591-5 (hc)
[1. Gomez, Evie (Fictitious character)—Fiction. 2. Friendship—Fiction.
3. Mexican Americans—Fiction.]
[Fic]—22. 2005933889
ISBN-13: 978-1-4169-1592-8 (pbk)
ISBN-10: 1-4169-1592-3 (pbk)

To those who live sixty miles north

Acknowledgments

A big, special thanks to the following people for all your unconditional support: Renay Garcia (Crafty Chestnut); Beagan Wilcox (Brown Bellisma); Bunny (Big Sis Brunette) Peter Brooks (Legally Blonde); Naygrita (Naturally Negra); Luis Guereca (Sugarbeat Black); Amilcar Serrano (Guerrero Sunset); my agent Lydia Wills (Savvy Sistah Blonde); for Spanish help and friendship, cuzin Lacy (Bako Brown) and Ana Tolentino (Central Cali Carmel); for letting me write in your wonderful home upstate, Laura Simon (La Loca Rubia); and especially to my patient, patient editor, Lynn Weingarten, the OG Honey Blonde!

1

Evie Gomez woke up on Saturday morning with two things on her mind. The first was that her best friend, Raquel Diaz, was definitely no longer just that, a best friend. Raquel had proven herself to be, as of 10:32 A.M. that late September morning, a 100 percent *pinche beyachee*. And why? Because after two weeks of no phone, no friends, basically no life, Evie wasn't under her mother's house arrest anymore for coming home a piddly-ass twenty (okay, maybe it *was* forty) minutes past her curfew. Her ankle bracelet had been officially clipped off, but did her girl Raquel bother to call so they could celebrate Evie's first night of freedom? *No*. Raquel hadn't even had the decency to return any of Evie's phone calls, text messages, or the desperate IMs Evie had sent to SexyMexy08. Raquel was no Sexy Mexy, Evie decided, but she was *definitely* a bitch.

The second thing Evie realized was how light her head felt. She ran her hand from the back of her neck and, yup, her long, dark brown hair was much shorter. All of it. She pushed up from her pillows and got a look at herself in her closet mirrors—her hair was now short, chopped in haphazard fashion with streaks of uneven blue. Cancún Blue No. 32 to be exact. But it should have been called *Abuelita Azulita* because it had come out the same exact blue tint you see on, well, *abuelitas*.

What had she done? She yanked down at the sides but they barely reached her shoulders. Who the hell cuts their own hair? Is this what happened to prisoners in solitary confinement? After being isolated from their peers for too long, did they eventually go mad and commit self-inflicted acts of hair assault with Ginghar craft scissors too? Evie looked hideous and she had no one to blame but . . . yes, Raquel. It was her fault that Evie had gotten grounded in the first place. Raquel had insisted they go to Tracy Tankerson's party two weeks ago. It was the first party on the first Friday of the new school year and Raquel promised she'd have Evie home by her curfew. But, as Evie should have known, by the time it was time to leave, Raquel was just getting her drink on. There was no way she was gonna get Evie home by her curfew, and she didn't.

Evie glowered at the sight of her reflection. Why, why hadn't Raquel just called her back last night? As a best friend, she *owed* it to her. When nine o'clock rolled around, it had become painfully obvious to Evie that she was going to spend another long night at home alone. And after clicking from one reality makeover show to the next, she realized it was she, not another midwestern housewife, who needed a change. She wanted something that demanded attention, respect. She wanted . . . hair the color of the Cancún ocean! And that's how *The Reinvention of Evie Gomez, Mex-treme Makeover, Friday Night Home Edition* came to be.

But as of now, Saturday morning, it was sadly evident that she had truly lost her senses the night before. Her rookie dye job screamed beauty-school flunk-out. The bleach she'd used to strip her brown wasn't dispersed as evenly as it should have been and now her head looked like a patchwork of beige, white, and blue, the national colors of . . . whatever country's flag was beige, white, and blue. She looked like crap.

"What do you think, Meho?" She toed her male tabby, nestled at the foot of her bed. "Punk rock, or goth-metal dork?" But Meho couldn't care less about her state of blue disrepair. He lifted up his hind leg and started to lick behind it.

"Cla-*see*," Evie smirked as she gave him a slight tap with the rest of her foot.

She heard Lindsay, the Gomez's housekeeper, turn up the volume of *El Mercadito* on the kitchen radio downstairs. Other than that, the house was quiet. She was sure her father, Ruben Gomez, had left hours ago for one of his several *panaderías* and her mother, Vicki, was probably in the pool doing her obligatory fifty laps.

Evie pulled her Dean Miller sheets up to her chin and looked blankly up at the ceiling. From her sister, Sabrina, who took eighteen credits a semester while maintaining presidency of the most prestigious Latina sorority at Stanford University to big ol' dopey Molesto (given name: Ernesto)—the Gomez's black Labrador, who demanded his pre-poop walk around the perimeter of the block every morning at 6 A.M.—the Gomezes were a very focused, ambitious family. They accentuated the *Go* in *Gomez*, all of them, that is except for Evie, who felt more of a personal connection to the lagging *z* as in Gomez*zzzzzzz*. . . . She yawned, lifted her Roxy T, and scratched her belly. It was now 10:45 A.M. Yeah, she could sleep a little bit more and deal with *las dilemas* later.

Just then the buddy alert on her computer dinged, signaling to Evie that one of her online buddies was available to chat. Raquel? . . . *Finally.*

Evie pushed off her blankets and went over to her desk. But it wasn't Raquel. It was Shaggy, who had already instant-messaged her.

ShaggyMA (10:46 AM): Hey, U up?
RioChica (10:46 AM): Yup. U just wake up, too?
ShaggyMA (10:47 AM): No. Just got in from surfing. Did Dawn Patrol this morning. Crazy. Surfer magazine was there and took photos of us.

Evie felt jealous. Did everyone have a more exciting life than she did? During her period of home internment, she had met Shaggy via a chat room for MASA. *No*, not *masa*, as in dough, but MASA as in the Mexican-American Surfing Association. Evie hadn't even known such a thing existed, but ever since she'd caught *Blue Crush* on cable with Raquel over the summer, she had become a mad active surfer. On the Internet, that is. Raquel wasn't so hot on independent study after seeing the film, so Evie researched all things surf on her own. How could she live in California and not surf? All those years as a kid at the beach and not once ride a wave? As a fourth-generation Cali girl she at least *looked* the part, from her sixty-dollar Hollister Ts to her Roxy hibiscus-print board shorts. Evie had even gone so far as to buy a surfboard, a white nine-foot, five-fin custom long board, especially shaped for her by the one and only Max of Santa Barbara. But truth was, Evie had yet to even get the pricey stick wet and, to be dreadfully direct, she could barely even manage a boogie board in waist-high white water. *Qué* scandalous, no?

RioChica (10:50 AM): What do you think of the color blue?
ShaggyMA (10:50 AM): One of my sticks is blue.
RioChica (10:51 AM): Cool enough.
ShaggyMA (10:51 AM): Hey, gotta go.
RioChica (10:51 AM): Sure, TTYL!

Sigh. Evie was alone, and bored, again.

Suddenly the latest Moz (Given name: Steven Patrick *Morrissey*) download, blared from her cell phone. Evie got up from her desk and grabbed the phone off her nightstand. She saw Raquel's face on the screen, her long hair pulled over in front of her shoulders and her chin drawn down. *Ugh.* Evie reluctantly flipped open her phone.

"Hello?"

"Heeey," drawled Raquel's gravelly voice. Apparently Raquel had gone out the night before. Without Evie. WTF?

"Oh, hey," Evie said trying to sound just as casual.

"So . . . ," Raquel started. Evie could sense a smile on the other end. "You got your phone back."

"Uh, yeah," Evie said. "I actually got it back yesterday, as of five P.M."

"Oh, yeah." Raquel paused. "That's right."

"So what happened?" Evie asked. "You said we were gonna do something, go out. I left you like a gazillion messages."

"Yeah." Raquel let out a moose-sized yawn. "Sorry about that. I completely spaced. My parents went out and then Jose came over with a six-pack. We ended up kicking it, watching *Fuel* all night. *Boring.*" The moose yawned again.

"Oh." Evie tried to sound calm, but she was burning up inside. "That's cool. Did Alex or Mondo go out?"

"Nah," Raquel said. "Nobody did nothing."

Evie relaxed. At least she hadn't missed anything, but that

didn't really surprise her. The five Flojos—herself, Alex, Mondo, Raquel, and her boy, Jose—shared one thing in common, and that one thing was the absolute, all-consuming, unending desire to . . . do absolutely nothing. Was it the cliché teenage rebellion against their workaholic fathers? Too many spins (and lyric interpretations) of Cypress Hill on Mondo's Technics turntable? Wherever they were, be it poolside or oceanside, and whatever you called it, trifling or chilling, the Flojos did *nada* together. Never mind Generation Y. The Flojos were in a generation of their own—Generation YBother?

Coincidentally, *flojo* (correct Spanish pronunciation: *flow-ho*) means "lazy" in English, but it's also what you call flip-flops (correct South Cali pronunciation: *flow-joe*) and as everybody knows, flip-flops are a pretty lazy excuse for a shoe. But the Flojos were hard-core when it came to their flip-flops and wore them 24/7/365. From high-end Havaianas ($118) to low-end plastic bin specials from Savon *(true* flojos, Alex claimed), nothing came between Flojos and their flojos.

But it wasn't just attitude or a common footwear philosophy that had brought the Flojos together. Evie and Raquel had been friends since growing up in Rio Estates and last year when they were freshmen, Raquel hooked up with Jose. He was a tall, lanky sophomore with the Mars Volta 'fro and black titanium chin labret piercing that gave him a devious look. Raquel fell for it hard. Once they started dating, his sidekicks,

Mondo (he who had a "delivery job") and Alex (he who actually did some surfing), came automatically included in the package. Of course, it was pure prestige points for Evie and Raquel to hang with upperclassmen. Besides, few students at Villanueva Preparatory High School were like them—rich kids whose family crests—that is, if they had crests—contained the letters *x*, *y*, or *z* (read: *Latino*).

Evie's family had a crest, sorta. If you counted the small, peach-tinted seashell logo for her father's successful business, Conchita's Bread. Years ago her father started Conchita's and thanks to his hard work (along with Evie's great-grandma Conchita's secret *pan dulce* recipes), the Gomezes had arrived where they were now: a big ol' Spanish-style house with a swimming pool in the back and her father's Escalade in the front. Not quite ransom-worthy rich, but the Gomezes, like a lot of the families in Rio Estates, were pretty well off.

"So," Evie continued. She took a deep breath. "I chopped off my hair."

"What?" Raquel said.

"My hair," Evie repeated. "It's gone."

"What do you mean?"

"I hacked it off. And . . ." Evie paused for dramatic flair. "I dyed it blue, sorta." Evie felt proud and a bit smug. She liked the idea that she'd done something so radical, on her own, and without consulting Raquel. It was so un-Evie of her.

"Yeah." Raquel yawned. "I dyed my hair blue one time."

"Really?" It was *so Raquel* of Raquel to try to outdo Evie. And Evie wasn't sure she was buying it. "When?"

"One time when I was up in the Bay Area, like two summers ago. It totally clashed with my complexion. Brownies can't be sporting blue. I changed it back the next day."

"You never told me that," Evie said, still suspicious.

"'Cause it was really no big deal."

Evie felt herself getting annoyed. "So," she said, changing the subject. "What's the plan for tonight?"

"Um." Raquel yawned again. "Jose heard about some party out near Bard. You in?"

"Definitely," Evie said. Actually, she had hoped they would drive down to L.A., do something covert, crazy. Rio Estates was just sixty miles north of Los, but it was still suburbia and, of course, painfully uneventful. Even though she was a Flojo, Evie had always felt the slight tug of wanting something more, wanting to do something outside of the 805.

But Raquel did say that the night's party was "out near Bard," so that could mean anything.

"As long as I'm home by twelve thirty," Evie reminded Raquel. "I mean, not even twelve thirty-two in the driveway. My mom will freak if I'm late again."

"Yeah, and we don't wanna freak out ol' Vicki," Raquel said in a tone meant to show she was so *over* mothers and curfews. "She must have crapped bricks when she saw your hair, huh?"

"Not really," Evie lied. "Like you said, it's really no big deal."

But Evie was starting to worry. What *would* her mother say about her hair? Vicki Gomez was known for possessing the legendary Gomez fury, unleashed when something didn't go her way.

Just then, someone knocked on Evie's bedroom door. She sank into her bed and quickly pulled the sheet over her head. Well, at least she wouldn't have to wait any longer—she was about to find out how her mother felt about having a Smurf for a daughter.

"Evelina?"

Whew. It was only Lindsay. "Are you awake?" she asked from the hallway.

"*Sí, sí,* Lindsay," Evie called out, making sure to keep her head covered. "Come in." She told Raquel she had to hang up.

"Oh, hey," Raquel started. "One last thing."

"Yeah?" Evie asked.

"Did you dye your pubes, too? 'Cause if you'd done your shrub, now, that woulda been *real* crazy ass."

"*Good-bye,* Raquel." Evie rolled her eyes and flipped her cell phone shut before tossing it onto the floor. Yup. No doubt about it. Raquel was definitely a bitch.

❋ ❋ ❋

"Oh," Lindsay said as she came into Evie's room and saw her in bed. "You're still sleeping."

"No, I'm awake," Evie answered, peeking out from under the covers. "I'm just laying here."

Lindsay looked around Evie's room and sighed. "*Ay*, Evelina. This is not good. Let me clean in here today. It would make your mother so happy."

"Lindsay, I really don't *care* what makes my mother happy. So," Evie changed the subject. "Did you buy anything off of *El Mercadito*?"

"*¡Ay, no!*" Lindsay took a seat at the edge of Evie's bed. "There was a foot, *¿cómo se llama*?" Her wrinkled hands made a rubbing motion across her Aerosole slip-ons. "A massager? But the lady wanted too much for it. No way." She turned around and looked above Evie's bed. "Why is all that scribble around that boy?"

Lindsay was referring to Paul Rodriguez, Jr. Evie had Sharpied elaborate red hearts on a poster of him skateboarding. So, he didn't surf, as far as she knew, but he did skateboard, which was close enough, and he did have a *z* in his name. Oh, come on, who was she kidding? P. Rod was *FAF*. She crushed him hard.

"Oh, that's—," Evie started to explain as she turned to look up at the poster. But when she did, her sheet slipped down, exposing her head.

"*¡Ay!*" Lindsay stood up. "Evelina, what did you do? Your hair!" She nervously fondled her gold chain necklace as though it was a rosary, protecting her from all decisions evil.

"Oh, I cut it." Evie nervously tugged at the sides, but it was no use. They remained short and stringy.

"Yes, I see that." Lindsay's face remained shocked. "But the colors. It's . . . does your mother know?"

"Well." Evie tousled her hair nervously. "She's always going on about money. So she should be happy that I saved her a hundred bucks by doing my own hair."

Lindsay's eyes widened. "You pay a *hundred dollars* to have your hair done?"

Evie immediately felt embarrassed and tried to explain. "It's not just for a cut. I mean, I get it washed, and they give it a blow-dry and style. Plus I sometimes get a one-on-one consultation, a lot of times with Viggo—he's the salon owner." But the more she said, the more Evie knew how shamelessly VH1 Diva it all sounded.

"Ay, Dios." Lindsay shook her head. "I just can't imagine what your mother will think."

"Think about what?" Vicki Gomez asked as she entered Evie's bedroom. Just out of the pool, Evie's mother looked effortlessly stylish in her magenta one-piece with a plush beige towel wrapped around her wet hair. There was no time to duck and cover.

"Oh, my God!" Evie's mother clasped her hand over her mouth. "Evie! What the hell did you do to your hair? You've got to be out of your mind! Did you forget that school photos are next week? Do you expect your father and me to fork over two hundred dollars to document *this*?" She towered over Evie and picked over her hair, like a grade-school nurse searching for head lice.

Evie looked shamefully over at Lindsay. *Yes, Lindsay, we also drop a few hundred for some measly school photos. Oh, but that does include wallet size!*

"What the *hell* were you thinking?" Evie's mother was furious. "I have a good mind to ground you for a month for this stunt!"

"What?" Evie pulled away from her mother. "Why? Just because *I* wanted to do something different to *my* hair?"

"No, because you don't think. That's the problem, Evie. You don't think about how your actions affect other people." She looked at Evie's bed and pulled the pillow out from under her. "Great. You stained the pillow, too. Did you even think to rinse out your hair or put down a towel?" Vicki Gomez looked around. "Oh God . . . look at this."

Evie looked beside her bed. Sure enough, a trail of small blue blotches stretched across the cream-colored carpet from her bathroom to her pillow. She hadn't noticed them before. There was even dye on the precious Dean Miller plastic-grass bed skirt she had begged her mother to buy her for her last birthday.

"Don't worry, Señora Vicki," Lindsay said, wiping the spots on the sheet as if they would magically go away. "I can get the stains out."

"Your father is going to be pissed!" Evie's mother continued to rant. "Do *not* make any plans this evening until he gets home and we can discuss this."

"You mean *tonight*?" Evie was horrified.

"Yes, *tonight*." Her mother knelt down and rubbed the stained carpet with her fingers.

"But Dad usually stays late on Saturdays and I told you I was going out with—"

"You'll just have to wait." Vicki Gomez stood up and handed Lindsay the pillow. After telling her in Spanish to work on it immediately, she stalked out of Evie's room. Lindsay followed silently.

No. There was *no way* that Evie planned to endure another night in the maximum security Gomez Penitentiary. She leaned over her bed, grabbed her cell, and speed-dialed her father.

He'll listen, she thought. Her father was a reasonable man, definitely much more reasonable than her mother. Evie knew she wouldn't survive another night of lockdown. *I'll go crazy, and who knows what I'll do?* she thought. *Maybe I really will dye my pubes blue.*

2

Within seconds, Evie was on the phone with her father. She pointed out that there were house rules for her recreational interests—how much time she could spend at Sea Street, the number of hours she was allowed to spend watching MTV2, how much alcohol she was allowed to drink (absolutely none!)—but no mention of cutting her hair and dyeing it blue. No rule, no violation, so no punishment, right? Surprisingly, her father agreed.

"*Ay*, Vicki." Evie handed her mother the phone, but she could hear her father talking to her mother through the receiver. "The color's not permanent and the hair will grow back. What teenager doesn't experiment with change? Remember when we were dating and you wanted to look like Teena Marie?"

And so Evie was sprung. She would have clicked her heels

with joy as she waited in the front driveway for Mondo to go to the party. If only she'd known how she'd finally slipped out of Warden Vicki's tightfisted control and was soon to be far, far away from the suffocating security gates of Rio Estates.

But eight turned to eight thirty, and eight thirty turned into nine. Evie grew impatient and then angry as she paced back and forth across the circular driveway. Where the hell was that Mondo? Finally, at nine thirty, his black Mercury Marauder slowly eased up the Gomez's driveway. Evie was ready to pop a fuse.

"What's the deal?" she snapped as she walked toward his car. "I've got a curfew, remember?"

"Oh, you know Mondo," Jose started to explain as he got out of the front seat and took over the back with Raquel and Alex. "He ain't called FedMex for nothing."

"That's right." Mondo smiled unapologetically into the rearview mirror. "When you absolutely, positively gotta be there on time, don't be calling me. Besides, beggars can't be—" He looked at Evie as she got into the front seat. "Whoa, what did you do to your hair?"

Jose actually snorted. "Hey, yeah. Blue's Clues!"

"More like Blue's Clueless." Mondo laughed. "Why'd you mangle your mane? It looked good before."

"You guys, shut up already," Raquel said from the backseat. Her eyes widened in bewilderment at the first sight of Evie's hair. "You can't help it if you screwed up your hair." She leaned over and stroked Evie's bangs. "Don't listen to them. We'll take you to Viggo and he'll fix you up."

"Man, Evie," Mondo said as he stroked his own long hair that went well past his shoulders. "You ain't never gonna get a hold of my hair." He motioned to her safety belt. "Hey, click it or ticket."

"Oh, like you are *so* concerned about breaking the law," Evie said as she fastened her seat belt and crossed her arms.

These were the so-called friends she was just dying to be with? She looked back at Alex and glared. "Don't even say anything," she warned him.

"Evie." Alex sighed. "I really don't care *what* you do with your hair."

* * *

When they pulled up to Bard Beach, Mondo killed the Marauder's ignition and announced, "Okay, just 'cause I drove does *not* make me the designated driver. Fulby should already be here and you guys can get a lift back from him if you need to."

"Dude, we can't all go with Fulby," Alex complained from the backseat. "He's got a truck."

"Yeah, a truck with a nice, wide flatbed." Mondo reached under his feet and lifted the floor mat to retrieve a rolled-up baggie.

The party was at Pacifica Abalone Farm, out at Bard Beach, one of the local beaches just west of Rio Estates. While Rio Estates was a planned residential community named to acknowledge the one and only river that ran through the county, Bard Beach was located near the river's mouth and was just as wild and unpredictable as the river itself. It was a part of town known for its hard living, where dime bags and Hawaiian Tropic were a way of life. This was perfect for Evie. She felt quite the *escandalosa* spending her first night out at Bard.

"Okay, okay, already." Evie was getting more impatient. "I'll take the friggin' bus back home if I have to." She pulled her corduroy jacket out from underneath herself. "Let's just go, already."

"Whoa, slow down, Blue's Clues," Mondo said. "There's no rush. We got our own party supplies here." He dangled the baggie in front of her. "And lemme tell you, this *mota* is *mean*."

"Yeah, just kick back, Evie." Raquel leaned into Jose and draped her arm over his shoulders. "We got all night to party."

"No." Evie opened the car door. "I *don't* have all night, and you know I don't smoke that shit. Forget it. I'll just meet up with you guys later."

"You're gonna go by yourself?" Raquel's question sounded more like a challenge than an expression of concern.

"Yeah," Evie said. "What's the problem?"

The problem was that the last thing Evie wanted to do was

enter some Bard Beach party by herself, scrappy blue hair and all. But of course, she wasn't going to admit it.

"No." Alex reluctantly sat up in the backseat. "You can't be walking around alone, especially out here. You've got Rio Estates written all over you. I'll go with you."

"I don't look all R.E.," Evie snapped defensively. She resented that Alex, who was also from Rio Estates, would say such a thing. Since when was he so "down"?

"You know what?" Raquel suddenly announced. "I'll go too. I gotta take a piss."

"What?" Jose looked at her. "But *you* were the one nagging for the new bud."

"Well," Raquel said matter-of-factly, "when you gotta go, you gotta go."

* * *

Evie followed Raquel and Alex down the sandy path toward the party. It was a typical fall evening in Southern California. The Santa Ana winds were kicking in, but the residue of summer was still in the air. Evie suddenly felt less irritated and more excited. *Yes,* she thought. *Tonight, the switch is ON!*

"I think everyone's at the other end of the farm, past these tanks," Alex guessed. "I can hear the band."

Evie stooped over one of the low concrete tanks. "What's in these things?" In the moonlight, she could just barely make out what seemed to be thousands of brown, rough-looking, quarter-sized organisms clinging to the tank's walls.

"Abalone spawn!" Alex deepened his voice. "Very dangerous stuff."

Raquel put her hand into the tank. "Man, this water's cold—oh my God!" Suddenly her whole arm was pulled into the bubbling seawater. Her expression changed from curiosity to sheer terror. "Oh my God! Evie, my hand!"

"Raquel!" Evie shrieked. "Alex! Oh my God! Help her!" She ran up behind Raquel to pull her arm out.

But Raquel just started laughing and then calmly pulled her hand out. Both she and Alex busted up.

"Man, you're such a sucker!" Raquel laughed harder and slapped her wet fingers on Evie's shoulder. "That was a good one!"

"You guys are such jerks." Evie tried to wipe her shoulder.

"It's just baby abalone," Alex said. "Look." He stooped over and picked something off the sand. It was a shell—small, but iridescent and perfectly intact. "Cool, right?"

Evie took the shell in her hand and nodded. "Yeah, it's pretty."

"Let me polish it up for you," Alex offered. "It'll look nice on a cord or something, I promise."

"You don't have to do that," Evie said.

"No, I don't mind. Think of it as a peace offering. Plus it would look good on you." He took the shell back from Evie.

"Yeah," Alex went on. "These tanks are like a little nursery for the abalone. Check it out—it takes like five years just to get one abalone full size."

"Five years?" Raquel said, looking over the tanks. "Damn, they must crank some bank here! If we got Mondo to cultivate this instead, we'd all be kickin' it, pimp style."

* * *

Alex was overreacting about Evie and Raquel needing an escort to the party, but that was Alex, always the overprotective gentleman. He wasn't as fine or tall as Jose, and he wasn't as funny as Mondo, but of all the Flojos, Evie guessed she needed someone like Alex around the most.

The crowd was sketchy but far from threatening. The Bard Boys and their crew were more AA than A-list, really just a bunch of tanned homeboys who liked to party. All had done their pre-requisite time in either County or rehab, or had spent endless days hustling on the beach. People might picture a California beach party as a bunch of fit, golden-tanned teenagers gathered around a bonfire, but no such postcard existed from Bard.

The three of them filled up at the nearest keg and Evie quickly took a gulp from her plastic cup. She didn't like beer, and the keg kind was the worst. Still, she felt she had some catching up to do.

"Hey, Evie."

She looked up. "Mikey?" At first Evie didn't recognize

Mikey Regalado. Evie hadn't seen him since they were both in grade school.

"Yeah, Mike." He pumped the keg and directed the spout into a waiting cup. "How are you doing?" He looked Evie over. "Check out your crazy-ass hair and shit."

"Oh, yeah." She felt slightly embarrassed. "I sorta messed it up."

Mikey's own head was now shaved. *Was he part of the Bard Boys?* Evie wondered.

"Nah, it looks good," he told Evie. "You've always been so crazy."

"Really?" She was sort of surprised by his comment. She didn't exactly feel exciting enough to ever be considered "crazy."

"Well, look at *your* hair!" She smiled as she took a reluctant sip from her cup. "Or should I say, lack of. Hey, remember—"

"E-*vie,*" Raquel interrupted. "I still gotta pee." She grabbed Evie's arm. "Come on, let's go find the little girls' room."

"Well, looks like I gotta go." Evie shifted her eyes toward Raquel to show Mikey her annoyance. "See you later, right?"

"Why not?" Mikey lifted his chin up toward her as he continued to pump the keg.

* * *

As Alex went to watch the band, Evie and Raquel left to look for an outhouse.

"With all the fine boys here," Raquel scanned the crowd, "I don't know why you have to flirt with some gang member."

"Gang member?" Evie raised her eyebrows. "Mikey? Not even. And, I was *not* flirting."

"Whatever."

Moments later, Raquel finally found the Porta Potti. She rattled the white plastic door. "Dude!" she called out. "Come on, already! You got a line out here!"

After a few moments the door unlocked and opened. When Evie looked up, she couldn't believe who stepped out: Alejandra, as in *de los Santos.*

While the Flojos were one of many "social groups" at Villanueva, there was actually another group that at least *seemed* similar to the Flojos. That group was the Sangros. The Sangros (short for *sangrona,* Spanish for full-blown bitch) were four girls from Mexico City. They were *born* in *Distrito Federal,* meaning they were *Mexican* Mexican, unlike the Flojos, who were born in California and were Mexican-American. While the Flojos were known for their flip-flops, the Sangros were known for their stripes, as in their perfectly calculated highlights—*blonde* highlights. Not blended or woven, but rather straight stripes the width of a straw that made for a severe contrast to their dark layered hair. Until Evie's newest look, Evie and Raquel had always thought the Sangros had the tackiest hair imaginable.

Alejandra de los Santos and her *ah*-migas, Fabiol*a*, Natali*a*, and Xiomara, were resident students at Villanueva. It took some hearty bank to be a resident student at Villanueva, but the Sangros had fathers who pulled powerful punches down in the distrito, so in addition to their green cards, the Sangros also flashed gold. Between their *papás'* piggy banks and the Flojos's ATM cards, it was the typical struggle between the haves and have *más*.

Even in the doorway of an outhouse (and even with those horrid stripes), Evie thought that Alejandra looked glamorous, a lighter shade of Beyoncé, ready to give a VMA acceptance speech. She sported the typical femmy Sangro look: knee-high leather boots, a low-cut frilly camisole, and, of course, *the hair*. In her Sanuk flojos and a tank top that she didn't quite fill out, Evie suddenly felt, *¿cómo se dice? ¿Sencilla? ¿Mierda?* Okay, bland.

"What are *you* doing here?" Raquel was already up in her face. "Shouldn't you be home watching *Sábado Gigante* or something?"

"What am *I* doing here?" Alejandra carefully stepped down from the outhouse. "Raquel, my second cousin Gabriel owns this farm. He *is* Pacifica Abalone. Shouldn't you be reading *Let's Go Mexico* and actually *go*?" She took her last high-heeled step onto the sand. "I've been coming to his parties for years." She ran her white-tipped nails through her blonde-striped hair. "I've never seen *you* here before."

Suddenly Evie felt nervous. Truth was, none of the Flojos were officially invited to the Bard party. Jose had snagged the info from a friend which, like so many of the evites he'd lifted for *pachangas*, led the Flojos to Bard Beach.

"Well, I gotta take a shit." Raquel gave Evie her beer to hold and pushed by Alejandra. "*Excuse* me."

She stepped up to the outhouse and shut the door behind her. Evie was now stuck alone with Alejandra. This was a first. Usually it was Raquel sister-necking a Sangro while Evie stood in awe.

"What did you do to your hair?" Alejandra asked. Her almond-shaped eyes were topped with a glittery green eye shadow. She looked straight at Evie.

"Nothing really." Evie smoothed down the front of her bangs. "It's no big deal."

"I guess not." Alejandra snapped her gum before spitting it into a piece of paper she got out from her pocket. "So, how's the doughnut shop?"

"Excuse me?" Evie tried to sound as fearless as Alejandra seemed.

"Doesn't your dad sell doughnuts or something?" Alejandra pulled out a pack of cigarettes from her suede bag.

"No, my dad *owns* a company." Evie knew that Alejandra was pretending to be naïve about her father's bakeries. Everyone in the whole county knew of Conchita's Bread. "His chain, all *four* stores, sells *pan dulce*, not doughnuts."

"*Pan dulce*?" Alejandra smirked as she lit her cigarette. "You gotta be kidding."

"No," Evie said. "Why would I be?"

"Well, I wouldn't know anything about fast food." Alejandra took her first pull off her cigarette. "My family's more scholarly, I guess. My father's the VP at U.N.A.M. in Mexico." She smiled smugly. "La Universidad Nacional—"

"I know what U.N.A.M. means." Evie's pride abruptly cut her off.

"O-*kay*." Alejandra pursed her lips. "So, as I was *saying*, I'm going to be doing an internship at Cal State Channel Islands this semester."

"Good for you, Alejandra," Evie answered, looking up at the outhouse. What was taking Raquel so long?

"Yeah." Alejandra blew smoke upward from the side of her mouth. "They're getting a new chancellor soon, Dr. Frank de LaFuente."

"*Frank* de LaFuente?" Evie asked.

"*Claro*. I might be working with him directly. Then I'm gonna apply for an internship at Yale next summer and—"

But Evie wasn't listening anymore. When she heard the name Frank de LaFuente, she felt her stomach drop *hard*. Frank de LaFuente was Dee Dee's father. Dee Dee had been Evie and Raquel's best friend when they were young girls growing up in Rio Estates. Raquel was Evie's official best friend now, but Dee Dee was actually the closest friend Evie ever had. Evie had practically lived at the de LaFuentes'. Evie hated to admit it, but when they were younger, she had always wished Dee Dee's mother were her own. Margaret de LaFuente didn't put on airs like her mom, and Margaret was always home, always around to talk, not like Evie's mother, who was always off chasing department store sales or focusing on older daughter Sabrina's accomplishments. But when Dee Dee was twelve, Margaret got sick, like, really sick, and died. Then Dee Dee and her father moved out of California and Evie hadn't heard from her in the last four years. Dee Dee never answered her e-mails or returned her calls. Evie still didn't understand exactly what happened. Just hearing Dee Dee's name gave her a stomachache.

Suddenly the Porta Potti door opened and Raquel stepped out, zipping her jeans.

"What," she said to Alejandra, "you still here?"

"You know what?" Alejandra bent her elbow to her side and held her cigarette out. "I think Gabriel would just *love* to meet some gate-crashers. Why don't you and your little blue *baya* stay put here by the toilets and I'll go get him?" She pushed by both of them.

As soon as Alejandra took off, Evie snapped at Raquel, "Why did you do that? You're gonna get us kicked out!"

"Nah." Raquel took her beer back and drank it calmly. "If it's the Gabriel I'm thinking of, and I'm sure it is, he won't kick us out. I've partied before with some older dude named Gabriel who said he had a fish farm out this way—it must be the same guy. Besides, I had Mondo get him the stuff and anyone knows that a first-rate delivery is definitely more important than some second-rate second cousin."

"Could you hear what Alejandra said?" Evie asked as they walked away from the Porta Potti. "About Dee Dee's dad, like, being at Channel Islands?"

"Yeah, I heard," Raquel said. "How come you didn't know?"

Evie shrugged. She felt foolish. "Doesn't your dad keep in touch with Dee Dee's?"

"We get Christmas cards," Raquel admitted. "With a pre-printed signature that you just know was sent by some assistant."

Evie's heart sank. Her family had received the same type of card for the past few years. She always looked for a handwritten note from Dee Dee but never found one. She brought her cup to her lips and tapped the last trail of foam into her mouth. This was not the kind of evening she had expected.

"Yeah, and I thought you were, like, best friends," Raquel continued.

"We were," Evie said. "I mean, all three of us were."

"No." Raquel shook her head. "You and Dee Dee were always tighter. I would've thought she'd call you right away."

"Yeah, I guess."

"So . . ." Raquel drank more beer. "You wanna go check out the band?"

Evie threw her empty cup on the ground. "Nah, not really."

She crossed her arms. She suddenly felt cold. "You wanna see if there's anyone else here from school?"

Raquel made a face. "Nah, not feeling it."

Evie looked around. She didn't know what to do. She didn't want to leave the party, but she sure as hell didn't want to stand around talking with Raquel, who was making her feel worse. Evie looked at her watch: 11 P.M. She still had an hour and a half. Really, an hour when you counted how long it would take to gather everyone up and make the drive back to Rio Estates.

"You know what?" Evie said. "Let's go back to Mondo's car."

"Mondo's *car*?" Raquel raised one eyebrow. "*You* wanna go back with Mondo and Jose? You know, they aren't just 'hanging out.'"

"Of course I know that," Evie snapped. "I'm not an idiot, Raquel."

"I'm not saying you are. It's just—"

"You know what?" Evie interrupted. "Tonight wouldn't be such a big deal if I hadn't just been grounded for two weeks and *that* was your fault. If I hadn't listened to you at Tracy Tankerson's party, I would've been home on time. And *then* you didn't even have the decency to call the first night I get to go out. Why is it such a problem that I want to have a really good time tonight?" Evie couldn't believe how utterly emo she was getting in front of Raquel.

Now both of Raquel's eyebrows were raised. "There's no

problem," she answered coolly. "I just didn't realize you were having such a lousy time, that's all."

"Well, I am. It's my first night out in weeks and I was all looking forward to being out with my friends and then I gotta find out all this about Dee Dee from Alejandra—" Evie stopped herself. "Let's just go back to the damn car."

"I ain't stopping you." Raquel inhaled uncomfortably.

"Okay," Evie said. "So, let's just go already."

And for once, it was Evie who grabbed Raquel by the arm and took the lead.

3

The next morning, Evie awoke to her mother bursting into her bedroom.

"E-*vie*!" she said. "Get up. It's late." She opened Evie's white wooden shutters, flinching when her fingers came away covered in dust. "Ewww! Evie, this is disgusting."

"Mom." Evie rolled over on her side and covered her eyes with her pillow. Her head was throbbing, and her mother's loud voice was making it worse. "Why do you have to break out with the negativity so early?"

"Early?" Her mother crossed the now sun-drenched room. She was carrying some kind of carpet cleaner. "It's already past eleven, and I've got to get in here to clean."

"Mom, *no*," Evie whined. "I don't want you rummaging through all my stuff. I can clean my own room."

"No, you can't." Her mother walked into Evie's bathroom and pulled a bottle of bleach from under the sink. "You know that Lindsay's off today and somebody's gotta work on these carpet stains." She came out of the bathroom and then spied something on the carpet. She crouched down and pulled up a ball of wax that had been embedded in the carpet. It had collected Molesto's long, thick black hairs; Meho's short, fine gray hairs; and God knew what else. "Evie, what *is* this?"

Evie rubbed her eyes and looked up."Oh, it's sex wax."

"Sex *what?"* Her mother immediately dropped the wad.

"*No."* Evie couldn't help but laugh. "Mr. Zog's Sex Wax. It's for my surfboard."

"Oh." Her mother didn't pick it up again. "The board your father paid almost a thousand dollars for and you have yet to use?" She wiped her fingers on one of the rags in her plastic bucket.

Fortunately for Evie, Moz blared from her cell phone.

"Evie," her mother began as Evie leaned over to get her phone from the pile of last night's clothes. "I told you I don't want your friends calling your cell when you're home. When you start paying—"

"Mom." Evie found her cell and saw Raquel was calling. "I have free weekend minutes and—" She flipped open the phone. "Hello?"

"Hey, it's me."

"Evie," her mother said as she finally headed out of the room. "Get up so I can get in here and clean."

* * *

"So I asked my dad about Dee Dee this morning," Raquel told Evie.

It took Evie a split second to remember what Raquel was talking about. "You did?"

"Uh-huh," she said. "And he confirmed it."

"Confirmed what, exactly?" Evie asked.

"That the de LaFuentes are definitely moving back to Rio Estates."

"And he knew?" Evie asked. "Why didn't he say anything? Why didn't he tell you?" Evie had cotton mouth and her head was pounding like a mofo.

"Oh, you know how ol' Charlie Diaz is." Raquel yawned. "*With his money on his mind and his mind on* . . . nothing else. My dad isn't concerned with long-lost family friends. In fact, he's actually known for weeks—he got an e-mail from Dee Dee's dad. And now my mom wants to have a little welcome-back party for them. She says it's the proper thing to do, especially to introduce Dee Dee's new mom to everybody."

"New mom?" Evie repeated. The Gomezes had received an announcement of Mr. de laFuente's sudden second marriage but knew nothing about his second wife.

"New *madre*?" Raquel asked. "Does that sound better?"

"I'm really not in the mood for semantics right now." Evie

turned to her other side and hugged her Hawaiian-print Mogu.

"So," Raquel said. "How are you feeling?"

"Totally dissed," Evie said.

"No, I mean after last night, with Mondo and Jose."

"Oh. Uh, okay, I guess," Evie told her. "It was totally not worth all the intrigue. Now, I'm just really tired. Like exhausted, and my head is killing me."

"That'll wear off," Raquel said knowingly. "Just drink lots of water. You want me to bring you some *menudo*?"

"No."

"But *ay, mi'ja,*" Raquel exaggerated her voice to sound slow and rickety, like a Mexican *vieja,* complete with a heavy Spanish accent. "*Pero,* you need *menudo. Mira,* I bring you a steaming hot bowl of *menudo* now, *¿sí?* I make it myself for you, fresh *tripas* and all."

Evie laughed. "No *thank* you, *Tía* Raquel."

"No, but seriously." Raquel changed her voice back. "You don't need anything? More of the *perrito* that bit you?"

"Ugh, no way," Evie moaned. "I just wanna sleep more but my mom came in like a Room Raider at the crack of dawn and now she's preparing to invade. I'm gonna have to take a nap in the friggin' pool house."

"Oh, yeah, that reminds me. My mom's gonna be calling your mom about the welcome-back gig," Raquel said.

"When's it gonna be?" Evie asked.

"Next Saturday."

"You mean *this* Saturday?" Evie asked.

"I thought it was too early for semantics," Raquel said. "But yeah, this coming Saturday."

"What kind of party?"

"Not really a *party* party," Raquel said. "It'll probably be just my parents, your parents, and some other Callaway-swinging golf goons from the SCC." She yawned again. "Just a little something."

When Evie finally hung up, she had a knot in her stomach. Dee Dee was coming back. They were going to be neighbors again and most likely classmates, but would they be friends again, too? All three of them—she, Raquel, and Dee Dee? It'd been over four years since Evie had heard from Dee Dee and, Evie thought as she looked at herself in the closet mirrors, people do change, blue hair and all.

4

RioChica (6:01 PM): Little party tonight. Should be fun.
ShaggyMA (6:02 PM): Have a beer for me!
RioChica (6:02 PM): I'm more into the bubbly, if anything.
ShaggyMA (6:02 PM): Sofisticated! TTYL

The following Saturday evening, when Evie arrived with her parents at the Diazes' home, it was clear that the "little something" Kitty Diaz had scheduled was going to be a full-blown soiree. Evie saw two valet parking attendants setting up a station near the Diazes' mailbox, and several caterers in crisp white *guayaberas* were lugging an oversized cast iron *comal*.

"Oh, look, Vic." Ruben Gomez nudged his wife. "They're gonna have tortillas *de maíz*. Handmade."

"Kitty's going all out." Evie's mother rolled her eyes. "Again."

"Yeah." Evie's father suddenly frowned. "I wonder why she didn't order any of my *pan*."

As he rang the front doorbell, Evie's mother looked her over. "Oh, Evie." She shook her head. "I wish you would take care of that hair. This is bad."

"Bad for who?" Evie asked. And actually, she *had* taken care of her hair, thank you very much. As Raquel had promised, she took Evie to see Viggo, who stripped all of the brown out and then dyed her whole head a nice shade of vivid blue. When Raquel suggested he also fix her cut, maybe add some extensions to fill in the thinned-out parts, Evie tallied the total bill in her head and declined. But Raquel pushed for the correction. "I can't have my best friend going around looking like a mauling victim," Raquel joked as she graciously paid the extra price with her credit card. "I have a rep, you know."

Evie's mother went on. "You could at least have put on some dress shoes."

"Dress shoes?" Evie asked. Did anyone even use that term anymore? "When have I ever worn *dress* shoes?"

"Well, you could have at least *dressed* appropriately."

Evie felt she was definitely dressed appropriately. Sure, tonight she wore flojos, but they were her fancy crystal Havaianas, and a secondhand blouse that she had found at a *segunda* downtown, cream-colored and lacy. It looked perfect with her vintage straight legs, and she had even put on the pearl stud earrings that her *Tía* Isabel gave her for her eighth-grade graduation. She knew Dee Dee would approve, especially of the blouse. As kids, they often went with Lindsay to the thrift stores downtown and loved trying on all the used bridal veils and *quinceañera* gloves.

"Vicki," Evie's father said, coming to her rescue. "Evie looks fine. Just drop it."

Evie's mother started to scowl, but rearranged her face into a pleasant smile as soon as Kitty Diaz opened the door.

"Ruben, Vicki!" Kitty welcomed Evie's parents into her house. "How are you? Thank you so much for coming early."

"Sure, Kitty," Evie's father said. "We are at your disposal."

"Hello, Evie." Kitty smiled at Evie. "Oh, look at you. Raquel mentioned that you colored your hair. You're a bluenette! *Very* creative."

"Thanks." Evie looked up at her mother and gave her a smug little grin.

Kitty Diaz resembled Evie's mother in appearance and style. Both wore minimal makeup and had no-nonsense haircuts intended to convey a career-woman image, but the similarities ended there. Kitty Diaz was chapter president of *Madrinas,* the National Latina Leadership Network, and she had also cofounded Hi Tech Aztec, the software company, with her husband. Evie's mother, on the other hand, rarely lifted a finger except to point to which Isabella Fiore bag or Via Spigas she wanted the salesclerk to ring up.

As soon as Evie and her parents entered the Diazes' foyer, Raquel called down from upstairs, "Hey, Evie! Come on up. We can hang out before the serious alkies arrive."

"Raquel!" Kitty looked up and threw her a stern look. "Act right! Remember, this isn't just some party for you and your friends."

"I know, I know." Raquel threw her mother an exasperated look. "I was just messin'."

Kitty led the Gomezes into the kitchen. "You are *not* going to believe how much this caterer is charging me for the last-minute job," she said. "The cake-cutting fee *alone* . . ."

Evie started up the stairs to Raquel's room. "My mom said that maybe your mom might need help. Maybe I should offer to cut the cake? At a discount?"

"What you could offer is to give her an elephant tranquilizer and . . ." Raquel spoke from the side of her mouth, "I'm sure she has one somewhere in that panic drawer of hers." Raquel let out an exaggerated sigh. "I don't know why my mother always insists on throwing these parties. They always make her so stressed out and bitchy." She looked Evie up and down. "By the way, 'scuse me, America's Next Top Model."

"What?" Evie asked.

"Nothing." Raquel brushed it off. "You actually look nice."

"*Actually*? What is that supposed to mean?"

"Nothing."

But Evie wasn't convinced.

"*Evie,* I'm serious. You look cute. Dang, you're so *sentida.*"

When they got to her room, Raquel shut the door and held up a bottle of champagne. "Check it out. Veuve Clicquot. Kitty Diaz is sparing no expense on *la familia* de LaFuente." Raquel started to uncork the bottle with precision know-how. "Oh, when I was sneaking it out, I forgot to get glasses. Looks like we'll have to take swigs. Not very sophisticated, huh?"

Evie sat on Raquel's vanity stool and took the first swig of champagne.

"Whoa, slow down," Rachel laughed. "There's plenty more where this came from."

Evie took a smaller sip before giving Raquel back the bottle. "I just wanna loosen up." She got up from the stool and flopped on her stomach on Raquel's canopied bed. She flipped through the *Kerrang!* magazine, Raquel's "favorite, favorite" rock zine, that was lying on it. "It's so *wrong* that Dee Dee's, like, back in Rio Estates and still hasn't called."

"Have you called her?" Raquel asked.

"No. Have you?" Evie suddenly felt awkward and found a loose cuticle that needed attention.

"I don't have her number," Raquel answered.

"Well, she has mine," Evie said. "I mean, at least my parents'. They haven't changed their number in years. She has no excuse for not calling."

"Ahhh." Raquel took a swig of champagne and looked up

toward the ceiling with a dreamy expression on her face. "And so the *novela* between the wayward friend and the forgotten woman left behind continues. *Dos mujeres, dos caminos . . .*"

"What's that supposed to mean?"

"Nothing, really," Raquel said. "I just think you're obsessing too much about Dee Dee."

"Obsessing?"

"Well, maybe not obsessing." Raquel took another swig from the bottle and passed it back to Evie. "But I mean, come on. What's the big deal about Dee Dee? Even when we were little kids, you always had to be around Dee Dee. You were like Mary-Kate to her fucking Ashley."

"That's not true." Evie pretended to be absorbed in an article about The Stanford Prison Experiment's latest CD.

"Don't take this wrong, Evie," Raquel said, putting on her authoritative voice, the one Evie knew all too well. "But maybe you just need a man." She pulled a bunch of her hair forward and mindlessly checked for split ends. "I was talking to Jose and—"

"You were talking to Jose about *me*?" Evie looked up at Raquel. "I can't believe you discussed my love life with him!"

"Oh, I didn't realize you *had* a love life," Raquel teased. "When did *that* start?"

Evie took a bigger swig from the bottle. "Raquel, do not talk about me to Jose. I know he's, like, the 'love of your life' and everything, but there's gotta be some boundaries."

"He *is* the love of my life." Raquel frowned.

"Well, you'd never know it," Evie said. "The way you two fight all the time."

"We don't fight," Raquel snapped. "Sometimes we disagree on things, sometimes our disagreements get heated, but we aren't fighting. That's what you call passion, Evie. Besides, you sure aren't one to judge a relationship. You've never even had one."

The room grew quiet, and Evie immediately felt put in her place. She *hated* that feeling. The last thing she wanted was to fight with Raquel, but it was always like this with her. It was Raquel's way or the *calle.* She was never open for discussion, debate, or compromise. Evie hated it when Raquel acted like such a know-it-all. But they'd been friends long before the Grandpapa Clause, meaning Raquel plain got away with certain behavior due to their history together. And you just can't mess with history.

Raquel stepped into her bathroom to switch on her flattening iron.

"So . . ." Evie continued to flip through *Kerrang!* and tried to change the subject. That seemed the only way she knew how to keep peace. "I wonder what Dee Dee looks like now."

"Yeah, I wonder," Raquel answered halfheartedly.

"Um . . ." Evie scanned Raquel's room hoping to find something, anything, for inspiration. She saw one of Raquel's fancy glass bottles filled with multicolored layers of sand. This one was in the shape of a genie's lamp.

"Remember when her mother had that Aladdin birthday party and insisted we all dress up?" Evie asked.

"Oh, yeah."

"Yeah," Evie continued. "She had just seen *Aladdin on Ice* or something like that, right?"

"Something like that." Raquel came back into the bedroom. "That party was the worst."

"I thought it was fun," Evie said. "You had on that really cute outfit, the harem pants and that halter."

"Hmm . . ." Raquel started warming up. "I guess at the time it was okay."

"Dee Dee's mom was so cool," Evie said. "She always threw the best parties."

"My mom throws good parties." Raquel frowned.

* * *

"Hey, Raq!" It was Jose, tapping on Raquel's bedroom door.

"Hey you," Raquel called. "Get in here, already."

Jose strutted into the room with an exaggerated pimp limp. Alex followed close behind. Both of them had on stiff baggy cords. Jose was in his usual Trunk Ltd vintage T, but Alex wore a button-up shirt. And when Evie hugged him hello, she detected the distinct odor of cologne, fresh and outdoorsy. Too cute.

"Hey, hey, hey," Jose said. "So this is where the pre-party

action is, huh?" He looked around and when he saw the Veuve Clicquot he instantly balked. "What, no *Cristal*? Girl, you going bourgie on me?"

"Messi-can, puh-*lease*." Raquel gloated as she went over to lock her bedroom door. "This is just the beginning. Once everyone gets bombed, we'll have the run of the place. Where's Mondo?"

"Mondo," Jose said slyly, "had a *very* important drop-off in the valley. He might be by later."

"Oh, he'll definitely be by later," Alex said. "He never turns down a party."

Jose looked Raquel up and down. "Damn, Rocky." He whistled slow, eyeing Raquel's low-cut black camisole. "You sure know how to rock a fella!"

"You likes?" She twirled around, the sheerness of her tiered cami exposing maybe more than she wanted.

"What do you think?" Jose gestured below his belt. "Check out the Miracle-Gro!"

"Jose!" Raquel snapped. "Why do you always have to ruin it?" She went to the bathroom and got her flattening iron. "I swear!"

"What?" Jose looked at her, then at Alex and Evie, perplexed. "That's a compliment. You want me to say you look ugly?"

"Just act right," Raquel reprimanded. She leaned against the bathroom doorway while she straightened her long, wavy hair.

Jose cowered a bit before taking over the window seat in Raquel's room. He looked out across the Diazes' backyard and whistled again. "Check out the fancy spread downtown."

"Didn't my mother just go crazy?" Raquel asked.

"Yeah." Alex sat on the edge of the bed, near Evie. "We saw some dude laying out flowers and some of those floating candles in the pool."

"Ooh." Evie went over to the window. "Lemme see."

They were right. The Diazes' backyard was pure swank. Their pool glowed in candlelight, and multicolor *papeles picados* hung across the yard between the Diazes' jacaranda trees.

"Are the cutouts custom?" Evie asked.

"Oh, yeah," Raquel said. "Each *papel* has, like, a little scene from when the de LaFuentes lived here. There's some cutouts of their first house here in Rio Estates, some from the summers we all stayed in Cabo, and oh, some of the Christmas we spent at Lake Tahoe. 'Member?"

"Hey, can I smoke out a little?" Jose interrupted, obviously bored.

"Jose." Raquel pursed her lips and gave him a look. "Quit acting stupid."

"What?" He pulled out some rolling papers from his back pocket. "I'm stupid just 'cause I asked a question? Remember what Mr. Mercer said in class today? There is no such thing as a stupid question, only stupid—"

"Boyfriends?" Raquel finished his sentence. "And don't

even get me busted by lighting up. If you wanna be high all night, you can just go home now. This is an important night—we don't want any drama. Right, Evie?"

"Right," Evie confirmed with an exaggerated single firm nod. She got back on Raquel's bed and lay on her side, propping her head up with one hand.

"Well." Jose opened the window and looked out again. "Maybe I'll get one of the bartenders to give me a lift home. Say, like maybe that sweet redhead setting up the bar?"

"What redhead?" Alex walked to the window and looked out.

"Ugh!" Raquel set her flattening iron down on the bathroom counter and went over to Jose. She dropped her body onto his lap. "Over my dead body."

Jose wrapped his arms around her waist. "Hey, I got nothing against necrophilia if you don't."

"My." Raquel dug her face into his neck. "Such a big word for a little boy."

"Dudes, get a room already." Alex rolled his eyes. "Oh, wait, we *are* in a room already."

Evie handed Alex the Veuve and he held it up to eye level. "This is dwindling," he said. "We're gonna have to get more." He took a short swig and handed the bottle to Evie. "But don't drink too much. Don't forget we're on Dawn Patrol tomorrow."

To Evie, getting up at dawn on a non-school day was entirely out of the question. But Dawn Patrol, as Evie had learned from Alex and Shaggy, was the time of day any serious surfer got to the beach. You staked out your territory long before the lineup got flooded with aggro locals (she, living in Rio Estates, was sorta a local, but far from aggro) and you nabbed hours of free parking, way before the meters inflated to weekend rates.

Alex was the only Flojo who surfed and he not only helped Evie pick out her long board but he had also promised to take her on DP with him. This excited Evie. She was not only going to learn to surf, but she was going on Dawn Patrol.

"Oh, no worries," Evie insisted. "I'm down for dawn."

"Yeah, that's what you *always* say," Alex said as he handed Evie the bottle. "But you have yet to go."

"Alex." Evie felt defensive. "I've been *grounded*."

"Yeah, yeah. But for two months now?" Alex rolled his eyes. "Anyway, so how long did this Dee Dee live in Mexico?"

"Almost four years." Evie took one last sip from the bottle. She was already feeling touched, and the memory of last weekend's hangover reminded her of a place she didn't want to visit again. "Dee Dee moved there when we were all twelve."

"Man, I'd love to live in Mexico." Alex got an excited look in his eyes. "Get my stoke on every day, down south, like Puerto Escondido."

"Well, Dee Dee didn't live in southern Mexico," Evie said. "She lived in, like, the Polanco District, right in Mexico City."

"Yeah, and you know she had to hate it." Raquel looked up from Jose's neck. "Dee Dee's a total bumpkin, afraid of her own shadow."

"Raquel!" It was her mother in the hallway. She jiggled the locked doorknob and spoke sternly. "Come out and join the rest of the party. We have guests. You are a hostess, and you are being rude."

"Oh, *shit.*" Raquel bolted up from Jose's lap and fanned his smoke out the window. "I better get out there." She called to her mother. "Sorry, Mom! Evie's just helping me pin my bra straps down. I'll be right out." Then she turned toward Jose and Alex. "You guys wait awhile and then come out and meet us. And remember, be as tolerant of Dee Dee as possible. She can be freaky shy. And you"—she looked at Jose—"stay away from that redhead."

* * *

Evie recognized many of the party guests from the SCC, the Saticoy Country Club. Others were colleagues of the Diazes, fellow Hi Tech Aztecs who'd also made their money through computers or some kind of software technology. A lot of men, robust in stature and liberal with the cologne, had families and homes in Rio Estates but held positions and, as Raquel claimed, *sanchas* up north, in their luxury Silicon Valley condos. Evie wondered, did that hefty new rock weighing down

Mrs. Coulhan-Reyes's finger have anything to do with some hefty new guilt weighing down on Mr. Reyes's conscience? *Qué* Kobe.

After they made the obligatory rounds of the party, the Flojos pretty much stayed to themselves. Evie anxiously watched the front door; Alex worked on sneaking more booze; and Jose tapped about every platter that came his way.

"What's with your mom serving all this Mexican food?" Jose asked Raquel as he took a quesadilla triangle off a passing tray.

"What do you mean?" Raquel asked. "What should she be serving?"

"I dunno, but didn't the de LaFuentes just come in from Mexico? Don't you think they've had their fill?"

"You are so *not* bagging on my mom," Raquel insisted.

"No, I'm bagging on her choice of food." Jose took a bite and immediately made a face. "Ugh. What is this?"

"Jose, don't be a jerk. It's a goat cheese quesadilla. Obviously too refined for your Taco Bell palate."

"Hey," he warned. "Don't *you* bag on the Bell."

Evie couldn't stop glancing at Alex's Nixon. It was already seven forty. The de LaFuentes were over half an hour late. Didn't anyone notice? Evie saw her mother with Mrs. Estes, admiring Kitty's new original Arturo, a sculpted metal art piece over the doorway. *Hmmm,* Evie thought, *maybe I'm the only one tripping over the de LaFuentes' rudeness?*

By eight o'clock, the appetizers of *minichalupas* and the aforementioned quesadillas were almost gone and everyone was toasty from an hour's worth of free booze. Charlie Diaz made an announcement to the crowd. "Okay, everybody, I just got a call from Frank." He was pink-faced from the heat and excitement. "They're on their way. They just turned on Camino Coral. They'll be here any second."

"What, did Frank forget how to get around his old neighborhood?" someone called out, and everyone laughed as if it were the funniest joke in the world.

A few minutes later, the de LaFuentes' car finally pulled into the Diazes' circular driveway, followed by a series of short car honks to announce their arrival. "Ah, man," Raquel nudged Evie. "*Qué barrio.*"

Evie's face started to grow hot. She quickly went to the bathroom to do a final check on her appearance and discovered that her anxiety was visible—there was a small sweat ring under each of her arms. *Crap.* That was the problem with vintage pieces—they were always made from some polyester blend that generated sweat and, worse, a mad stink. Evie grabbed one of the monogrammed guest towels hanging from the chrome towel bar and reached under her blouse, patting each armpit dry. She looked for deodorant in the Diazes' bathroom cabinet and discovered that Kitty, just like Evie's mother, bought the Trader Joe's natural stuff, which *naturally* didn't do jack. Evie heard shouts and greetings. She quickly rubbed on the deodorant anyway and raced back to join the party.

When Evie returned, Frank de LaFuente, Dee Dee's father, was already standing in the Diazes' foyer. Next to him was a short, smartly dressed woman. Evie's and Raquel's parents were cooing over both of them. Frank de LaFuente looked a lot like Evie remembered: the same broad smile and thick, bushy eyebrows that were now a bit grayer. He still wore a three-piece suit and silk tie, his standard classic uniform.

"*¡Bienvenidos!* Welcome!" Evie's father exclaimed. "Frank, it's been too long!"

"Yes, yes!" Frank de LaFuente agreed excitedly. "It's so wonderful to be back! To be home."

"Look." Evie's father pushed her forward as if she were a prop or something. "Here's Evie!"

"Oh, Evie!" Frank de LaFuente took her hands in his, stood back, and beamed. "*Mi'ja*, let me look at you! Such a beautiful young lady you've become! Look at this hair. *Como* the ocean!" He looked over at Raquel, who was standing next to her. "And Raquel, *¡tú también! ¡Qué bonita! Mira,* I want you both to meet my wife, Graciela."

Graciela was a stout, fair-skinned woman with dark eyes and dark hair cut in a short bob. Two large, ornate earrings swayed like ship lanterns from her ears.

What Dee Dee's father offered in warmth, Graciela definitely cooled down with her own ice. Her *brrr* factor was cranked high as she offered a lukewarm hello, surveyed the Diazes' home, and asked Kitty Diaz, "Is our Lexus going to be safe with those men outside?"

"Oh, yes, of course." Kitty put her arm around Graciela's shoulders. "We've used this valet company for years."

"*Buenas noches,* Graciela," Evie said with her best Spanish accent. "*Soy* Evie. Dee Dee and I have been best friends since we were little kids."

"Yeah," Raquel added. "We've all been friends since we were, like, seven years old."

"Really?" Graciela looked them over. Evie suddenly felt like a piece of silver-plated jewelry she wouldn't even bother to try on. "What did you say your names were again?"

"Uh, I'm Evie," Evie started awkwardly. "And this is—"

"Evie?" Graciela asked. "What kind of name is that?"

"Well, my real name is—"

"Where's Dee Dee?" Raquel interrupted, looking around Graciela.

"You know how you girls are," Frank de LaFuente said as he reached over and took his wife's black sequined wrap. "We couldn't get her off her cell phone—she has been on that thing since we arrived. She's going to drive over herself in a little while."

"Oh?" Evie's mother looked over at Kitty disapprovingly. "Well, I do hope she arrives soon. Kitty ordered a *tres leches* especially for—"

"We're all just excited to see our little Dee Dee," Evie's father said quickly. "Especially Evie."

"Dee Dee has her own car?" Evie directed the question to Frank de LaFuente, but looked at her mother.

"Of course." Frank de LaFuente put his arm around her. "We got it for her the first week here. *Pero*, no worries, *mi'ja*. She'll be here soon."

Evie felt confused. Why hadn't Dee Dee just come with her parents? Why didn't Graciela know who she or Raquel was? But most important, she wondered as she discreetly sniffed to the left and then to the right, why hadn't she put on more deodorant?

* * *

By 9:30, Dee Dee still hadn't arrived and the party was dying down. The singer from the band, *un trío* that Raquel's father had hired, had shaken her *maraca* one last time and the caterers were gathering up the dessert dishes and what was left over from the *tres leches* cake.

"This is very rude of Dee Dee," Evie overhead her mother say to her father as she scratched the side of her neck. "Very inconsiderate."

Evie was surprised to find herself in full agreement with her mother. She couldn't believe that Dee Dee was being so thoughtless on this night of all nights. Evie felt that Dee Dee wasn't just blowing off the party, she was blowing *her* off. Evie's eyes started to burn with anger.

She walked around the party again and was relieved to finally spot Jose and Alex in the Diazes' great room. They'd get her mind off Dee Dee's absence. She immediately went over to join them. They were chatting it up with some older female guest and a server. Both women were laughing and speaking Spanish.

As the server left to gather more plates from other guests, the guest switched to Spanglish. "But *ay*, no," she insisted to Alex. "Aren't you ever afraid? What about sharks? And those waves are so big. *¡Tan grandes!*"

Her bangs were blown up high and her neckline was low. She had on a black (was that Lycra?) minidress and, in bold contrast, wore light blue, almost white, contacts.

"Well, I wouldn't say I'm a *big-wave* surfer," Alex said, not noticing Evie had just joined them. "I mean, I'm no Laird Hamilton, but—"

"¿Quién?" the woman asked.

"Oh." Alex waved a hand dismissively. "He's just some surfer."

Some surfer? What was Alex saying? Laird Hamilton was, like, Alex's idol.

"Yeah." Jose smiled. "We should take you out with us sometime."

"We?" Alex ribbed Jose. "Dude, you can't even float." He

turned his attention back to the woman. "I'll take you out and you'll be totally safe. I'm a lifeguard at the pool. At the country club."

Yeah, Evie thought, *in the kiddie section.*

"But I don't even know how to swim." The woman gave a helpless giggle and tugged on her tight mini, which was riding up her thighs.

"Oh, I can help you." Alex shook the ice around in his empty glass. "I'll have you doing a few basic strokes in no time."

"Yeah." Jose grinned. "I'm *sure* he will."

"You"—the woman playfully slapped Jose on the chest—"are gonna give me problems. I can see that already."

Evie was being blatantly ignored and her patience was wearing thin. She finally offered her hand to the woman. "Hello, I'm Evie."

"Evie?" The woman's piercing white eyes penetrated hers. "Evie Gomez?"

"Uh, yeah . . ."

"*¡Ay!* Evie!" The woman set her dessert plate on a chair and wrapped her arms around Evie. She was suffocated by flesh, hair, and putrid flowery perfume. A lot of perfume. "Evie!" the woman exclaimed. "I've been asking everyone where you've been!"

"Excuse me." Evie felt lost. "But have we met?"

"Evie! It's me! Dela!"

"Dela?"

"Oh." The woman threw an embarrassed sideways glance over at Jose and Alex. "Okay . . . Dee Dee?"

"Dee Dee?" Evie couldn't believe what she was seeing. This . . . this was Dee Dee?

"Oh my God, Evie," the woman went on. "Look at you! Oh my God. Your hair! You are so crazy with your *pelo azul*!"

She put her arm around Evie and turned to Jose and Alex. "This girl is the friend I was telling you about. Right here, little Evie Gomez. *Ay*, Evie, you are *so* cute. You never got any taller, did you?" She actually patted Evie on the head.

"Um." Evie's voice came out like a squeak. "Dee Dee, uh . . ."

"*Ay, mi'ja*," she said. "I'm so sorry I'm late. Don't be mad. I just could *not* get off the phone with *mi novio* back in D.F. He hates that I am here and he gets so possessive. *Ay*, I mean, *posesivo*. I hope American boys aren't that way." She gave Jose and Alex a coy smile.

"Nah." Alex smirked. "We let our women go as far as our leashes let them."

"*¡Ay!*" Dee Dee gave him a sideways glance. "Now you too?"

"Um, Dee Dee . . . ," Evie tried again.

"No, no." She put one finger over Evie's lips. "*No one* calls me Dee Dee. *Por favor*." She frowned knowingly at Jose and Alex.

"So, Dela." Alex was still all smiles. "I bet you've got some funny stories from when you and Evie were kids."

"Oh, yes, I—" Dela snapped her fingers to get a server's attention. "Over here," she called, holding up her glass. "I'm done here." She turned her attention back to Alex. "Let me tell you, she was my best, best friend. We did everything together and—oh, wait, I want you to meet Graciela, my stepmother. *'Ama!"* she called. "*'Ama*, here's the friend I was telling you about. This is Evie."

"Oh, yes." Graciela looked Evie over again. "I met her earlier this evening. Very nice." She turned to Dee Dee. "Listen, *mi'ja*. Your father and I are getting tired. We are going to head home."

"Already, *'Ama*?"

"Yes, yes. I'm still not used to the time change and the food." She put a palm over her abdomen. "It's not sitting too well with my stomach."

"Ah." Jose smiled. "The goat cheese quesadilla? Am I right?"

"*¿Mande?*" Graciela looked at him, confused.

"Oh, *'Ama*," Dee Dee said. "These are my two new friends. This is . . ." She looked at Alex. "I'm sorry, what is your name again?"

"Uh, Alex," he said, looking embarrassed.

"Alejandro?" Graciela asked.

"No. Just Alex."

"You mean Alexander?" Graciela asked again.

"No, Alex," he repeated, uncomfortably. "*Just* Alex."

"Okay, *'Ama,*" Dee Dee interrupted as she gave her stepmother a quick peck on the cheek. "I'll see you later tonight."

As Graciela started to leave, Evie saw Raquel slowly swagger up to them. Oh, man, where had she been this last hour or so? Somewhere, obviously, that granted her an all-access pass to a steady flow of liquor. She looked trashed.

"Uh, Raquel," Evie started to warn her.

"Raquel?" Dee Dee smiled widely and patted Raquel's tummy. "*Ay, Pancita!* Look at you!"

"*¿Pancita?*" Jose laughed. "Oh my God. You used to be called *Pancita*?" He looked Raquel over. "Yeah, I can see that."

Raquel looked at Jose, then hard at Dee Dee. "Who the *hell* are you?"

"It's Dee—" Evie tried to inform her. "I mean Dela. Dee Dee."

"Yes, it's me, Dela!" Dee Dee held her arms up and wiggled her body.

Raquel squinted. "Whoa, what the fuck happened to your eyes?"

"What?" Dee Dee asked. The wiggling stopped.

"Your eyes," Raquel said again. "Oh, shee-yat!" She placed her fist over her mouth and looked at Jose. "I feel like I'm talking to a wolf! No, no, one of those huskies. A Siberian husky!"

"Excuse me?" Dee Dee fumed.

"Oh God." Raquel suddenly put her hand on her forehead. "I feel sick. Whoa, whoa . . . I feel really sick."

"Raquel, why don't you come with me to the bathroom?" Evie suggested.

"It's okay." Jose put his arm around Raquel. "I'll take her."

"But I don't wanna go . . . we gotta wait for Dee Dee," Raquel whined. "Evie's dear little Dee Dee. Right, Evie? Your best friend?"

"Oh, man." Alex looked away. "Here it comes."

"*¿Qué es su problema?*" Dee Dee demanded.

"Nothing," Jose said. "She's just had too much to drink. Sorry 'bout this . . ."

"*Sorry?*" Raquel pulled away from Jose and glared at Dee Dee. "Why you telling *her* sorry?"

"Well," Dee Dee started, "we *were* having a nice conversation before you—"

"Oh," Raquel said slowly. "Did *I* interrupt you? You macking on *my* boy? You were always this way, Dee Dee. Even back in Mr. Harrison's class when you knew I liked . . ." Raquel covered her mouth and groaned again. "Ooh, I'm really gonna be sick. Oh, Jose, don't let me get sick."

"Well, baby, you're gonna have to be sick before you can get better." Jose led her toward the bathroom.

"What, so she's like an alcoholic now?" Dee Dee asked.

"No, it's just been a long night," Alex said.

"Yeah," Evie said, coming to Raquel's defense. "It's been a long night and we've been waiting . . . all night."

"Oh, so it's my fault she's all *borracha*?" Dee Dee asked.

"No, I'm just saying that we've all been excited to see you, and it's been years, and we hadn't even heard from you and now—"

"Wait, don't put it all on me that your friend has a drinking problem."

"My friend?" Evie raised her voice. "Dee Dee, I thought Raquel was *our* friend."

"You know, Evie," Dee Dee said angrily, "it's obvious you're having a bad night, and I'm not gonna let you ruin my party."

"Ruin it?" Evie snapped. "Dee . . . Dela, this party's been over for hours."

Dee Dee looked over at Alex. "Alejandro, can you take me home?"

Evie also looked at Alex. *No, no, no.*

"Uh, yeah," Alex said hesitantly. "But I thought you drove here."

"I did," Dee Dee said firmly. "But I just don't feel like driving right now. Isn't there somewhere we can go? Like for a drink or something?"

"Well, it's not like Mexico," Alex said slowly. "You gotta be twenty-one to drink here."

"No, I know that. I was thinking of a coffeehouse or something?" She looked around. "Hey, why don't you take me to Sea Street."

"Sea Street?" Alex asked.

"Yes, Sea Street." Dee Dee pulled out a silver compact from

her purse. Evie noticed the initials D.D. on it. "I haven't been there since I was a kid." Dee Dee flipped the compact open and checked herself in the mirror, patting the corners of her eyes with light beige powder. "I'm going to say good-bye to my father, and then I'll be waiting . . . outside." Dee Dee snapped her compact shut and turned to leave. She made sure her eyes didn't meet Evie's.

"Well," Alex said uncomfortably. "I guess I better take her, huh?"

"What?" Evie balked. "Are you out of your mind? You are *not* taking her to Sea Street."

"Well, where should I take her?"

Where should he take her? Evie thought. *God, Alex, are you totally* tonto?

"I mean," Alex said awkwardly, "I feel like it's sorta my obligation. She is a guest."

"So then just go, *Alejandrrro.*" Evie dismissed Alex with a wave of her hand. "I didn't *realize* you were the goodwill ambassador for Mexico."

❋ ❋ ❋

But as soon as Evie watched Alex go out the front door to meet Dee Dee, she didn't feel quite so tough and dismissive. She felt horribly betrayed. She felt like . . . nothing.

"Would you like a slice?" It was the same server that Evie had seen earlier with Dee Dee. She had a piece of *tres leches* on her platter and was now offering it to her.

"Uh, no. No, thank you," Evie said.

"Your friend." The server smiled playfully. "*¿Qué mala, no?*"

"Uh, which one?" Evie asked.

"*La sangrona,*" she teased as she looked after Dee Dee and Alex.

"The *sangrona*?" Evie repeated. "No, she's not *that* bad." *But who am I kidding?* Evie thought. Dee Dee seemed to have become a Sangro, just like Alejandra and all her little *ah-migas*, which, according to Evie, was *mala. Muy, muy mala.*

"You know what?" Evie told the server. "I will take that piece."

After Evie took the slice, she took a big bite. The sweet, milky moistness flooded her mouth, but she still couldn't shake off the bitterness that seared her whole body. What had happened to Dee Dee? When had she turned into this . . . stranger? Was there anything of the old Dee Dee behind the fake contacts and tight clothes? She took another bite and tallied up the evening's score. Sangros: one, Flojos: zero. And Evie? More than anything, she didn't want to be in the game.

5

Like most Californians, Evie knew that shake and bakes (Ca-lingo for the earthquakes that occur during hot weather) are most likely to occur early in the morning. So the next day when Evie woke up to her glass-top nightstand rattling, she started to panic, only to discover it was her cell phone. She had left it on vibrate.

When Evie reached over and saw Alex's face on the screen, she was surprised. That was big of him, she thought, to actually call after being such the a-hole the night before.

She also saw on her cell that it was already 11:03 A.M. The operative word here was *already.* When he'd left the party with Dee Dee, Evie knew that Dawn Patrol was definitely off. Besides, she thought as she looked at her vibrating cell, dawn had cracked almost five hours ago. So why was he even calling? But as soon as the vibrating stopped, Evie couldn't help but feel a pang of regret. Maybe she should've answered it. Maybe Alex wanted to apologize, beg for her forgiveness, and admit he'd been a lousy friend at the party last night. Maybe . . . but then Evie stopped herself. Who was she kidding? It was *already* three minutes after 11 A.M. If he was so sorry, he would have called much earlier.

She tossed her phone on the covers and curled onto her side.

She looked at her Max long board in the corner of her room. How could Alex have taken Dee Dee to Sea Street? What had even happened to Dee Dee anyway? The big buildup of excitement about seeing Dee Dee crumbled into one tremendous Malibu-like landslide. For one thing, Dee Dee didn't look even remotely like the best friend Evie remembered. No more long brown hair, freckles, or the skinny chicken legs that had gotten her the nickname, *Popotitos*. But suddenly Dee Dee, Sangro look and all, was back in Rio Estates and, most likely, would be going to Villanueva. How was Evie going to deal with this, this . . . Dee-*lemma*? She looked at her cell. It was much too early to call Raquel, who would undoubtedly be snoring off a hangover.

Just then Evie heard the doors of the linen closet in the hallway swing open, followed by the heavy sigh she knew so well. She got up and went over to the doorway to her bedroom.

"Hey, Linds," Evie said. "What are *you* doing here?" She peered out from behind her door, in her cotton cami and cheeky hipsters. Lindsay had seen her in various states of undress hundreds of times, but she was feeling oddly modest for some reason. Maybe because it was a Sunday, Lindsay's day off.

"Oh." Lindsay turned away from the closet. "*Good morning,* Lindsay. How are *you* this morning, *Lindsay.*"

Evie upped her playful challenge and said, as quickly and confidently as she could, "*Buenos días,* Lindsay. *¿Cómo estás? ¿Por qué estás aquí?*"

Lindsay smiled, but turned back to the closet. "Your mother called me early this morning and asked me to come in, for the brunch."

"The brunch?" Evie wiped the sleep from her eyes. "What brunch?"

"Just a little one, for the de LaFuentes." Lindsay looked at her watch. "In about an hour."

"*What?*" Evie felt her forehead crease involuntarily. For all the times her face had gone into shock over the last forty-eight hours, she figured she'd need some major wrinkle cream in three years, by her eighteenth birthday. "The de LaFuentes are coming *here?*"

"Uh-huh," Lindsay answered. "You should go ask and see if your mother needs anything. She still has a lot to do."

"Is Dee Dee coming too?"

"I don't know, Evie." Lindsay answered halfheartedly. Her only concern at the moment was choosing the right color of soap for the guest bathroom.

Evie slipped on some sweat-shorts and her favorite Havaiana flojos, and headed downstairs. Hadn't last night's welcome-back party been enough? As a kid, Evie had always watched her mother trying to keep up with, well, not the Joneses, but the Diazes and the de LaFuentes. Sure, Vicki Gomez's husband owned a few bakeries, but she could host a get-together just as good as the wife of a scholar (i.e. Graciela de LaFuente) or the CEO/owner of a software company (i.e. Kitty Diaz) and she always felt like she needed to prove it. Was her mother back to her old competitive ways?

When Evie entered the dining room, she had her answer. For one thing, the dining table was free from clutter. Ordinarily their California mission-style table was littered with paperwork; Ojai spa bills, Santa Clara Church donation requests, catalogs from PawPrints, the *only* guide for high-end pet accessories. This morning, everything had been cleared away, and positioned dead center was an oversized clay vase filled with eucalyptus leaves and birds of paradise. A definite sign of impending company, or as Evie feared, an oncoming collision. What would she say to Dee Dee when she showed up?

Evie went into the kitchen and found her mother slicing and juicing oranges. Her short hair was wound in small hot rollers and she had a strip of Jolene cream applied above her top lip. Just how intimate was this brunch gonna be?

"What's going on?" Evie picked up Meho, who was rubbing against her calves.

Her mother looked up. "Maybe I should be asking you that."

"What do you mean?" Evie immediately felt her guard go up.

"I mean, what went on last night? With Raquel?"

"What do mean, Raquel?" Evie scratched Meho behind his ears.

"Evie, *quit* answering my questions with questions." Her mother brushed her forehead with her arm to wipe away nonexistent perspiration.

Oh, please. Evie rolled her eyes. The AC was more like FF—friggin' freezing—and how hard is it to place half an orange on a juicer?

"Raquel was throwing up all night," her mother continued. "Kitty was worried sick wondering if she had alcohol poisoning and—"

"Alcohol poisoning? Mom, come *on* . . ."

"Do *not* interrupt me, Evie. How did Raquel even get the liquor? I'd better not find out that you were drinking."

"Me? No. And who even says it was alcohol?" She struggled to protect Raquel, as well as herself. "Maybe the milk in the *tres leches* was bad or—"

"Evie! Stop it. When your father gets back I'm going to have him talk to you." She pulled a paper towel from the roll hanging under the cabinet and wiped the Jolene off her upper lip. She went back to juicing, shaking her head. "I don't know, Evie," her tone softened. "Your best friend is back and I would think you would have wanted to make a better impression. Granted she was rude, late to her own party, but we could be the more gracious ones. Dee Dee has gone through a lot, Evie. Losing her mother, moving to another country . . . and that Graciela's no consolation."

Evie took over one of the red sponge-painted stools at the kitchen counter. She knew her mother was *partially* right, but she wasn't about to admit it. Yeah, she, Dee Dee, and Raquel had once been the triple threat of Camino del Rio—three cute little rich girls who lived side by side at the end of the cul-de-sac. But when Dee Dee moved away, only Raquel and Evie remained close. And after last night, Evie had come to realize that Dee Dee had changed a lot, and not for the better. She had become the type of girl Raquel and Evie despised—the helpless giggling blonde, with the too-tight "hot" clothing. And those colored contact lenses!

Lindsay came in from the backyard through the French doors, carrying a plastic bowl filled with more oranges. "Okay, *señora,*" she told Evie's mother. "I got the last of them. I even checked around the trees, on the ground."

"Oh, thank you, Lindsay. I think this'll be enough," Evie's mother took the bowl and placed it in the sink. "Kitty doesn't really drink mimosas anyway."

As soon as Evie heard Raquel's mother's name mentioned, she stiffened.

"*The Diazes* are coming too?" she asked. "You said just the de LaFuentes."

"I didn't say that," her mother said calmly. "Everyone is coming . . . maybe not Raquel. We all didn't get much time together at the party last night and I thought a more intimate brunch would be nice. I didn't think of it until this morning, but fortunately everyone can make it."

"Except," Evie tilted her head, "maybe not Raquel."

But before her mother could say anything, the front door opened and Evie's father came in from the front room with Molesto clumsily trotting behind him. Great. Now, here came the lecture: "The Importance of Teen Sobriety" by Ruben Amílcar de Miguel Gomez.

But Evie's father had other things on his mind.

"I got 'em!" he announced excitedly as he threw his car keys on the kitchen counter and placed the large flat box on the dining table. "I was beginning to worry this whole morning was gonna be a bust."

The box had come from one of the Gomezes' *panaderías*. Evie had grown up with the white bakery boxes, each one with the image of a shell stamped on top. Evie went over to the table and lifted the box's lid. She inhaled the aroma of fresh bread, but the *pan* looked no different from the sweet bread her father brought home practically every night.

"You got what?" she asked. "More *pan dulce?*"

"No lard," her father corrected.

"Huh?" He took a crispy *oreja* from the box and broke a piece off. "None of these have *manteca*. Taste it."

Evie took a bite. The *pan* was still warm, but tasted bland, like the Jenny Craig dietary loaves the whole family had to tolerate when her mother was in a no-carb phase.

"What do you think?" her father asked eagerly.

"I think it's good . . . for someone who needs to lose weight."

"What's that supposed to mean?" He frowned.

"I dunno," Evie confessed. "It tastes weird."

"*Ay*, you *don't* know." Her father waved her aside. "Lindsay will tell me. She'll be honest."

Yeah, as honest as her yearly bonus allows her to be.

"Come here, Linds," he called over to Lindsay. "Try this."

Lindsay stopped slicing oranges to take a bite into the same flat, flaky *oreja*. She immediately smiled. "*Ay, Señor* Gomez," she gushed. "This is good. Really. I can't even tell the difference."

And of course, Evie's father just beamed, which made Evie wonder: When was the last time *she* had done or said something that made her father's face light up like that? It was always someone else who made her father glow. Like Sabrina, with all her achievements at Stanford; Molesto, chewing up all the Gomezes' unwanted junk mail; Meho, who purred on command; and now Lindsay, with her little *cumplimiento insincero*. *Blah*. Evie rumpled her lips.

"Hey, Vicki." Evie's father carried the box over to the counter. "Do we have a nice plate or something to put these on?"

"I am already one step ahead of you," Evie's mother sang as she pulled down a wicker basket from the top cabinet.

"Oh, that's nice. Real traditional. Hey, Linds," Evie's father started, "you need some coffee with your *pan*? Sit down. I'll get it for you."

"Oh, thank you, *Señor* Gomez." Lindsay pulled up one side of her skirt and apron and took a seat at the kitchen counter. She looked over at Evie and smiled.

"Can I do anything?" Evie found herself asking meekly.

"Actually, yes," her mother said. "Go out and look over the lawn. Make sure Molesto didn't leave anything behind."

"Wouldn't Arnie have done that yesterday?" Evie asked, referring to the Gomezes' gardener. He was meticulous about maintaining their Marathon sod lawn and the last thing she wanted was to go outside and scoop Molesto's torpedo-sized turds.

"Evie." Her mother raised an eyebrow and motioned Evie to the backyard. "Just do it."

"Come on, Evie," her father chimed. "Just do the doo!"

"Yeah," her mother added. "It's the call of doodie!"

And of course they both laughed. As they did *every* time they repeated the same corny jokes about Molesto's overly productive intestinal tract. Times like this made Evie wish they had gotten that aquarium like her mother had wanted.

So while the comedic duo collaborated over how to showcase an array of sweet bread, while a happy housekeeper got a mandatory impromptu coffee break on her day off, Evie pulled the pooper-scooper out from the kitchen utility closet and headed for the backyard. Little did any of them know that no matter how much she cleaned up after Molesto, it wouldn't matter. Now with the Diazes coming, a real shitstorm was on its way.

❋ ❋ ❋

By noon, the Gomezes' foyer was taken over by Spanish, Spanglish, and what Evie called *"Ay qué* speak."

"¡Ay, quééé guapo!" Evie's mother complimented Frank de LaFuente in his stylish white Cuenca Panama hat. Seconds later, Kitty followed with a reprimand to her own husband. *"¡Ay, quééé malo!"* She playfully slapped his back when he claimed that the only reason Frank de LaFuente wore such a hat was to cover his expanding bald spot.

A slightly jaundiced-looking Raquel was with her parents, but Dee Dee was absent. Evie was partly relieved, but also concerned. Just how pissed off could Dee Dee be? And why did Evie even care so much? If anything, it was Dee Dee who owed *her* an apology, or at the very least, an explanation. It was Dee Dee who hadn't kept in touch while she lived in Mexico. It was Dee Dee who hadn't even bothered to call when she arrived at Rio Estates and it was Dee Dee who took her sweet-ass time arriving to her own party, and when she finally showed, humiliated both Evie and Raquel. Yeah, it was Dee Dee who had some explaining to do. Mos def.

As Evie's mother led the adults outside to the Gomezes' deck, Evie pulled Raquel aside. "So, did you know about this?" she asked.

"Nuh-uh," Raquel said. "My mom just yanked me out of bed and insisted that I come. Like I had to make up for my so-called inappropriate behavior from last night." She rubbed her temples in annoyance. "I am so *not* in the mood for idle chitchat and greasy *chorizo*."

"We're actually having eggs Benedict," Evie told her.

"Did your mom or Lindsay make them?" Raquel asked.

"My mom."

"Well, I guess idle chitchat won't be so bad." Raquel half-smiled.

* * *

The parents sat down on the back deck and sipped mimosas while playfully arguing over who could offer the de LaFuentes better floor seats to the Lakers. Evie hung back in the kitchen while Raquel tried to recuperate. If she knew her mother, it would be at least half an hour before Lindsay served brunch.

Evie filled one of her mother's red and white kitchen towels with ice cubes and poured a can of warm ginger ale into a glass. She placed both of them on the counter in front of Raquel.

"You need aspirin?" Evie asked.

"Nah." Raquel took the towel and held it to her forehead. "I'll see how I feel in the next hour. I don't like overdoing it."

"Yeah." Evie pulled up a stool to sit next to Raquel at the counter. "You proved that last night."

The morning marine layer of fog that often plagued coastal towns like Rio Estates had burned off, making the afternoon, and the kitchen, sunny, warm, and bright.

"Ugh . . ." Raquel groaned as she pulled her Aviators over her eyes and placed her head down on her crossed arms on the kitchen counter. The sun's rays bounced off the counter's white tile. "What's with your mother's opposition to some simple kitchen blinds?"

"It's more like an opposition to, like, discretion or something," Evie said, referring to the large ornate baylike windows that overlooked the Gomezes' lush lawn, bountiful citrus trees, and tiled swimming pool. "My mother likes to see what she's thought up and put together."

Raquel looked out onto the deck. "Look at them. Just like back in da day, minus the OG Sangro," she said, referring to Graciela.

"Speaking of Sangros . . ." Evie lowered her voice. She had been dying to bring it up just as soon as the parents were out of earshot. "What did you make of Dee Dee?"

"What did I make of her?" Raquel grimaced. "She's such a friggin' FOTB Sangro, that's what I make of her."

Evie knew very well, of course, that the de LaFuentes, fresh or not, hadn't taken a boat to travel back to California. If she knew the de LaFuentes, they flew back to Cali on Mexicana Airlines, first class, and *not* by cashing in frequent flyer miles, thank you. But did Raquel really think Dee Dee had become a Sangro? Well, as much as Evie didn't want to admit it, if it giggles like a Sangro, squeals like a Sangro, wraps tight Lycra 'cross the ass like a Sangro . . . it was, definitely, a Sangro.

"Do you know that Alex took her to Sea Street?" Evie asked.

"Sea Street?" Raquel looked up. "When?"

"Last night. After the party. She practically ordered him."

"Stupid Alex." Raquel shook her head in disgust. "That dude be dense. Sea Street is Flojo Zone only. It's a good thing she didn't tell Jose to do anything. I'd have beat her ass." Raquel put her head back on her folded arms. "We gotta steer clear of her. I mean it, Evie. She's not the same friend we thought we knew."

"It seems that way," Evie reluctantly agreed.

"Seems?" Raquel lifted her head up again. "As if there was any suspicion she wasn't? Evie, you have to realize that she *was* a friend, *used to be* a friend, but times, obviously, have changed. We gotta have each other's backs."

"I *know*, Raquel."

Fortunately, just then, Evie's mother announced that brunch was ready. Evie welcomed the interruption and got up to go outside with Raquel.

Evie and Raquel took seats at the smaller patio table that was pushed up against the end of the main table, where all the parents sat. Evie noticed that Lindsay had included an additional place setting for Dee Dee.

* * *

"Besides, what do you even need ol' Dee Dee for?" Raquel continued as she poured some orange juice for herself. Evie started to put some melon salsa on her plate. "Hey,"—Raquel flashed a goony larger-than-life smile—"you got me." Evie knew, in Raquel's condition, it must have just killed her head. "Look," Raquel went on. "I'll even remove all this little nasty avo for you." She started to pick out the cubes of avocado from Evie's plate.

"Hey," Evie playfully pushed her fingers away. "Get your grubby paws outta my food!"

As soon as Lindsay had placed individually prepared servings of eggs Benedict in front of everyone, the brunch officially began. Evie's father welcomed the de LaFuentes back to Rio Estates for the umpteenth time and then Evie's mother got on her own pedestal.

"I'll have you know," her mother proudly pointed out with a champagne glass in her hand, "that just about everything on the table came from our own backyard—the tomatoes, the *aguacate*, and oh, even the orange juice. We squeezed it this morning."

"*¡Ay!*" Raquel's father feigned pain and pretended to spit an orange seed into a napkin. "And these *semillas, también*? I think I broke a crown!"

Everyone laughed, minus Graciela, who just smiled.

"So," Frank de LaFuente asked as he passed the carafe of orange juice. "How's Sabrina? How is she doing at Stanford?"

"Oh, just great," Evie's father said, cutting into his eggs. "She made the dean's list and was just elected president of her sorority."

"See," Frank de LaFuente knowingly addressed both tables, using his fork to make his point. "That girl was always a go-getter. She did things right, stayed on a path. There are Mexi-cans and Mexi-can'ts. And she's definitely a Mexi-*can.*"

The adults laughed, except Graciela, who just continued to smile.

"What," Charlie Diaz asked Frank de Lafuente, "you writing for *Mind of Mencia* now?"

Raquel nudged Evie and rolled her eyes. "If that's the case, *can* this Mexi-*can* change the channel?"

* * *

While Sabrina's accomplishments impressed everyone, the debut of Ruben Gomez's *pan dulce* garnered the most attention.

"*Ay*, no," Graciela winced after her first bite into a fluffy *banderilla*. "With all respect, Señor Gomez—"

"Grace, please," Evie's father interrupted. "We're like family. Call me Ruben."

"Oh, well . . ." Graciela looked at her husband uncomfortably. "My family calls me Graciela. Anyhow, as I was trying to say, I understand your intent, but . . . I don't know how to say this, but *no lo mete*."

"*¿Mande?*" Evie's father looked genuinely confused.

"Let me say it this way," Graciela continued. "The heart, *el corazón* of *pan dulce* is the *manteca*. It's what holds the *pan* together, literally and figuratively. In Mexico, a *panadero* would never dream of playing with tradition."

"Can you believe she's calling your dad out in his own house?" Raquel whispered over to Evie. "*Nerve*."

Evie sat up in her patio chair. Raquel was right. Her father would *definitely* have something to say about this.

But before Ruben Gomez could defend his beloved bread, a voice called out from the Gomez's kitchen.

"Dad? Graciela?"

Raquel sat up in her chair. Not nervously, but aggressively. Ready for combat.

"*¡Ay, mi'ja!*" Frank de LaFuente directed his attention, and thankfully everyone else's, away from the *pan dulce* to Dee Dee, who was coming out from the kitchen. "*¡Aquí!*" he called out. "We're out here!"

Dee Dee, in huge, green-tinted sunglasses and a blouse tied high to expose a pale stomach, came out onto the Gomezes' deck. She wore her blonde hair pulled into a ponytail and carried a large paper bag.

"Oh, Vicki." She went over to Evie's mother and gave her a hug. "I am *so* sorry I'm late. I overslept. It was *such* a long night last night."

Raquel nudged Evie, "And an even earlier morning . . . with Alex, I'm sure."

"Plus," Dee Dee gathered a fake yawn together, "I'm still so jet-lagged. It always takes me so long to get over it when I travel. But look, look." She held up her bag of Noah's Bagels. "I brought some bagels."

"Oh, Dee Dee." Evie's mother stood up and took the bag. "How thoughtful. You didn't have to do that." She passed them on to Lindsay without saying anything, which meant that the bagels would remain in the kitchen for the rest of the morning. After Graciela's negative comment, the *pan dulce* needed no more competition.

"Um," Dee Dee looked over the two tables uncomfortably. "Where should I sit?"

"Sit wherever you want, *mi'ja*," Evie's mother said. "But I think Lindsay already made a place for you." She gestured to the only available seat, across from Evie and Raquel. Dee Dee pulled out a patio chair and reluctantly sat down.

"So, what did I miss?" She kept her sunglasses on and

focused her attention on the adults. She didn't look at Evie and Raquel.

"Here," Evie's father passed the basket of *pan* over to her side of the table. "Try some of my new bread from the *panadería*. It's fat free."

"Fat free?" Dee Dee looked appropriately surprised. "Are you serious? Wow." She eyed the last *hornito* in the basket.

But Raquel, seeing Dee Dee's interest, waited until the parents had gone back to discussing Ruben Gomez's new business venture, grabbed the remaining piece of *pan* and tore a bite off with her mouth. She crossed her arms and looked defiantly at Dee Dee. *Not* Raquel's most mature move.

"Ay, qué glotona." Dee Dee casually brushed her hair back with her fingers. "It's a good thing it's fat free, *Pancita*, 'cause the last thing you need is any more fat."

Evie looked over at her parents but they were clueless to what was starting up or, actually, what was continuing from last night. She sank into her deck chair and said nothing, and neither did Raquel. Actually, how could she? What with her mouthful of soggy, semi-devoured *hornito*.

"I'd rather . . . be . . . a glutton," Raquel finally responded, cramming the last bits of the *pan* in her mouth, "than some . . . *pinche puta* . . . right, Evie?"

Evie said nothing as she pretended to be engrossed in her melon salsa.

"¿Puta?" Dee Dee narrowed her eyes at Raquel.

"Yeah," Raquel continued, shifting her attention between Dee Dee and the parents. "Ordering Alex to take you to Sea Street, you being all up on Jose at the party. Evie and I were just talking about you, before you showed up late, *again*. Right, Evie?"

"Oh, really?" Dee Dee looked at Evie wide eyed. "Is that what you were you saying, Evelina?"

The earnest way Dee Dee asked made Evie feel guilty. It was one thing to agree with Raquel's smack in private, but quite another to speak smack right in front of Dee Dee. Besides, Dee Dee seemed so defenseless. Was it the lack of her alien-looking colored contacts that made her suddenly seem more vulnerable, more human? Dee Dee's brown eyes patiently waited for Evie's answer.

"Well . . . " Evie tried to find her voice. "Last night was bad. I mean, it was late and everyone was tired. And you were just saying yourself that you get jet-lagged and—"

"*What?*" Raquel spat under her breath. She looked over at the parents, but they were not paying attention. "Evie, how can you fucking say that?"

"I'm not saying anything," Evie tried to backpedal. "I'm just agreeing that last night was craziness and that—"

But Raquel wasn't listening. She pushed her chair back and stood up. "Mom, I gotta get home." She looked down, toward Dee Dee. "I feel nauseous."

"Nauseous?" Evie's father was immediately concerned. "From

what?" The last thing he wanted was the suggestion that Raquel's nausea was linked to his forward-thinking, progressive *pan dulce.*

"Raquel." Her mother looked at Raquel firmly. "Sit down. You are being rude. We came together, we are leaving together."

"*What?*" Raquel challenged. "You mean we need to *cross the street* together?"

"Raquel—," Her father started.

"Oh, Kitty," Evie's mother interrupted. "If Raquel still isn't feeling well, she's more than welcome to leave. I won't be offended." But Evie knew that her mother didn't want the notoriously moody Raquel around in the first place. God forbid she got all *asco* on the teak furniture.

"You heard her, Mom," Raquel said. "Vicki doesn't mind." She got up and tossed her crumpled napkin on her plate. But before she left she made sure to lean over and give Evie a minor earful. "I knew you'd be weak. Thanks a fucking lot, *Evelina.*"

* * *

"Oh, I am so sorry," Kitty Diaz started to apologize as Raquel left. "She's never been a morning person."

"Or afternoon or evening. . . ." Charlie Diaz looked upward in exasperation.

"And who isn't a little tired the morning after such a wonderful celebration?" Frank de LaFuente said as he tried to smooth over the situation. He looked at Kitty and winked. "*¡Y qué fiesta!* We can't thank you enough."

"Oh, you are so welcome, Frank." Kitty smiled before looking at her watch. "Oh, but you know, that reminds me." She looked over at Evie's mother. "I hate to do this to you, Vicki, but we should get going. We have the rental company coming over to pick up all the tables and chairs from last night."

"On a Sunday?" Evie's mother sounded suspicious.

"Well, if they don't come today, we'll be charged an extra day."

"We should get going, too." Frank de LaFuente slowly pushed away from the table. "We still have a lot of unpacking to do."

"But it's still early." Evie's mother struggled to keep her brunch alive. "Why don't we at least take our drinks down by the pool? It's so nice out."

"Oh, it is." Raquel's father looked about. "But, *ay*, Vicki, it's gonna have to be another time. Kitty's right. We should get home to meet Party Rents."

"Actually," Frank de LaFuente started, "Graciela wanted to see that *talavera* in your bathroom. It's similar to the tile we want for ours. Could we take a look at it?"

"Oh, of course," Kitty Diaz smiled. "Come on over."

"And we still have some *tres leches*." Charlie looked over at Evie's father playfully. "Some nice, sweet, fattening *tres leches*. No more *pan dull*-ce, eh, Ruben?"

* * *

As the Diazes and the de LaFuentes left to cross Camino del Rio, Evie actually felt sorry for her parents. She could see the dejected looks on their faces. Their only consolation seemed to be that Dee Dee, strangely enough, stayed behind.

"I'm not leaving, Vicki," Dee Dee announced sweetly, still seated at the patio table scooping up melon salsa with hollandaise sauce. "Do you need any help? Cleaning up?"

"Oh no, Dee Dee," Evie's mother smiled weakly. "That's so nice of you. But it's not necessary. I've got Lindsay today."

"And I really want to try the *pan dulce,*" Dee Dee assured Evie's father. "I used to love going to the bakery, especially the original one on Colonia Road. Your *pan* is even better than what I had in Mexico."

Great. Evie thought. *Add one more to the list of Ruben Gomez's* culo-*kissers.*

"Nah . . ." Evie's father shook his head, but then, "*Really?*"

"Yes, really." Dee Dee smiled, assuringly.

And with that, Ruben Gomez practically tripped over himself as he rushed to the kitchen phone. He wanted to make arrangements for someone from his bakery to deliver more *pan dulce, sin manteca.*

"That is so sweet of you to say," Evie's mother told Dee Dee during her husband's phone call. "Ruben really needed to hear that."

"But I didn't just say it," Dee Dee insisted. "I meant it. I guess growing up in California, in Rio Estates, I just thought that's how all Mexican things should be. Does that make sense? Even if it's not considered *auténtica?*"

"It makes perfect sense." Evie's mother laughed as she took a seat next to Dee Dee. "Who's to say what is authentic or not? Even in Mexico, you're not gonna find a fish taco in Oaxaca that tastes like one in Ensenada, right?"

Dee Dee wrinkled her nose. "Uh, I don't really know. I don't like fish tacos."

"Oh, uh," Evie's mother didn't know what to say. "So, you must have had some fun experiences, adventures in Mexico City. I've always wanted to go there."

"Oh, you have to!" Dee Dee gushed. "People always talk about Paris or some other European place being so great and cultured and all, but nothing compares to D.F. You've never been?"

"No," Evie's mother admitted. "Before we had the girls, Ruben and I would always take trips down to Baja and then, as you know, we all went to Cabo . . . when your mother was alive." Evie's mother suddenly got a glassy look in her eyes. "We always had so much fun."

"Yeah, we did." Dee Dee winced, but managed a wistful smile. Her face softened and for a brief moment Evie saw past the blonde hair and mascara-laden lashes and caught a glimpse of the Dee Dee she remembered from when they were kids. Evie's father was right—the de LaFuentes *were* like family and Dee Dee *had* been like a sister to her. Dee Dee made for a better *Plácida Dominga* than the *Sábado Sangro* from the night before. Dee Dee and Evie's mother let out a laugh and Evie felt like an outsider. The way her mother acted toward Dee Dee—so calm and caring and attentive—reminded Evie of a side of her mother she hadn't seen in a long time. Why, Evie wondered, was it always other people who brought out the best in her parents?

"Well," Evie's mother patted Dee Dee's arm as she got up from the table, "I'd better go help Lindsay in the kitchen. It's her day off and I know she'll want to get out of here as soon as possible."

"Are you sure you don't need my help?" Dee Dee looked up.

"Oh, no, *mi'ja*. It was just so nice to catch up with you. I knew it would be good to have this brunch, right Evie?"

"Uh . . ." Evie was caught off guard. "Right."

When her mother left to join Lindsay in the kitchen, Evie realized she no longer had a buffer. It was she and Dee Dee, one-on-one.

"So." Dee Dee pulled out her cell phone and checked to see if she had messages. "It's nice to see Lindsay. Remember we used to have a crush on her son, Alfredo? He must be, like, married by now, huh?"

Who was Dee Dee trying to fool, acting all casual like last night never even happened?

"So," Evie crossed her arms firmly. "What happened at Raquel's? At the party?"

"Yeah." Dee Dee still didn't bother to look at Evie. She was using her thumbs to type out a text message. "That *Pancita* has always been so bossy and aggressive, especially to you, Evie. I don't know why she attacked me the way she did."

"Well, for one thing, you were macking on her boy."

"I was what?"

"You were flirting with her boyfriend."

"Her boyfriend?" Dee Dee looked up from her cell phone. Her eyes widened. *"¿Quién?"*

"Jose," Evie said matter-of-factly. "You know, the guy with Alex."

"I didn't know that was her boyfriend. He actually came up to me and started saying all those silly things first." Dee Dee paused for a beat. "Is . . . is Alejandro *your* boyfriend?"

"Alex? No. We're just friends. All of us, me, Raquel . . . there's another guy, too. Mondo. And," Evie added, "Raquel doesn't like being called *Pancita*."

True, Raquel had been chubby as a child, and four years later, well, what could you say? *Real Women Have Muchas Curves*?

"Oh," Dee Dee waved her hand aside, "I was only teasing. In Mexico, a little name like that would be taken as an endearment."

"Dee . . ." Evie almost corrected herself, but then continued. "We're not in Mexico. And you know what? I'm already tired of hearing about Mexico. Was Mexico so great? Was that the reason you never called? Or answered my e-mails? I mean, the whole universe doesn't revolve around Mexico. You never cared about Mexico when we were kids, growing up. Now it's all Mexico this and Mexico that."

"Well," Dee Dee went back to fidgeting with her phone. "I've *had* to care. I had no choice. And you know, it was actually nice to get away."

"Get *away*?"

"Evie," Dee Dee continued, "I hate Rio Estates. When my dad told me we were coming back, you don't know how horrible I felt. To leave my school, my friends . . ."

"Well," Evie could feel herself getting more agitated, "I am so *sorry* Rio Estates doesn't compare with the cosmopolitan life you had in D.F."

"Evie, no." Dee Dee's voice softened and she finally put her phone down. "It's just being back here, in Rio Estates, in this neighborhood. It's hard. It reminds me of . . . my mom."

Evie immediately felt horrible. "Oh, Dee, Dela, I'm sorry. I wasn't even thinking. I didn't mean it that way . . ."

"I know you didn't, it's just . . ." Dee Dee's voice got dry and sounded as though it was about to crack. "You know, I don't want to get into it, but maybe I did come on too strong last night. But I *was* excited to see you, Evie. Really." Dee Dee tried to regain her composure. "When I heard about the party I thought about all the ways I could surprise you and Raquel. I didn't know that right before the party I was going to get into a big fight with Rocio, my *novio*, and—"

"*Novio*? You're engaged?" Evie interrupted.

"Huh? Oh, no. In Mexico . . . " Dee Dee stopped herself, realizing she'd referenced Mexico again. "I mean, *novio* can also mean boyfriend." She suddenly laughed to herself. "I couldn't be engaged! My father would kill me. Remember that time I had a slumber party and Pete Galindo and all his friends came over to crash it? My dad was ready to pound them with a golf club!"

Evie laughed.

"Oh, Evie," Dee Dee said. "I'm so sorry we got off on the wrong foot. You will always be my best friend. Even in Mexico, I always, always, talked about *mi amiga mejor* in California. Really."

"Really? You're not just saying that to get Gomez points?"

"Really." Dee Dee giggled. "You are *not* your father."

Evie laughed again and then she and Dee Dee got up from their chairs and hugged. And unlike the hug from last night's party, this one was *auténtica*.

6

Monday morning, Evie decided to ride to school with Dee Dee. Raquel hadn't answered any of Evie's phone calls or text messages on Sunday evening and she wasn't feeling exactly thrilled about sharing a ride to school with her in Mondo's car. Villanueva was a good thirty minutes northeast of Rio Estates. Which would be worse? The silent treatment or a tongue-lashing from Raquel? Either one would be long and excruciating.

But as soon as Dee Dee beeped the horn of her VW Beetle five short times in a row ("*¡Qué barrio!*") and Evie ran out of the house to meet her, she immediately regretted her decision. Dee Dee's iTrip blasted *reggaetón* from the speakers. If that wasn't bad enough, the overwhelming stink of a highly fragrant rose sachet, hanging from the rearview mirror, took over the front seat. What was this? An FDS commercial?

"Hey, *chica*!" Dee Dee gave Evie's shoulder a squeeze. "*Qué* cute you look! Your skirt matches your hair."

"Oh, thanks," Evie said. She didn't think that she was wearing anything especially cute, just her silver metallic Havaianas and a batik skirt she'd found at Tilly's in the Esplanade, but she would take an early-morning compliment just as quickly as the next sophomore girl who questioned her cute quotient.

"I was so worried." Dee Dee held a lit cigarette out the driver's window. "When my dad and Graciela told me I'd be going to Villanueva I thought that I'd have to wear a uniform or something. In Mexico, you have to wear one if you go to a private school. But we can wear anything at Villanueva, huh?"

"Yeah." Evie looked over Dee Dee disapprovingly. "Anything."

From her too-tight designer denim to the super-sized hoops that practically pulled her poor earlobes past her shoulders, could Dee Dee be any more Sangro? Evie caught a glimpse of herself in the side mirror. *Could you be any more judgmental?* What if all the students at Villanueva did have to wear uniforms? They'd be sporting midnight black and *puta* pink, the school colors. ("Garter belt colors," Raquel always quipped). With a school dress code, even the Flojos would have to wear shoes every day (gross), and how long would it take for any of them to figure out who was worth each other's time? Would someone like, say, Mondo, truly be Evie's friend?

"So, what are the people like at Villy?" Dee Dee took a pull from her cigarette. "Lots of cute boys, like Alejandro?"

"Uh, not really." Alex *cute?* Evie guessed some girls might think he was. No, Evie took that back. Alex *was* a cute boy, but then again, he was *Alex*.

"He was never your boyfriend?" Dee Dee asked. "He seems to really like you."

"Oh, that's just how Alex is. He's just a friend."

Dee Dee giggled and tapped the tip of her cigarette in the car's ashtray. "In Mexico, I didn't have any male friends. As soon as I met Rocio he didn't want me hanging around other boys."

"Are you serious?" Evie asked. "I wouldn't stand for that."

"Well, you don't have to worry about it."

"Why?"

"'Cause, *Evelina*." Dee Dee bowed her head sideways at Evie. "You don't even have a man!"

Evie playfully tapped her and grinned.

"Man." Evie looked over the dashboard and backseat of Dee Dee's Beetle. "You're so lucky you got your own car. I'm really hoping when I turn sixteen and get my license that I get a car."

"Yeah, it was pretty easy for me," Dee Dee said. "I mean, I just cried and cried about leaving Rocio, and my friends, and about moving, so what could my father really do?"

Evie continued to look around Dee Dee's car and noticed that the vase on the Beetle's dashboard held a bunch of unlit incense sticks.

She ran her finger over the tips of them. "You've always liked the girly scented things."

"Yeah, I guess." Dee Dee nonchalantly took another drag

from her cigarette. "But it's also so my parents don't suspect. They would kill me if they knew I smoked. So would Rocio."

"When did you start?"

"Oh, I don't know. Maybe when I first moved to D.F.? I don't smoke too much. Really, just socially."

"Oh." Evie threw her a sideways glance. "And driving to school is a social event? Wait, when you *first* moved? Dela, you were still, like, twelve!"

"Was I?" Dee Dee played naïve.

As Dee Dee's VW Beetle exited the 101 Freeway and merged onto Highway 33, reality finally bit Evie hard . . . right in the ass. And a disturbing image popped into her head: Raquel's face, contorting in anger, getting ready to shout at Evie. Evie was going to *school* with *Dee Dee.* What could she be thinking? This was so not gonna fly with Raquel, a card-carrying member of the grudgeholder's guild. Right between her fake ID and jambacard, you could actually see a laminate that logged long, hard, residual resentment. The last thing Evie wanted were personalized squares on Raquel's shit list. After twelve punch outs who knew what could happen?

"So," Dee Dee started as though she had just read Evie's mind, "have you talked to Raquel since yesterday?"

"Nuh-uh," Evie admitted. "I called her twice and sent her a text message, but I haven't heard back from her . . . yet."

"Yet?" Dee Dee questioned. "It'll probably be a while. You know what a grudgeholder Raquel can be."

Evie looked out toward the lemon groves that lined Highway 33. She definitely was not ready to make a grand entrance at Villanueva with Dee Dee. Maybe she could fake sick and ask Dee Dee to drive her back home. Suggest they both ditch and head out for a day at Sea Street? *Hmmm*. That was something Raquel would be down with, but with Dee Dee? She wasn't so sure. Could she ask Dee Dee to drop her off on the edge of Ventura Road so she could walk up to school by herself?

Highway 33 soon turned into Ventura Road, a two-lane highway lined with hand-painted signs advertising local produce and homemade apple cider. "Wow," Dee Dee observed as they drove through Ventura Road. "Nothing here has changed. It's still the same as when we came up here as little kids. Remember when my mom took us horseback riding?" she asked.

"Oh yeah," Evie said. "That was always so fun. Oh my God, remember that horse, the white one you always got? What was his name?"

"*Her* name was Blanca."

"Oh, right. *Duh*. She was so sweet," Evie said. "Oh, except that time when she bucked Raquel off. Ew, remember that?"

"Ooh." Dee Dee scrunched her face. "Yeah, that was bad.

"Yeah," Evie went on. "Raquel's hated horses or anything outdoorsy like that since then. Rocky couldn't believe it. She really threw Raquel off—I mean, right on her ass—but she didn't even cry or anything."

"Yeah," Dee Dee remembered. "That's right."

"In fact," Evie continued, "now that I think about it, I've never seen Rocky cry. Ever."

"Really?" Dee Dee took another long, slow pull off her cigarette and looked over at Evie. "Never?"

"Uh, no," Evie said. "I don't think so."

"Hmmm . . ."

"What?" Evie asked.

"Nothing."

Evie realized they were already driving up the main road to Villanueva.

Dee Dee put out her cigarette in the car's ashtray. "Wow." She looked ahead. "I almost forgot how beautiful Villy was."

"Beautiful?" Evie spent most of her waking hours stuck at Villanueva. To her, Sea Street was beautiful, her cozy bed on a Sunday morning was beautiful, even the cheap-looking, white-plastic dome that capped the Pacific View Mall was beautiful. Any place was more beautiful to her than *school.*

"Yeah," Dee Dee said. "In D.F. you don't get all this scenery, the fields, the oak trees, *y más*. Everything is so cramped and on top of itself. When my mom used to bring us up here to the stables, we'd always pass Villanueva. Who knew we'd actually be going to school here together?"

"Not me," Evie admitted. "With my GPA, I'd have been lucky to get into a C school."

"So how did you get into Villy?"

"Let's just say," Evie confessed, "my father donated a *lot* of dough."

"I'm guessing not the same kind he uses for his *pan dulce.*" Dee Dee smiled.

"Exactly."

"¡Ay!" Dee Dee suddenly cried out. *"Día de los Muertos?"*

"Huh?" Evie asked. "What are you talking about?"

"There." Dee Dee pointed her chin toward the front of the school.

Evie looked up and recognized two seniors, Amelia Cleary and Laura Simon, from student council. They were on the ledge of the school's main marquee, straightening out the large, black block letters that announced Villanueva's upcoming annual Day of the Dead celebration and dance.

"Oh, yeah," Evie didn't see what Dee Dee's alarm was about. "They have it every year."

"I can't believe you're going to have a dance for *Día de los Muertos.*" Dee Dee giggled to herself. *"¡Qué chiste!"*

"Why is that so funny?" Evie asked.

"In Mexico we wouldn't have a school *dance* for *Día de los Muertos.* It's sorta weird."

"Why is it so weird?" Evie felt defensive even though she didn't really go to the dances. "We know tradition, but that doesn't mean we don't know how to have fun."

Sure, Villanueva had its own spin on *Día de los Muertos,* and maybe it wasn't the same way *Día de los Muertos* was celebrated in Mexico. Students were encouraged to dress as their favorite dearly departed, which could be a beloved great uncle who died from heartbreak or a famous playwright who committed suicide after a career-killing review. But nobody at Villanueva was ever that romantic or original. Everyone just went as either Kurt Cobain or Marilyn Monroe.

"Of course," Dee Dee tried to explain, "it's just that in Mexico, we have church ceremonies, processions . . . to *really* reflect on the holiday, you know, to remember and honor the dead. By November second, the streets are flooded with *cempasuchitl.*"

"Zempa-what?" Evie asked.

"Marigolds." Dee Dee smiled as she drove through the rows and rows of parked cars of the student parking lot. "*Ay, Dios,* we are never going to find a space."

"Welcome to California." Evie smirked. "Or should I say, welcome *back.*"

Only a small percentage of Villanueva's student body had resident status; the rest were day students, like Evie and Dee Dee. So most students who owned a car wanted the opportunity to flaunt their identity, even if that meant a D.A.R.E. (Drug Abuse Resistance Education) sticker on the back bumper. "The best way," Mondo claimed, "to throw the cops off."

Dee Dee finally found an empty spot and pulled in. But when Evie looked over, she saw that Dee Dee had parked her Beetle dangerously close to Mondo's Marauder and Alex's truck.

Evie could see the three of them—Mondo, Jose, and Alex—leaning casually against Alex's truck, hanging out before first period like they always did. Evie immediately regretted that she hadn't returned Alex's calls. She could have used an ally right about now. He had called two more times on Sunday and he sounded so concerned in his message, but her pride wouldn't allow her to phone him back. Saturday night's fight was the first official argument they'd ever had and she wondered if it had bothered him as much as it did her.

Evie got out of Dee Dee's Beetle and couldn't help but notice Raquel. She was stretched out in the front seat of Mondo's Marauder, casually twirling strands of her hair with her fingers and reading something. Was it just *Kerrang!*, or could it be a DIY manual on how to snuff out a former friend?

Evie kept her head down as she grabbed her backpack from the backseat. Her plan was to pull Dee Dee the opposite way, around the other row of cars, to avoid meeting up with Raquel and the other Flojos. But as soon as Dee Dee got out of her Beetle, she started walking right in their direction.

"Hey," Evie quickly tugged at her arm. "Let me take you the scenic route."

But it was too late. Dee Dee had already seen Alex.

"Alejandro!" she called out. "Hey!"

What could Evie do but follow? Alex looked over and seemed genuinely confused to see Evie with Dee Dee. *Yeah, I know.* Evie felt sheepish. *I gave you hell at the welcome-back party and now look who called the tortilla flat.*

"Hey, Alex," Evie said, apprehensively.

"Hey, Blue's." Alex smiled. So maybe Saturday night's war of the words had not been on his mind.

"Heeey." Mondo gave Dee Dee the once-over. "Who's the new *fresita*?

"Oh, Mondo, *please*," Evie struggled to get her backpack on. "This is my old friend, Dee, I mean, Dela. She just moved back from Mexico City." She then looked over at Raquel and lowered her voice. "She's Raquel's friend too."

Raquel heard her name and popped her head up to look over the Marauder's dashboard. She squinted her eyes and when she saw Dee Dee and Evie, she immediately got out of the car.

"Yeah." Raquel slammed the car door with her hip. "She's old, but she ain't my friend."

"Raquel." Dee Dee tilted her head innocently. "What have I ever done to you?"

"Oh," Raquel said slowly. "So now my name is Raquel?"

"Oh, yeah," Jose smiled. "Mondo, check it out. Raquel used to be called *Pancita*!" He pinched Raquel's side and she immediately slapped his hand away.

"Yeah." Mondo looked Raquel over with a half smile. "I can see that."

"Dude," Jose laughed, "that's exactly what *I* said!"

"Shut up, you two. You're such idiots." Raquel turned her attention back to Dee Dee. "Dee Dee, don't you have a nail to file?"

"Raquel—," Evie started.

"Don't you have one to pull out of your ass?" Dee Dee shot back.

"Oooh," Mondo said. "These kitties have claws."

"Yeah." Jose rubbed his palms together. "Maybe they'll kiss when they make up!"

"That must have been some party Saturday night." Mondo looked Dee Dee over again. "Sorry I missed it."

"You didn't miss nothing." Raquel put her arm around Jose protectively. "And there's nothing to see here. Just another sloppy Sang-*ho*."

"A *what*?" Dee Dee raised her eyebrows.

"Raquel," Evie finally stepped in. "Come on. Please. We used to all be friends."

"'Used to' is the key word," Raquel bit back.

"That's actually two words," Jose put in.

"How about these two words?" Dee Dee looked at Raquel. "Fuck *you*!"

"Fuck *me*?" Raquel spat. "Hey, you're the one waltzing in with your blondie locks and your little *lenses fakos*, pretending to be a friend. But you know what? We didn't miss you, *Dee Dee*, and we definitely don't need you."

"Well." Dee Dee didn't say anything for a moment. She finally looked at Evie. "Well, thanks for the welcome wagon. I can't say you didn't try." She then looked at Alex and then huffed away.

"Dela," Alex called after her. "Wait!"

"Oh, don't try and be all Mr. Boy Scout," Raquel said. "What, you got a complimentary BJ when you took her out to Sea Street after the party?"

Mondo looked at Alex with a wide grin on his face. "Dude, you took *her* to Sea Street? After the party?" He held up his hand for a high five, but Alex didn't reciprocate.

"Can you be any uncooler?" Alex looked at Raquel.

"Actually, yeah. I can." Raquel smiled. "You want to time me?"

"You guys, stop it!" Evie yelled. "God! Why are you acting so lame?" She glared at Raquel and then looked after Dee Dee.

"Dela," she called out. "Wait up!"

"Yeah, Evie," Raquel smirked. "Go after your little best friend."

Evie looked at Raquel. She started to open her mouth, but didn't bother when she realized she had no clue what to say. Evie held the straps of her backpack and sprinted after Dee Dee, through the parking lot and up the stone steps of Del Norte Hall. By the time she had pushed by all the other students and reached Dee Dee at the top, she was out of breath. "Dela," she huffed. "Wait. Please!"

Dee Dee turned around. Her face and neck were flushed with tension.

"*What?*" Dee Dee snapped.

"Well, for one thing,"—puffs of air came out from Evie's nostrils—"you're going the wrong way. Unless your first class is boys' P.E."

"Huh?" Dee Dee looked around Del Norte Hall. She looked flustered and confused.

"Dee Dee," Evie started. "Look, try not to trip. Raquel's just being a c-bag. You know it, I know it, *everybody* knows it." Evie was surprised how rational she sounded when inside her stomach was churning. "It's just . . . look, let me just take you to the ad building. It's way on the other side, but I can help you get set up and we'll get you an official class schedule."

"Is there any way I can officially not have *Pancita* in any of my classes?" Dee Dee exhaled. "In my life?"

"Dee, uh, Dela, you gotta stop calling her that. You are only making it worse."

Evie led Dee Dee down Del Norte Hall, the main hall of Villanueva, among all the other students. It was already October, the second month of a new school year, but everyone's clothing still exuded that freshly cut tag smell. Most of the students slugged along, talking to friends or entranced by their iPods. When the first bell rang, everyone scattered. Soon it was just Dee Dee and Evie walking down the empty hall. The *tap tap tap* of Dee Dee's high-heel boots and the flip-flopping flop of Evie's flojos reverberated from the tile and off the walls, making it very clear that they were alone. Neither of them said anything to each other.

Evie glanced over at Dee Dee. Under her perfectly patted beige foundation, Evie could detect creases of strain on Dee Dee's face.

Evie took a deep breath and continued to lead her to the ad building. Maybe it would be good if Villanueva had a dress code, despite what Dee Dee thought. Something like California Casual meets High Drama, a lightweight, knit blend of steel armor. That would be perfect, Evie figured, because it was obvious that Raquel had already declared war.

7

Dee Dee was right. Villanueva was a nice-looking campus. If anything, it looked more like a Spanish-style five-star resort hotel than a mere high school. Small classes were held in charming stucco bungalows with red brick tile roofs and just about every window had a panoramic view of the Topa Topa mountain range. Villanueva also boasted an Olympic-sized swimming pool (a three-million-dollar renovation since the San Fernando earthquake of 1971) and beautiful, beautiful guests (er, students) checked in from all over the world. Headmaster Covarrubias took pride in a school that reflected "a well-rounded and diverse student body that didn't tolerate intolerance." At least, that's what the catalog claimed.

During lunchtime students were free to come and go as they pleased, but since Villanueva sat tucked so deep in the southeast hills of the county, and had only one road that led to one town that led to one Wendy's, most students just remained on campus. The thirty-minute trip took too long for a forty-minute lunch period. And really, how many square-shaped burgers can one person eat in a school year?

Evie calculated that between her first class, Spanish II, and fifth-period lunch, she had exactly 238 minutes to organize and strategize. How could she continue to be friendly with Dee Dee while not causing more of a rift with Raquel? Dee Dee, her past, had caught up with Raquel, her present. Could they all have a future together? She looked up at the classroom's clock. She now had roughly 235 minutes. Evie yanked harder at her blue locks.

"Hey, Evie." Stephanie Elizondo, another sophomore who sat next to Evie in Spanish, looked over. "You fixed your hair."

"Oh, yeah," Evie replied. She didn't bother to say thank you. After all, Stephanie didn't say it looked good, just that it was "fixed."

"Who was the girl I saw you with this morning?" Stephanie started to open *Dos Mundos,* their textbook. "Is she new?"

"Oh, yeah, her name's Dee—" Evie stopped herself. "I mean, Dela."

"Oh, is she, like, an exchange student?"

"Exchange student?" Evie frowned. "No, she's from Mexico. I mean, she's from here. She used to be my neighbor, but she's been living in Mexico City for the last four years. We used to be best friends."

"Oh, she's really pretty."

"Uh-huh," Evie said. "That's what *everyone* thinks."

Everyone, Evie thought, but especially Mondo. Evie would have to put him in his place before things got out of hand. She kept an eye on Mr. McDaniel-Galván as she pulled out her cell to text Mondo.

U r a perv. B Nce!

But Mondo, who lived for texting, didn't text back once the whole rest of the morning.

* * *

By lunchtime, Evie didn't have any big ideas or well-thought-out plans on how to make peace between Raquel and Dee Dee. She slowly trudged down to Veranda Hall, where the majority of lockers were assigned to sophomores. This fall semester, Evie didn't have any classes with Raquel, but they always met Alex, Jose, and Mondo for lunch under Juniper's Tree. Juniper's Tree was a humongous oak with a commemorative plaque that claimed that Father Juniper Serra himself, along with local Chumash Indians, had actually planted the tree back in 1782. It was the same plaque that Jose put out his cigarette butts on and near where Mondo had demostrated community pride by carving R x E, as in Rio Estates, on the ancient trunk. So much for historical preservation and *respeto*.

But after the morning's parking lot incident, Evie was sure

she wouldn't be so welcome at Juniper's Tree. Besides, would she even want to go?

She found Dee Dee and Alex waiting for her at her locker. She was relieved to see that Dee Dee didn't seem as jolted as she had earlier. She was chatting enthusiastically with Alex, who was propped against the lockers. He had one thumb hooked inside the front pocket of his jeans. He held his books in the other hand. He leaned toward Dee Dee and seemed to be listening intently with a big smile on his face. And it hit Evie: *Wow, he* is *into her.* Of course, Alex was into girls, and when he was with Mondo and Jose, he could mack like crazy. But as long as she had known Alex—well, all of last school year and over the summer—he had never had a girlfriend. But now, after remembering that they did go to Sea Street, alone, after the party, and seeing the way he was with Dee Dee, Evie thought maybe that was going to change. She really didn't know how she felt about that but she did know that her cheeks grew hot at the sight of them.

"Hey, Blue's." Alex straightened up as soon as Evie appeared. "We were just waiting for you. I still gotta drop my books off, but I'll see you two at the tree, yeah?"

"Claro, ¿por qué no?" It was Dee Dee who answered, as she squeezed his arm. "Thank you again, Alejandro, for all your help."

As Alex had walked away, Evie thought, *at the tree*? Was he kidding? Was his brain logged from an early surf session that morning? God, Raquel was right. Dudes can be dense.

"So," Evie said as she turned the lock on her locker. "How's everything working out?"

"Everything is going great!" Dee Dee held her spiral notebook to her chest. Evie could see the names and numbers of a few students already scrawled across the back. When Evie first started Villanueva she had felt incredibly lucky when Raquel teamed up with Jose. It gave her three more names to add to her cell directory—Jose, Mondo, and Alex, an instant doubling of social contacts.

"I have Alejandro in two of my classes," Dee Dee continued. "He is *so* sweet, really helpful. And one of my teachers," she looked over her course sheet, "a Mr. Guereca, actually lived in the Polanco District, my old neighborhood. *Qué chido, ¿no?*"

"Yeah, cool." But Evie couldn't really pay attention. All she could do was worry about lunch and how that was going to pan out. "So, since it's so nice out," she started, "I was thinking we could grab some grub and head out to the Art Den." It was the only secluded area of campus she could think of, occupied only with horrible student renditions of Che Guevara and the Ventura coastline.

"The Art Den?" Dee Dee asked. "We're not going to meet Alex at the tree?"

"Nah, the tree is so played out." Evie crammed her books in her locker.

It was only the second month of school, but already it was cluttered with issues of *SG*, Raquel's *Kerrang!* magazines, and useless accessories from her former long hair days. "It'll be basically him and Mondo gabbing gears."

"Gabbing *what?"*

"Talking cars," Evie said. "The Art Den's our student art garden. It's really peaceful. You'll love it."

"Yeah." Dee Dee put her forearm next to Evie's as they walked toward the cafeteria together. "I want to work on my tan. I am so pale! That's one thing I missed in D.F., going to the beach. Remember we went so much as kids?"

"Oh, yeah," Evie remembered. "And Raquel had that amazing beach umbrella? The orange and white one that her father got in Rosarito Beach?"

Dee Dee didn't respond. Instead, she focused on looking around the quad at the other students, taking it all in. More than a handful of interested guys rubbernecked at her while, Evie noticed, more than a handful of annoyed girlfriends tapped the back of their heads for realignment.

"Hey, Evie." Robert Karimi was walking toward them, but his eyes were on Dee Dee. Rob was a senior and rarely talked to Evie, but this afternoon he had all the time in the world.

"Is this your friend from Mexico?" he asked as he adjusted his square-frame glasses. "Alex mentioned her to me."

"Yeah, Dee—Dela," Evie started. "But she's actually from here. She just lived in Mexico." She introduced him to Dee Dee. "This is Robert Karimi. He runs the student TV show."

"Oh," Dee Dee smiled and shook his hand. "*Mucho gusto.* You have your own TV show? *Qué chido.*"

"Just a small one." Rob tried to play it down, but Evie could tell his ego was about to take off. "It's local, but it's the number one student-run show in the tri-counties. You should come on some time." Rob looked at Evie, uncomfortably. "You know, so, we could, uh, get her perspective on what it's like being a student from Mexico, that uh, used to live here."

You are so stretching.

"So." Rob smiled coyly."Your name's Deedela?"

"No," Dee Dee smiled back. "My name's Dela. Dela de LaFuente." She looked over at Evie. "Evie just gets sloppy."

"Yeah, well let me know if you need any help with anything, like a tour guide or something."

"Oh!" Dee Dee squeezed his arm. "You are *too* sweet."

Evie didn't remember anyone being so willing and helpful when she was a freshman, navigating the large campus, which at the time appeared totally overwhelming. She quickly checked herself. *Don't* hate!

As soon as they left Rob and walked into the cafeteria, Evie and Dee Dee were assaulted with central air and G-rated hip-hop. Evie surveyed the scene. She didn't see any of the other Flojos around and because it was a nice day (*duh,* California), all of the students were outside. That is, except for one group: the Sangros. They were at their usual table, at the far end of the cafeteria, in the corner. Alejandra, as usual, was the ringleader of *chismeando*. She sat up on the cafeteria bench, while the other Sangros—Natalia, Fabiola, and Xiomara—sat hypnotized by her. Last year Raquel had nicknamed their table "the Stable." "They sit around like a bunch of horses, preening and combing their manes," Raquel had said. "And doesn't Fabiola have a big ol' ass, just like a horse?"

"Oh, God," Evie lowered her voice to Dee Dee as they started to pass the Sangro Stable. "You have to watch these girls. They—"

"¡Ay, Dios mío!" Dee Dee suddenly cried out. "Alejandra?"

Huh?

Alejandra looked up at Dee Dee and actually squealed. *"¡Ay, chica!"* Then all seeming six feet of her rose from the Stable. *"¡¿Qué onda, mujer?!"*

She gave Dee Dee a double air-kiss as she hugged her. "I thought you said you didn't know which school you'd be attending." She slapped Dee Dee's arm. "Why didn't you shoot me a thread, *puta*?"

"Don't be mad," Dee Dee pleaded playfully. "*I* didn't even know what was going on. Seriously. But I'm here now. Right? *Mira.*" She put her arm around Evie. "You must know Evie."

Evie wondered if there was any way she could morph herself into the cafeteria's linoleum floor. Anything so she wouldn't have to be a part of this Divas de D.F. reunion.

"Yeah." Alejandra looked over Evie and then back to the other Sangros, who smirked in unison, tilted heads and all.

"We know Evie." Alejandra leaned over and ran her hand quickly through the top of Evie's hair. "*La Loca* with the blue hair. Where are your friends, *Loca? ¿Dónde están los otros Flojos?*"

"The who?" Dee Dee asked as Evie jerked away from Alejandra.

"*Los Flojos,*" Alejandra repeated.

"The Lazies?" Dee Dee asked Evie. "What is she talking about?"

"Oh," Evie started slowly. "She just means me and Raquel and, you know, Jose and—"

"But why are you called the Lazies?" Dee Dee covered her mouth and giggled. "What are you, like, a gang?"

"No," Evie tried to explain. "*Flojos* 'cause of our flip-flops. Remember when we were kids, we called them flow-joes?" She lifted her foot and waggled her silver metallic Havaianas in front of Dee Dee. "Remember?" But as she explained, it suddenly all seemed so juvenile to her.

"Ay, ¡qué naco!" Dee Dee clapped her hands. "That's right!"

"So." Evie tried to sound calm and composed. "How do you know Alejandra?"

Dee Dee linked arms with Alejandra. "From Mexico. Her father is VP of U.N.A.M." She looked up at Alejandra and grinned. "He helped my dad get the position at Channel Islands. She's the reason I'm here!" Dee Dee playfully squeezed her arm. "Thank you, Alejandra!"

Of course. Alejandra did say she might be interning with Dee Dee's dad at Channel Islands. How could Evie be so *tonta*?

"So, Dela." Alejandra turned her full attention back to Dee Dee. "You must sit with us." She patted the cafeteria bench. "You have to meet my friends. *Otras chicas de D.F.*"

"¡Ay, muy chido!" Dee Dee looked at the girls and quickly took a seat at the table. "You don't mind, do you, Evie?"

"But I thought you wanted to work on your tan!" Evie asked.

"Blah!" She waved her hand in the air. *"Ay, no quiero trabajar hoy. Ni siquiera en mi bronceado."*

The Sangros all giggled, throwing their heads back in synchronized precision and then immediately smoothing their hair back into place. Evie didn't understand the joke or the translation. Dee Dee didn't want to work today? Not even on her tan? What was so enormously funny about that? And since when did Dee Dee decide to break out with the Spanish V? Yes, it was the perfect time to bail on El Stable.

"Hey." Evie didn't take a seat, but rather looked around and placed her hand flat on her belly. "So, I'm gonna go get something to eat. I'm starving."

"Yeah, yeah," Dee Dee answered distractedly. "Go get some *comida.* I'll be there in a bit."

"Yeah, why don't you get us something too, while you're up?" Natalia said. "Don't they sell your dad's *pan dulce* in the vending machine?"

"Yeah," Alejandra added, mocking Evie. "Or does he own the vending machines? Like maybe all *four* vending machines?"

More laughter.

As Evie left, her face burned with embarrassment. Who

did the Sangros think they were, making fun of her? And how could Dee Dee be so flippant and naïve? Raquel would *never* allow them to talk to her that way.

Evie escaped to the salad bar. Unlike most of the architectural design at Villanueva, the salad bar was not Spanish style. It was actually constructed like an idealized California surf shack, complete with bamboo siding and a grass roof. The selections were also stereotypical Cali—lots of fruit, greens, and sprouts—but Evie's choice for comfort? Mini meatballs and shredded orange cheese stuffed in taco shells. She quickly got a plate and picked two shells from the metal tray.

"Nice friends you got there."

Evie looked up and saw Raquel. She was on the other side of the salad bar, picking croutons directly from the bar with her fingers and popping them into her mouth. She didn't look at Evie, but just glared over at the Stable.

"Raquel—," Evie started.

"I've been watching the whole thing." Raquel spoke slowly between bites. "It's so obvious that you used me just as a fill-in for Dee Dee. As soon as she moved away, I was 'suddenly' your new best friend." She used her fingers to mimic quotes when she said *suddenly*.

"What?" Evie couldn't believe what she was hearing. "That's so not true."

"Even Jose agreed with me."

"Raquel . . ." Evie was losing her patience. "Why do you

always have to have Jose validate things about me? About us? What, like he's some expert on, like, human behavior?"

"What are you saying?" Raquel finally looked at Evie. "That he's stupid?"

"No, I'm just saying—"

"You know what, Evie?" Raquel clutched the strap of her shoulder bag tightly, distressing the distressed leather even more. She faced Evie. "It doesn't even matter what you *say* because you've been *showing* what a lousy friend you really are . . . at the party, at your mother's little brunch, and now today. You show up to school with *her*? How do you think that makes me feel?"

"Raquel, she asked me if I needed a ride. What was I supposed to say? It's her first day of school and the way you just took off yesterday, I didn't think I had a ride with you and Mondo. You never called me back. I called you twice last night."

"Why should I have called you back?" Raquel huffed. "You know, Evie, yesterday we agreed, *agreed*, that we would have each other's back. You said that she was not the friend we used to know. But as soon as she showed up at your house, batting her plastic blues, you fell for it. Just like always."

"Fell for *what*, exactly?"

"Evie, she's been this way since we were little kids. She always had to get her way, she always had to have your attention. I was always the odd one out and you never cared."

"Oh my God, Raquel, what are you even saying? And if you wanna talk about the odd man out, I mean, what am *I*? It's always you and Jose, or Jose and you. *Or,* it's you, Jose, and Mondo and I'm just tagging along. Besides, you haven't even gotten to know Dee Dee."

"Why should I?" Raquel clenched her bag strap still tighter, her fingers revealing more tension and strain. "Evie, people don't change. But you know what? I don't know why I even care if you prefer Dee Dee over me."

"Who said I prefer Dee Dee over you?" Evie asked. "Who? Jose?"

But Raquel wasn't listening. She turned sharply away from Evie and stormed off, almost shoulder-slamming Alex, who was approaching both of them.

"Whoa." Alex looked after Raquel as she pushed by him to leave. "Looks like you're up to your elbows in suds."

"It seems that way," Evie sadly agreed. It *was* all becoming a soap opera. She was tempted to call out after Raquel, but what was the use?

"You know how Raquel can be," Alex said comfortingly. "You want me to wait for you?"

"Nah," Evie half-smiled. "I'm not that hungry." She dumped her empty taco shells in the nearby trash and nervously scratched the side of her neck. "I gotta study for a test anyway. I'm gonna hit the library."

"The library?" Alex looked out the cafeteria's windows. "On a day like this?"

Evie looked up at him. "Alex, I have my whole life to work, even on my tan."

"Huh?"

"Nothing." Evie patted him on his shoulder. "Just go out to the tree. I'll meet up with you later." Of course, she had no intention of doing so.

"Are you sure?" he asked.

"Totally." She tried to brush it off. "*No problema.*"

But it was a *problema*. It was her big *problema*. She could tell Raquel was angry, but that didn't give her an excuse to act like such an outright c-bag. What was Raquel thinking? She and Evie had been best friends for years; the fact that Dee Dee was back in the picture didn't take away from that. Besides, if she remembered right, it was *Raquel* who started it all, by making fun of Dee Dee's blue contacts at the party.

Evie looked over at Dee Dee, who was now laughing it up with Alejandra and the other Sangros, as if *they* were the old best friends finally reunited. She definitely didn't want to go back and intrude on that little *comadreanda*. She looked around the cafeteria once more. *Nadie*. Nobody she really wanted to hang with for the remaining thirty minutes of lunch.

Maybe she really would go to the library, she thought, and maybe she would get a book on Mexico and see for herself just what was so "*muy chido*" about all things south of the border. But then again, she thought, looking over at the Sangros, maybe she wouldn't.

8

Evie tried to remember how the battle between the Sangros and Flojos had even started. As a freshman, Raquel had heard that Alejandra had been with Jose at some Sangro party, just a month before she, herself, hooked up with him. Jose had completely denied the whole thing, claiming it was just an ego-driven rumor that Alejandra had started. But according to Jose, Alejandra was hot for him; always throwing looks his way, leaning her body over his desk to ask a simple question in class, seductively nibbling the end of her pencil while her eyes burned a hole in the zipper of his pants. These candid reports from Jose drove Raquel crazy, of course. She immediately issued a threat to Jose, Evie, and all the Flojos: If any of them ever associated with Alejandra, or any of her fellow slutty Sangros, there would consequences. And Evie, being a wide-eyed freshman—but, more importantly, Raquel's best friend—agreed.

* * *

After their episode in the cafeteria, Raquel continued to ignore Evie's calls and text messages. On Wednesday, Evie decided to call Raquel at home, on the land line, one last time. But she was curtly told by the Diazes' housekeeper, Vanessa, that Raquel was *"ocupada."*

Evie didn't believe her. She could hear the Hidden Hand blasting in the background. Since when did Vanessa do her housecleaning to political heavy metal?

Evie also soon discovered that Raquel must have enforced a talk-block on Jose and Mondo. Whenever Evie text-messaged "Sea St 2day?" to either of them, her messages went unanswered. Suddenly Evie felt like she couldn't even go to Sea Street anymore. Like Raquel had said, Sea Street was Flojo zone and after a few hours of surf lessons, she'd only have to paddle ashore to deal with Raquel and her newly appointed velvet-rope henchmen—Mondo and Jose. *"You can glance at Ms. Diaz, but do not speak, touch, or look her directly in the eyes. Keep your eyes drawn down at all times." Mucho* bummer.

Alex was not fazed by the Raquel-induced drama. He was, however, concerned that Evie was going to give up her interest in learning how to surf.

"How are you ever gonna learn?" he asked on the phone one night that week. "You gonna be like everyone else in California, with the old-school Señor Lopez pullover and that texturing surf paste in your hair."

"I don't wear surf paste!" Evie patted the top of her hair. Was it that noticeable?

"You might as well." Alex clicked his tongue.

"Why can't we go somewhere else?" Evie asked.

"We can try somewhere else if you want," Alex suggested, halfheartedly. "But Sea Street has the best break and baby sets for beginners like you. But if you are so afraid of Raquel . . ."

"I'm not afraid of Raquel," Evie insisted, if only to hear herself say it.

Yes, Evie was, in a way, afraid of Raquel. But thankfully Alex didn't bring it up again. And so the opportunity for a surf lesson fell by the wayside and her expensive long board, shaped by the one and only Max, collected dust bunnies in the corner of her room.

* * *

Days passed and Evie and Raquel continued to avoid each other. And, because Jose and Mondo followed suit, she didn't have a ride home.

Evie started to wait for Dee Dee after school to get a ride back to Rio Estates and as they walked out to the student parking lot, she would always try to make it look as though they were engaged in super-heavy conversation. But out of the corner of her eye, she couldn't help but watch the Flojos prepping for Sea Street, remembering a time when she'd been right there with them. Alex would remove his long board from Mondo's car, where he had it locked up during the day, and place it in the back of his truck. Raquel would tie up her long hair and apply Hawaiian Tropic to her face and arms. And then they would all drive off as if it had always been that way, as if they were forgetting nothing and no one. Each time she saw them pull away, she felt her stomach sink. She was losing her friends, and she was losing access to the one thing she had actually begun to feel motivated about—surfing. Would she *ever* step into *líquido*?

* * *

But as Evie soon found out, she wasn't the only one jonesing to get all up in water.

"I *have* to learn to swim," Dee Dee insisted as they were leaving Villanueva after school one Friday. "You won't *believe* what happened today in swim class."

"I didn't know you were taking swimming," Evie said.

"I got transferred in." Dee Dee pointed her car's remote to her Beetle and clicked the alarm off. She and Evie got in. "And guess who was there? In my class?"

"Who?"

"Pancita."

"Oh yeah?" Evie tried to sound nonchalant, but her stomach was turning. She remembered what Alex had said about her being in the middle of a soap opera and she didn't want to make things any worse. "Hey." She unzipped the side pocket of her backpack. "You mind if I hook up my iPod?"

"You don't like Don Omar?" Dee Dee frowned.

"No, it's just I'm sorta in the mood for something else."

"Okay. I guess." But Dee Dee didn't sound too happy as Evie unplugged her iTrip from the radio deck. "So, yeah," she continued, "Miss Riley brings me in and tells me to stay on the steps, until she can work with me and there's *Pancita, also* on the shallow end."

"Yeah." Evie smiled. "I'm sure she was crying cramps." She knew Raquel's gym excuses all too well.

"Exactly," Dee Dee nodded. "All whining of cramps *y más* and then when I come in, she suddenly feels better. Enough to tell me, in front of everyone, that I look like a prostitute in my bathing suit!"

"A prostitute? She actually called you a prostitute?"

"Well, she said, 'So where's your pole and plastic heels?' In front of *everyone*."

Evie couldn't help but laugh, but immediately stopped when Dee Dee threw her a look.

"It wasn't funny, Evie," Dee Dee said. "Everyone laughed at me. Then I told her that she could only dream of wearing a bikini like mine and then—"

"Wait, you wore a *bikini* to swim class?"

"Well, it was more of just a two-piece. Miss Riley said our

suits only had to be a solid color. She didn't say one piece or two. Why?"

"Nothing," Evie looked out the window so Dee Dee wouldn't see her smirking. "Go on."

"So, I told her, 'Poor *Pancita*, Americans have such a problem with their weight. Maybe that's why your man is always eyeing me.'"

"You said that?" She twirled her iPod wheel till she found Priestess and cranked up the volume. *Nice.*

"Yeah, 'cause it's true, Evie. That Jose *es un catrín*. Mondo too." Dee Dee pulled out onto Ventura Road and talked louder over the music. "Did you know that they are *both* always hitting on me?"

"Who, Jose?"

"Yes, *Jose*. Eyeew, with that ugly spike in his chin. *Qué cochino.*"

"Oh, he's just stupid," Evie said. "You gotta just ignore him."

"Well, *Pancita's* gonna find out sooner or later," Dee Dee predicted. "So anyway, before I know it, she just starts slamming water at me. I mean, not just splashing, like when we were kids playing Marco Polo or something. She was totally out of control. Thank God Miss Riley came over and made her get out of the pool. That *Pancita está loca.*"

"Slamming water into you? Are you sure you aren't exaggerating?"

"No, ask anyone. She totally freaked out."

"I dunno, Dela. Even for Raquel that sounds a little bit crazy."

It was all Evie wanted to say. She didn't want to get into it with Dee Dee.

"I am not exaggerating," Dee Dee insisted. "And I cannot bear another day sharing the kiddie end with her. I *have* to learn how to swim." She checked her side mirror and sped up on Highway 33. "*What* are we listening to? It sounds like Marilyn Manson on crack."

"It's Priestess," Evie bragged in a rock-snob manner. "They're from *el otro lado*."

"Oh," Dee Dee suddenly looked interested. "*Mexico*?"

"No," Evie smiled. "Canada, the *other otro lado*."

Dee Dee shook her head and rolled her eyes. "So, anyway, I asked Alejandro over tonight. He is so sweet. He's going to teach me to swim."

"You asked Alex over? To your house?" *She* hadn't even been to Dee Dee's house yet.

"Yeah, around seven," Dee Dee said. "You should come over too. My parents are going to the opening of the Hispanic Heritage Museum in Santa Barbara, so we'll have the whole house to ourselves."

When did she and Alex get so chummy? Sure, he had offered to teach Dee Dee to swim at the welcome-back party, but she didn't think he was really serious. She felt a little left out. Dee Dee had already asked Alex, knowing they would have "the whole house" to themselves. Evie was just an afterthought.

"So, Dela," Evie asked, continuing to twirl her iPod's click wheel, not really looking for anything else in particular, "how are things with you and Rocio?"

"Rocio?" Dee Dee looked over. "*Bien.* Why?"

"Just wondering. You haven't really mentioned him lately."

"Well, I've just been busy," Dee Dee said. "I mean, it has been my first week of school, but I still e-mail him every day and we talk every Friday night, and—" She looked over at Evie suspiciously. "Wait, what is this all about? Do you think I like Alejandro?"

"No, not at all." Evie felt caught. "I was just asking."

"Evie, I *have* a boyfriend, back in D.F. Sounds like someone is a little *posesiva,* no?"

Evie shook her head quickly, "Me? With Alex? Please!"

"Evie," Dee Dee started cautiously. "Don't take this wrong . . ."

Uh-oh. Here we go again.

"But have you had a boyfriend yet?"

"I've had boyfriends." Evie got more defensive.

"I'm not talking Dean Paulger in fourth grade. I'm talking like a real boyfriend who you actually go out with."

"No," Evie said. "I know what you mean. I actually met a guy, just this summer and—"

"What guy?"

"Well, if you let me finish." Evie tried to think. What was ShaggyMA's real name? What *did* the MA stand for? For all she knew he could be Shaggy Married Already or Shaggy Mal-Adjusted. Or worse, Shaggy Mammoth Monkey Ass. *Eew.*

"His name is Sean." Evie made up the easiest name possible. "And he lives in Santa Cruz." There. Did that sound convincing?

"Santa Cruz?" Dee Dee's face turned sour. "Evie, that's, like, five hours north of here. How can he even be a real boyfriend?"

"Dela," Evie said. "You're one to talk. Rocio lives in friggin' D.F."

"Yes, but we were going to the same school long before I moved. We're totally devoted to one another and we've been together and we've already scheduled all our school vacations so we can be even more together. Have you even *been* with this *Sean*?" She threw Evie a quick glance.

"*None* of your business," Evie said.

"When we were kids, you and Raquel always tagged me as *la inocente*." Dee Dee smiled smugly. "Guess I proved you two wrong."

"Okay, Dela. I get your point."

"You know, Evie," Dee Dee continued. "I was talking to Alejandra about your—"

"*What?*" Evie became livid as soon as she heard Alejandra's name. "You were talking to her about *me*? Dee Dee, *don't*. You shouldn't be talking about me to anyone."

"Okay, okay . . ." Dee Dee heard Evie loud and clear. "You don't have to get your *chones* in a bunch!"

* * *

Just to prove she wasn't so *posesiva,* Evie passed on Dee Dee's invitation to go swimming at her house.

"Are you sure you can't come?" Dee Dee asked again later on the phone. "I was thinking you could sleep over and we could make elephant eyes for breakfast. Like we used to do as kids."

"No, I can't," Evie lied. She didn't want Dee Dee thinking it mattered to her what she or Alex did. Especially since she was so confused herself as to why she *did* care. "I'm really tired. Besides, I owe some e-mails."

"Oh, to *Sean?*" Dee Dee teased.

* * *

When Friday evening came around, Evie logged on to her computer to check her MySpace account just to reassure herself that she did have people in her life. "RioChica has 120 friends." *Yeah, right. So where are they now?* As she looked over the photos in her "friends" network, what did it really matter? She was, after all, home on a Friday night and she wasn't even grounded.

But Evie's mood lifted once she went into her favorite chat

room—Bonfire 13. Shaggy was in the same chat. So she didn't have a man in her life, but a little male attention never hurt anyone. Shaggy was innocent enough. He lived far away and seemed only interested in early-morning surf reports.

ShaggyMA: Hey chica, long time no hear. Sup?
RioChica: School, drama, the usual. How's surf in Norcal?

"Evie?" It was her mother, bringing in folded clothes. Meho was at her heels. "You're not going out tonight?"

"Nuh-uh." Evie didn't look up from her screen. "Dela asked me to sleep over, but I'm just gonna stay in." She anxiously waited for ShaggyMA's response.

ShaggyMA: 4 ft. Cold as balls.

Okay, so his netiquette could use some work.

"How is she getting along at Villanueva?" Her mother put the clothes beside her on the edge of the bed where she sat, uninvited.

"Who?" Evie asked.

"Dee Dee," her mother said.

"Mom, I told you she wants to be called Dela," Evie answered. "And she's doing just fine."

Dee Dee *was* getting on divinely at Villanueva. She had a renewed friendship with Evie, her stable of Sangros, Alex's attention, and she didn't even seem to give a rat's ass about Raquel or the inner turmoil she was causing Evie because of it. Yeah, *qué* fine.

Evie looked at her computer screen. Someone named LadyLeche had just entered the chat. *Ugh.* Evie was a hater of sexed-up screen names. Milk Lady? What was *that* supposed to mean?

LadyLeche: I got something to warm you up!
ShaggyMA: I bit u do
LadyLeche: U wanna bite me? Where?

"We should really have her over again," Evie's mother continued. "She's grown into one very lovely young woman."

"Uh-huh," Evie said absentmindedly. She tried to regain Shaggy's attention.

RioChica: You should come to Sea St. You'd love it.

"You know . . ." Evie's mother got up. "Sabrina called for you again. You should call her."

Evie rolled her eyes. The last thing she wanted to do was phone her sister and hear all about her super-sized social life—her dozens of sorority sisters, all the frat boys who were totally in love with her, and how she was oh-so-terrified that her precious GPA was dipping to a 3.96. She waited for Shaggy's response.

"I'll send her an e-mail," Evie said.

"Evie." Her mother's voice lowered. "An e-mail's not the same as a phone call. You should call your sister. She sounded a bit homesick."

Well, I'm homesick too. Sick of this home!

But ShaggyMA was already in the throes of LadyLeche's fleshy language. They both simultaneously logged off, indicating to Evie that they'd probably taken their conversation and libidos to a private chat room. *Ew.*

She felt deflated. She couldn't even attract the attention of an anonymous online male. Was her font style or size not alluring enough? Should she upgrade from Times New Roman to something with more cleavage and curves?

"Okay." Evie turned around to face her mother. "I'll give Sabrina a call."

"She'd like that." Her mother smiled as she finally left the room.

But just as Evie was about to log off, she heard her buddy list alert go off again. Shaggy? No. Evie was surprised to see it was SexyMexy08. What was Raquel doing on her computer on a Friday night at—Evie looked at the screen's clock—9:13 P.M.? She was always, *always*, with Jose on Fridays. It had been a full week of school and neither one of them had spoken to each other except for their confrontation at the salad bar. Evie was sure that Raquel knew that she was online. They were on each other's buddy lists. She waited. Maybe Raquel would send her a message? In boldface angry CAPS.

Evie waited and waited, but no message from SexyMexy08. Evie finally figured she would have to be the one to say hello.

RioChica: Hi

Too *cas*? She deleted the message and started over.

RioChica: Hello Raquel

Too formal. Maybe something more upbeat and silly? That'd be more Raquel's style. And after their argument on Monday, it might be a better icebreaker. She deleted and started over.

RioChica: Oh-lah, chica! Qué onda?

Oh my God! What was she thinking? Super Sangro! She quickly deleted the whole thing. Sweet and sentimental was the way to go.

RioChica: Hey, Rocky, I miss you.
Remember the time—

But it was too late. Raquel logged off. *Shit!* Evie had taken too much time thinking of the perfect message. What was the quote Mrs. Mattis had used in lit class? "He who hesitates is . . . ?" Well, something about how wasting time was not good.

Evie turned of her computer and grabbed Meho off the floor.

"It's just you and me tonight, precious." Evie snuggled her face into his fluffy gray fur. "Let's go get us a snack."

She carried Meho and headed downstairs to find a snackita when she noticed Lindsay in the den. She was folding more laundry and watching her favorite TV show, *La Tormenta*.

"Hey, Lindsay," Evie started. "You're here late." She looked at the TV. "What's happening now?" Not that she was so interested, but when you're barging in on someone else's *novela*, it's just polite to ask.

"I'm taking tomorrow off and I want to get this done." Lindsay didn't take her eyes off the den's plasma-screen. "Oh, wait. Shhhhh—tell you at commercial."

Great, even Lindsay had her own Friday night gig going. Evie moved some laundry to the side and stretched out on the couch.

"You're not going out with your friends?" Lindsay finally asked when a commercial came on starring Esai Morales with "an important announcement regarding home insurance." She turned down the volume with the remote.

"Nah." Evie dangled a sock in front of Meho. "Raquel's mad at me."

"Imagínate," Lindsay clicked her tongue sarcastically. "That's nothing new."

"Yeah, she's in hater mode."

"¿Mande?"

"She's all mad 'cause I'm friends with Dela, Dee Dee. She's a playa hater."

"*Playa*? Why does she hate the beach?"

"No." Evie laughed. "Playa, like player, like . . . a popular person."

"Oh." Lindsay still seemed not to understand. *"¿Y Dee Dee?"*

"She's hanging out with Alex," Evie said as she finally clued in on Meho's disinterest. He was not going to exert energy over some average gym sock.

"Oh, on a date?"

"No," Evie said. "They're just hanging out."

"But it's a Friday evening," Lindsay pressed.

Maybe it was better to leave Lindsay alone, engrossed in her soap.

"Lindsay . . ." Evie was getting irritated. "Just because a guy and girl spend time together, doesn't mean they're on a date. It's not like that here. Nowadays."

"Hmmph," Lindsay said before turning the volume up. *La Tormenta* was back on. "O-*kay*."

But Evie suddenly felt it wasn't simply okay. Was there something she didn't see that Lindsay did? And what did she care if Alex and Dee Dee were becoming more than friends? She should be happy for them. She was happy for Raquel when she hooked up with Jose, right? Even if she did feel like the third wheel at times.

Evie gave up on Meho's finicky mood and before she knew it, she herself was caught up in the torment of *La Tormenta*.

The night's episode was about a beautiful, big-breasted, wasp-waisted brunette who had consistently ignored the advances of a dapper banker. He was the owner of pinstriped suits and a thick, furry moustache. He had offered her his unconditional love, sparkling jewels, and even a house by the sea, but the beautiful, big-breasted, wasp-waisted brunette wasn't interested in any of it or in him. One night the dapper banker was alone, drinking sherry in front of the grand fireplace of his mansion. He was distraught that he would never win the love of the beautiful, big-breasted, wasp-waisted brunette, but then, all of a sudden there was a tap at his door. What was this? Was it she, the beautiful, big-breasted, wasp-waisted brunette? No, it was a new neighbor who had just moved in down the road. She was a beautiful, big-breasted, wasp-waisted blonde and she needed help. His help. She couldn't light her pilot light on her new stove. *"¿Puede usted ayudarme con el fuego?"* she asked in husky *español*. By the end of the episode, the dapper banker with the moustache and the pinstriped suits had fallen head over heels in love with the beautiful, big-breasted, wasp-waisted blonde. And the beautiful, big-breasted, wasp-waisted brunette? She was forever alone . . . to lead the life of an old maid, with her unloving, inattentive cat.

"Ay," Lindsay sobbed. *"La tormenta . . ."*

Evie looked up at Lindsay, then down at Meho.

"Mom!" she cried out in a panic. "Can you drop me off at Dee Dee's?"

* * *

When they were all kids, the de LaFuentes' house was on the end of Camino del Rio, right between the Gomezes and the

Diazes. But now, four years later, the de LaFuentes' new home was on Calle Cortez, a somewhat more posh street in Rio Estates. On Calle Cortez, the house addresses were actually hand-painted on oval ceramic plates and two large royal palms at the street entrance made for a grand introduction to the tree-lined cul-de-sac.

Evie's mother pulled up to the de LaFuentes' house. A number of shiny late-model sporty cars were already parked in the driveway.

"Well." Her mother looked up in surprised envy. "I knew Frank had done well in D.F., but *this* well?"

She was right. The de LaFuentes' new home was large, with two prestigious columns on each side of a custom hand-carved front door. In the middle of their circular brick driveway, spotlights lit a three-tiered fountain. The de LaFuentes' old house, like the Diazes and Gomezes, had been painted adobe beige, but their new home was a light peach stucco, fresh and different from all the other houses. There was also enough foliage on the front lawn to re-create an entire native Mexican desert. From five-gallon agaves and sago palms to Mexican grass trees still packed in wooden shipping crates, the plans for a future landscaping extravaganza were definitely in the works.

"This must all be Graciela's doing," Evie's mother suggested with a slight air of disapproval. "Margaret was never so show-offy with appearances. All this desert stuff . . . didn't Frank say she was from the North?"

"I dunno," Evie answered. Her mother was getting wound up over a few measly plants?

Because there wasn't any room in the driveway to park her Saab, Evie's mother ending up parking down the slope on Calle Cortez. She looked up at the de LaFuentes' home again and turned off the engine. "Maybe I should go in and say hello," she thought out loud. "I haven't really talked to Frank since my brunch."

"Mom, *no*," Evie pleaded. She knew her mother just wanted to check out their new digs. Besides, she didn't want her to know that Dee Dee's parents were out for the evening. "I'm already late. Please, can't I just have some time with Dela? By myself?"

"Okay, Evie." Her mother put her key back in the ignition. "*Okay.*"

Evie grabbed her overnight bag and sprinted up to the house as quick as her Havaianas could take her, before her mother could change her mind.

* * *

The de LaFuentes' doorbell announced Evie's arrival with the somber sound of churchlike chimes. Moments later, a young woman in jeans and a Garfield sweatshirt opened the door. She was in her mid-twenties and Evie assumed she was the de LaFuentes' housekeeper.

"Hi," Evie greeted. "I'm here to see Dela."

"¿Quién?" The woman's eyebrows creased downward.

"Oh," Evie corrected herself. "Dela? Dee Dee?"

"Oh, *sí,*" the young woman nodded as she let Evie in. *"Soy Marcela."*

Evie soon learned that Marcela didn't speak much English. But she didn't really need to vocalize her feelings. Her face conveyed annoyance as she led Evie through the de LaFuentes' home. Hundreds of cardboard boxes of every size covered the newly waxed wooden floors and the stairway. The only piece of furniture in the great room was an oversized white leather sofa still covered in plastic. A large framed portrait of a younger Graciela, with heavily lined eyelids à la the sixties had yet to be hung and was propped against a wall which, like all the other walls in the great room, were dotted with Spackle, waiting for paint. Evie also noticed a lot of indoor foliage in terra-cotta planters and containers, large and expensive-looking. Graciela *must* have a green thumb, Evie thought, if not from planting things herself, then from counting out all the green to pay for interior plant maintenance.

As Evie followed Marcela through the kitchen, she noticed puddles of water on the beige tile floor, evidence that Dee Dee and Alex must have been roughhousing earlier in the evening. No wonder Marcela seemed aggravated. What housekeeper wants to work a Friday night, mopping up after some careless kids? Evie found herself a bit annoyed. Judgmental, maybe?

When they reached the back door, they both heard a scream. Evie jumped back. Marcela, however, just looked up in more annoyance. The scream was quickly followed by muffled laughter and Evie realized that Dee Dee and Alex weren't the only ones out in the backyard. Perhaps Dee Dee's parents decided to stay in? But when Marcela pulled the blinds to one side and slid the sliding glass door open, Evie gasped. The backyard was full of tall, boobs-pushed-up, striped-haired . . . *Sangros.* All four of them, there, in Dee Dee's backyard. Fabiola, Xiomara, Natalia, and Alejand-*rra.*

Evie felt her jaw drop to the concrete. Her first instinct was to sneak back into the house, call her mother, and make her drive back and pick her up as fast as her speedometer allowed.

But it was too late. Dee Dee had already seen her.

"Evie!" she called out. "You came! Come join the party!"

"Well, I just came by to—," Evie started. But it was no use. She couldn't think of a reasonable excuse quick enough. Marcela had already shut the sliding door behind Evie and pulled the blinds back into place.

Dee Dee sauntered over. Like all the other Sangros, she was wearing a micro bikini (hers hot pink) and large, gold hoop earrings. The suit was *so* small, practically child size, and for a minute Evie thought that maybe it was the same Garanimals bathing suit that Dee Dee had worn as a kid.

"Mira." Dee Dee held up a bottle in a paper bag and smiled slyly. "Natalia brought some Patrón Silver. You want a shot?"

"Uh, not really." Evie could detect a tinge of liquor on Dee Dee's breath. "I really can't stay long."

Dee Dee looked over at Evie's Weekender bag and tugged on the canvas strap. "But what's all this for? Aren't you staying over?"

"Well . . ." What could she say? Her mother had already left.

"I thought Alex was here." Evie scratched the side of her neck nervously and looked around.

"He is. There, with Xiomara." Dee Dee motioned with her chin. "She can't swim either." Alex was in the shallow end of the pool with Xiomara, who wore a metallic gold bikini. Metallic gold? She looked like she belonged in a Mystikal video. Xiomara flailed about in the water as Alex desperately tried to balance her with his arms under her back. Evie did a double take. *Wow, Xiomara's C-cups overfloweth.* And Alex? His neck was bright pink. That's one thing that Evie knew about Alex—when he got nervous, his neck turned the color of her old Hello Kitty diary.

"Nice suit, Flojo." Alejandra approached Evie and Dee Dee. She was swirling the ice in her Styrofoam cup.

Evie instantly felt dwarfed between the towering, platform-heeled Dee Dee and Alejandra. Evie glanced down and wished she had put on her nicer flojos. Her green Havaianas were comfy, but totally did not fit in with this swim lesson cum pool party cum beauty pageant. She also noticed that the blue nail polish on her toes was flaking off. Maybe she was truly a Flojo—too lazy to even touch up her toes. Flojo. Sigh. She could only imagine how Raquel would react in the same situation.

"Now, you be nice," Dee Dee reprimanded Alejandra with a sideways glance. "This is my house and my friend." She threw her arm around Evie. The half dozen or so thin gold bracelets clinked on her wrist. "I told you that Evie's been my best friend since forever. My very, *werry* best friend," Dee Dee cooed in baby voice. She pressed her cheek against Evie's. Was it the Patrón that was making Dee Dee lay it on so thick? All Evie could do was smile uncomfortably.

"Yeah, yeah." Alejandra clicked her tongue. "You know I was only teasing."

"Ay," Dee Dee peered into the bottle of Patrón and saw that it was empty. "*No más*, Evie." She made an exaggerated sad face. *"Lo siento, mi'ja."* She then turned to Alejandra. "Ally, be a *chula* and go get Evie some Patrón."

Alejandra gave Dee Dee a look.

"Oh, it's okay," Evie reassured Dee Dee. "It's no problem." She didn't need no Sangro doing her any favors.

"Al-*leeee*," Dee Dee cried. "Just goooo. Be nice."

"Okay, okay." Alejandra grabbed Evie's arm. "Come on, *chica*."

She took Evie to the pool house where another bottle of Patrón was stashed, away from the possible tattletale eyes of Marcela.

As Alejandra started to twist off the cap she looked sharply at Evie. "No offense, Flojo, but . . . ," she started.

Uh—oh. Evie thought. Here it comes.

"But just out of curiosity," Alejandra continued. "Why do you always dress like a boy?"

"A *boy*?" Evie was offended. "You think I dress like a boy?" Sure she had on baggy board shorts, but she often wore skirts to school. And she did shave her legs. She wasn't, like, *Nor*Cal.

"I *told* you not to take offense," Alejandra reminded her. "It's not like you're ugly or anything." She took a swig from the bottle and winced. "Actually between Raquel and you, you are definitely the prettier one and I don't know why—"

"Alejandra, Raquel is my friend."

"Oh, really?" She raised her already arched eyebrows. "I don't see you two hanging out as much anymore."

"Well, she *is* my friend." Evie held up her cup. *Can I just get what you dragged me here for?* "If anything, I'm just a board girl."

"¿Qué?" Alejandra poured a small amount of soda into Evie's cup before adding the Patrón. "*¿Aburrida?* With what?"

"No, not *bored.*" Evie half-smiled. "Board, b-o-a-r-d, as in surfboard, skateboard, snow . . ."

Was she really explaining herself to Alejandra de los Santos?

"Aaah," Alejandra said. "*Sí.* I know. You like all that stuff." She poured more Patrón into her own cup. "So you actually surf? You stand up and everything?"

"Of course," Evie lied.

"So I'm sure you've been to Puerto Escondido."

"Nuh-uh," Evie admitted. "My family, we usually go to Cabo."

"Cabo?" Alejandra giggled. "Are you serious? *¡Qué naco!* My family has a house in Puerto. It's supposed to be the best place for surfers."

"So I've heard." Yeah, someday she would actually ride a board and go. Maybe even a surf trip with Alex. He had mentioned Puerto Escondido. Evie took a sip of her drink. *Yikes.* No wonder Dee Dee was loopy. The Sangros were concocting a lethal syrup with the soda and Patrón. Evie took another drink, already beginning to feel warm and toasty inside. "So," she hesitated slightly, "you really think I'm prettier than Raquel?"

"¡Ay!" Alejandra put the cap back on the Patrón and giggled more. "Dee Dee is right!"

"Right about what?"

"You're funny."

"Oh, thanks." It was all Evie could say. So far she'd been called "funny" and "pretty" in the course of one night. That was more than she sometimes heard over the course of one year from Raquel, who had supposedly been her best friend.

"Hey." Dee Dee came over with Alex to join Evie and Alejandra. "Alejandro's leaving."

"What? Already?" Evie hadn't even said as much as hello to Alex.

"Already?" Alex said. "What are you talking about? I've been here since, like, seven."

"Yeah, but I just got here." Evie took a sip of her Patron. She didn't like the idea of spending the rest of the evening with the entire Sangro posse with not one fellow Flojo around.

"Yeah, well, I wanna get up early, to head out to Sea Street." Alex looked at Evie. "You wanna go, Eves? You can finally try out that board of yours."

"Tomorrow?" Evie got excited. There was no way Raquel would be at Sea Street so early on a weekend morning. "Uh, yeah, should I leave with you now?"

"Evie!" Dee Dee cried. "*No.* You promised. You said you were staying over. I have everything planned."

"Everything planned?" Evie looked at her. "You didn't even know I was coming over until I showed up."

"Yeah, but, you're here now, and now you are going to leave because you have better plans? That is *so* rude."

"Yeah, but Dela," Evie tried to explain. "I really wanna go to Sea Street. I haven't been in, like, forever."

"Evie," Dee Dee insisted, "you can go to the beach anytime. This is my first slumber party in my new house and now you are just going to leave?"

"Slumber party?" Evie asked. "You didn't say you were having a slumber party."

"Yes, I did. All the girls are staying. Right, Alejandra?"

"Claro," Alejandra agreed. She took a drink from her cup.

"Oh." Alex grinned suggestively. "Maybe I should stay too."

Dee Dee smirked. "No. Sorry, Alejandro. Girls only. You're already being a bad influence, trying to lure away my best friend."

Dee Dee was sure playing up the best friend angle. But Evie had to admit, it sorta made her feel, how would you say, *muy especial*?

Evie took a large gulp of her Patron. "Yeah, okay," she said slowly. "I guess there will be plenty of other times to get to Sea Street."

"Good!" Dee Dee smiled. "It will be just like the old days."

"So, you're not coming?" Alex asked.

"No," Evie said reluctantly. "I guess not."

Dee Dee was right. It was her first slumber party in her new home and Evie should be there. Unlike the Diazes' welcome-back party, this was a party for Dee Dee and Evie needed to position herself as Dee Dee's "very, *werry*" best friend and to make sure the Sangros didn't try to bite "the old days" away from her.

* * *

After Alex left, Evie couldn't believe that she was spending an entire Friday night, alone, with the Sangros. What would

Raquel think? Friday night was usually a night set aside for her and her fellow Flojos, time to just zone out in front of the plasma, or drive out to Sea Street to hang out. Well, maybe not every Friday night. As Evie sorely remembered, the first Friday night she was free from being grounded, Raquel hadn't even called her. The pain hit Evie again. Yeah, maybe it was time she did things her way.

* * *

"Okay, *chicas*," Dee Dee called out. "He's gone!" She put her her arms around her back and unclasped her bikini top.

"Shit," Alejandra smirked. "You were waiting for *him* to leave? I couldn't care less." But she did care less. That is, not only did she take off her top, she peeled off her bottoms.

"What about you, *azul*?" Alejandra challenged Evie. "Does your top match your bottom?" She eyed Evie's hair and then her board shorts.

Evie took another sip from her cup. She had never been fully naked in front of anyone else before. In P.E., all the girls had to undress to shower, but it was just a short walk to the shower stalls and she was usually covered with a gigantic Hang Loose beach towel that she'd gotten in Hawaii. There wasn't any running, swimming, or actually hanging loose involved. And there had never been any Sangros in her gym class to judge her.

"I'm on the rag," Evie lied as the other Sangros did away with their bikini tops. Only Alejandra got totally nude. She flaunted her confidence as she waltzed to the de LaFuente's swimming pool slide. She climbed up the ladder, crouched down at the top and then slid briskly down the plastic slide into the pool.

Ooh, that's gotta hurt.

Dee Dee laughed. "Ay, *chica*!" she yelled out. "Don't leave behind any skid marks!" She put her arm around Evie. "I'm *so* happy you stayed."

"Yeah, me too." Evie didn't know how else to answer. She crossed her arms over her chest.

"You know," Dee Dee said, her slur getting stronger, "I just want us all to be friends. Everyone. I just want a fresh start."

A fresh start? Evie wondered if that meant Raquel wasn't going to be included. Was she considered an old finish?

Evie watched Alejandra get out of the pool. She didn't want to stare, but she couldn't help but notice that she had a prominent mark on her left breast. She looked again and saw that it actually looked like a tattoo.

Evie lowered her voice and asked Dee Dee. "Is that a tattoo on Alejandra?"

"Mmm-hmm." Dee Dee nodded lazily. "They all have it."

"Who?" Evie asked. "Have what?"

"Xio, Fabby . . . Natalia . . . they have DF tattooed, near their hearts."

"What?" Evie looked over at the other girls and saw the same little imprint. "That is the stupidest thing I've ever heard."

"I don't think so," Dee Dee said. "What's wrong with being proud of where you are from?"

"Nothing, but come on! A tattoo? On your booby?"

"I'm thinking of getting one . . . ," Dee Dee said.

"Of what?" Evie demanded to know.

"Of DF, of course," Dee Dee answered nonchalantly.

"*What?*" Evie said. The thought of Dee Dee aligning herself with the Sangros and some foreign city crushed Evie's heart. "But you're not even *from* Distrito!"

"But my soul is," Dee Dee said. "And that's all that matters. I'm gonna move back the first chance I get. You don't know what it's like, Evie. It's the most exciting, amazing city in the whole world."

"Like you've been all over the 'whole world.'"

"I don't need to go around the whole world," Dee Dee said. "DF is the world to me, my world, and I can't wait to get back to it."

Evie took another sip of her Patrón. She felt the pit of her stomach in the back of her throat. "*The first chance I get*"? Dee Dee was already planning to move away again. How could she want to leave? She had just returned to Rio Estates and to Evie's life. Evie took another gulp from her cup. She looked at the tattoos on the other Sangros and discreetly placed her forearm on her own left breast. What could that possibly feel like, getting the tattoo right there on the booby? Evie didn't have any tattoos, but Raquel had a few. Evie just couldn't believe someone would be so devoted, dedicated to a particular identity to make a permanent mark on their body. Blue hair was one thing, but a tattoo? No way.

9

The next afternoon, all the girls were lying around in Dee Dee's room having a typical lazy Saturday. Nobody awoke until noon and nobody got out of bed until after one. By three, everyone was still lounging in their matching cotton camisoles and boy bottoms, listening to the beats of Daddy Yankee (iPod), following the saga of *Laguna Beach* (TiVo), and enjoying the satisfaction of elephant eyes (DiVoured).

"I can't believe I ate three eyes." Evie put her fist to her chest and let out a long, low, eggy belch, less from necessity than to shock the room.

Dee Dee crinkled her nose and waved her hand in front of her face. "Evie, gross! How can I work under these polluted conditions?"

"Polluted?" Evie asked. "You're the one who lived in D.F. You should be used to dirty air."

"And L.A. isn't polluted?" Alejandra took offense at Evie's comment.

"We don't *live* in L.A.," Evie reminded her. "This is Rio Estates."

"Yes," Alejandra said with an air of city arrogance. "Unfortunately."

* * *

Amid spiral notebooks, loose papers, and a few school books, Dee Dee lay across her chenille bedspread, redoing Evie's Spanish homework. That was one of the perks of having Dee Dee back from Mexico. Not only did Evie get another best friend, but she got a best friend who had similar enough handwriting to hers and superior conjugation skills to whip through her Spanish II homework.

"Hey," Dee Dee asked Natalia, who was sitting on the carpet painting her toenails. "Would I use *por* or *para* in this sentence?" She read the sentence out loud.

"*Por,*" Natalia answered off the top of her head, no pause, no guessing, no nada.

While Dee Dee started to conjugate verbs, Evie looked over all the single framed photos of Dee Dee and Rocio on the bedroom dresser. One photo in particular caught Evie's interest. It showed Dee Dee in a black knee-length skirt and pointed heels. Rocio was in a sport coat and had binoculars and a program in his hands. They were posed, arms around each other, on the steps of a fancy building, with the blur of other people rushing about behind them. Evie picked up the framed photo and studied it.

"Where was this picture taken?" she asked Dee Dee.

"Which one?" Dee Dee looked up.

Evie held the picture up to show Dee Dee.

"Oh, that was at *Bellas Artes,*" Dee Dee said. "We had just seen a ballet. I can't remember the name of it."

"If it was *Bellas Artes,* it was probably *El Flor de Xochimitlco.*" Alejandra was going through Dee Dee's lipstick supply. "That's *always* there."

"So," Evie said putting the photo back on the dresser, "how did you and Rocio hook up?"

"What exactly do you mean by hook up?" Dee Dee didn't look over. She kept conjugating.

Best friend and, yes, a diligent cheater, too!

"She means," Xiomara said, flipping through a magazine, "when did you first fuck him?"

"Oh, *that.*" Dee Dee looked up and smiled coyly. "It was right away and then, after that, all the time. I think we even did it that night, at *Bellas Artes.*"

"If I know you," Natalia said smiling, "you did it with him in the bathroom, right in the men's stall."

If I know you? How well did Natalia think she knew Dee Dee? Evie was the established longtime friend and this was all news to her—Dee Dee's supposed crazy sexual exploits.

"Natalia!" Dee Dee wrinkled her nose again. "Gross! I did

not!" She sat up from her bed, stretched her shoulders and looked at the photo. "No, but really, it was love right away with me and Rocio. That's how you know it's real. We practically read each other's thoughts. Also, he comes from a great family."

"That seems really important, huh? In Mexico, I mean," Evie asked. "Family."

"It is to me," Fabiola interrupted. "I don't want to be dating some *Indio pata rajada."*

Barefooted Indian? What did *that* mean? Evie wondered. No wonder the Sangros looked down on Evie. In her flojos, she *was* practically barefoot.

"You know," Evie thought out loud, "I don't think Raquel's even met Jose's parents and they've been going out for over a year."

"Well, I'd keep her hidden." Alejandra smirked. She had just outlined her already thick lips with a dark pink pencil. She then pressed her lips together and rubbed them in front of Dee Dee's large oval bedroom mirror. "Jose's too good for her. I don't know why he's so into her."

Evie suddenly felt awkward. Why did she say that about Raquel? She didn't want to start capping on her in front of the Sangros. She still, in a way, had an allegiance to her Flojo-hood.

"So, Evie," Dee Dee interrupted. She had a tone that suggested she had something else on her mind. "Have you thought about a touch-up?"

Evie looked down at her exposed toes. She was hoping no one had noticed. The chips of blue paint from last night were now specks. God, what had she left floating in the de LaFuentes' pool? "Yeah, I guess I am in need of a paint job."

"No." Natalia laughed when she saw Evie looking at her feet. "She means your hair."

"My hair?" Evie touched the side of her head as she looked at herself in Dee Dee's mirror. Her hair had been blue for a few weeks and she had a good amount of black roots showing. She turned her head to one side. "I hadn't really noticed."

"Well, it's *very* noticeable." Alejandra looked at her through the mirror. "Your hair grows really fast."

"Yeah," Dee Dee agreed. "How about not just a touch-up but something completely cool and *en la moda*?"

"*En la moda?*" Evie asked. She didn't like the sound of that. "I can tell you right off I am *not* getting braid extensions."

"No," Alejandra said. "We're not talking about those cheap *trenzas* that *turistas* get in Acapulco." She fluffed the top of Evie's hair. "But what if you went with a different color? Right, Dela?"

"Like *what*?" Evie became more suspicious.

"Some highlights?" Dee Dee offered cheerfully.

"*No.*" Evie pulled her head away from both Alejandra and Dee Dee. "No way." At Villanueva, highlights were the bona fide mark of a Sangro. It was one thing getting to know the Sangros, accepting the Sangros, but to look like one of them?

No way. She had her own style, her own fashion sense. Besides, Raquel would have a fit and really never speak to Evie again. "I'm *not* going blonde. You gotta be kidding."

"Not really blonde," Dee Dee assured her. "We could dye your hair back to brown, a light brown, and then give you some highlights, just like a half crown, and overall, it would look—"

"Blonde," Evie said matter-of-factly.

"But not just blonde," Alejandra tried to persuade her, "like those bland *blanquitas* at the Pacific View Mall, but *más* exciting. You're a surfer, right? Don't you want to be blonde?"

"Like blonde supposedly defines a surfer?" Evie said. "Alejandra, OG waveriders were brunettes. Besides, blonde stands for everything Raquel and I—"

"Who?" Dee Dee interrupted.

"No one. Just me," Evie finished. "Blonde stands for everything *I'm* against."

"Oh?" Dee Dee raised an eyebrow. "And blue stands for everything you are *for*?"

Just then, Graciela tapped at the side of Dee Dee's bedroom doorway. "Dela," she asked. *"¿Están ocupadas?"*

"No, *'Ama,"* Dee Dee called out. *"Entra."*

Graciela walked in. She was dressed in a narrow dark skirt and sweater with three-quarter sleeves. A short strand of pearls completed her very polished look. Evie wondered where she was off to in the middle of the afternoon dressed so formally.

"Hola, Señora de LaFuente." Alejandra moved away from the mirror. She gave Graciela a quick peck on the check. It was obvious that she had been spending time at Dee Dee's and had gotten to know Graciela better than Evie had. She wondered if Graciela had DF tattooed on her left booby. *"Ay."* Alejandra looked at her pearls. "I love your *perlas.*"

"Gracias, mi'ja." Graciela touched her strand and smiled at Alejandra. She looked around the room. *"¿Se están divirtiendo, muchachas?"*

"Oh, *sí,*" Fabiola answered for everyone. "Lots of fun. Thanks for having us over."

"*Sí*, anytime. It's nice to see Dela happy, with her friends," Graciela looked at Dee Dee. "I'm leaving on errands, *mi'ja. ¿Necesitas algo?"*

Errands? Evie was surprised as she looked at Graciela. When her own mother ran errands she wore a simple sweat suit and T-shirt. Sure it was a Juicy Couture velour sweatsuit, and an eighty-dollar Anne Klein T-shirt, but still.

"Are you going to Long's?" Dee Dee asked.

"Long's?" Graciela opened her black leather handbag and shuffled things in it. "What do you need from Long's?"

Dee Dee nonchalantly patted her stomach. "Oh, just a First Response? You know, *un* pregnancy kit."

"¡¿Mande?!" Graciela looked up from her handbag, her eyes and mouth stretched wide in horror.

"Ha!" Dee Dee laughed. "Just messing, Gracie!"

"Ay." Graciela playfully slapped Dee Dee's arm. *"¡Qué mala!"*

The whole room giggled. Evie couldn't quite believe that Dee Dee talked that way to Graciela. She used to be playful with Margaret, her mother, but Graciela didn't seem the type to take such jokes lightly.

"No." Dee Dee threw her arm around Graciela's shoulders. "We just need hair color." She looked at Evie defiantly. "Right, Evie?"

"Dela . . . ," Evie started.

"Come on, Evie," Alejandra joined in. "You'll look great . . . you'll be *¡un taco de ojo!*"

"A taco *de what?"*

"Ay." Graciela clicked her tongue and looked over Evie's scrappy blue mop. *"¿Por qué no?"*

"See?" Dee Dee chimed. "Gracie knows. She used to work in television and knew all the top stylists and hairdressers, right, Gracie?"

"*Graciela,"* she corrected Dee Dee as if she'd had to a million times before.

"You are *not* coloring my hair," Evie said as if *she'd* had to correct Dee Dee a million times.

"Yeah," Dee Dee said. "I guess Raquel wouldn't like it."

"It has nothing to do with Raquel," Evie insisted. "This is *my* hair."

"Okay, okay." Dee Dee didn't sound convinced. "I'll drop it. Never mind *'Ama,"* she told Graciela. "We don't need anything."

As Graciela left the room, Dee Dee looked Evie over one more time. "I really wish you'd rethink it, Evie."

"Well, I won't, thank you." Evie was adamant. She joined Xiomara on the carpet and started to go through Dee Dee's supply of nail polish. The least she could do is cover up her tacky toes. Dee Dee had dozens of bottles; at least eight of them were different shades of pink. Evie finally decided on the lightest shade, cleverly labeled "Lightest Pink."

Dee Dee walked over to Evie and Xiomara and reached down under her bed. "Hey, I have something for you."

"For me?" Evie looked up.

"Yeah."

"Dela, you ain't gonna bribe me."

"*No seas terca,*" Dee Dee said. "I was gonna give this to you later, but I want you to have it now." She pulled out a small flat package.

"Hey." Fabiola looked at the gift. "What about me?" she teased. "I'm the one with the birthday next week."

"Oooh." Evie eyed the package. "Seriously, I can open it now?"

"Yeah." Dee Dee handed it to her. "You know it's not like you haven't been blonde before."

"Huh?" Evie was confused.

The Sangros huddled around Evie as she started to unwrap the foil paper. The gift was a picture frame. When Evie flipped it over, she saw the photo.

"Is that you?" Natalia asked.

Evie immediately covered her mouth. "Oh my God!" She laughed. "This is so funny. I totally remember this day!"

The photo was of her and Dee Dee, both nine-year-olds in costume for the Marina Park Beauty Contest. Just about every girl, including the two of them, had dressed as the Coppertone girl. They all sported blonde wigs pulled into pigtails and tied with blue ribbons. Dee Dee and Evie each wore a blue two-piece bathing suit.

"I still don't understand why we didn't win." Dee Dee smirked as she looked at the picture. "I mean, our tans were for real and they gave first place to a *gabacha*!"

Evie laughed. She actually looked cute in the blonde wig. She looked at Dee Dee, who had gone back to her bed and continued doing Evie's homework. Dee Dee *was* a really good friend, she thought. A very good friend. She then looked at her own hair in Dee Dee's mirror. Blonde? *Nah*. Then she looked at herself again. Oh, what's a few highlights really gonna do anyway? They *could* be done to look natural, as if she had spent a few days at the beach. They might even look cool. Raquel would *freak*, that's for sure.

Besides, Evie thought, wasn't it every girl's dream to be a *taco de ojo?*

10

The next morning, Monday, when Evie got up from her bed and went to her bathroom, she startled herself in the mirror. She had forgotten about what she had committed the night before. Treason. Her hair was now blonde.

She groggily leaned over the bathroom sink and squinted. Oh God, who *was* that squinting back at her? What had she let herself get talked into?

"Aaah," Alejandra had raved when Dee Dee and Xiomara were finalizing the blown-dried touches on Evie's hair the night before. "I wish I had done my *pelo* this shade. Honey Blonde . . . *Qué* cool!"

But now, the morning after, neither Dee Dee, Xiomara, nor Alejandra was around to fluff her hair or her ego. Evie looked herself over and wondered if she truly looked *qué cool.* She tilted her head from side to side and grimaced. Never mind Sangro stripes—she was *all* blonde, 100 percent Honey

Blonde chica blonde. Maybe it was too early in the morning and too early in the process to embrace such change? And in the back of her mind, a little thought was nagging at her: *What will Raquel think?*

When Evie came out of her bathroom, she could hear that Monday morning life was going on as usual for the rest of the Gomez household. *El Mercadito* was on the kitchen radio and she could hear her mother downstairs, talking to Lindsay. This was going to be her mother's first chance to see Evie's new look. Last night, after Dee Dee had dropped her off at home, she'd gone straight to her room. Thankfully, her mother and father were catching up on their TiVo in the den. But that was last night. What would her mother say this morning?

"Well," she said yawning as she pulled on some drawstring pants, her silver Havaianas, and headed down to the kitchen. "Here goes *nada*."

Lindsay, pulling a *bolillo* out from the toaster oven, was the first to see Evie. "Evelina!"

"Hey, Linds." Evie tried to sound confident as she took over one of the stools at the counter.

Evie's mother was still in her pool robe, her hair wet from her morning swim. She looked over at Evie. "Evie!"

Here it comes—the Gomez *furioso*.

But to Evie's surprise, her mother smiled. "When did you fix your hair?"

"Oh." Evie timidly played at the sides with her fingertips. "Last night at Dela's." Then she quickly added, "It was her idea."

"I like it." Her mother sipped coffee from the oversized mug she held with both hands. "Dee Dee did it? I'm impressed."

Which were the golden words? Evie wondered. "Dee Dee did it" or "It was Dela's idea"? She would definitely make a note of that. *But Dela thought it would be okay to take your Saab into Tijuana so we could go nightclubbing, and then when we met those men, they were just so nice that we decided to share a hotel room with them. Don't worry, it was Dee Dee's idea!*

"You know," Evie's mother said as she smoothed her own damp hair, "I used to be blonde."

"I remember Dad saying something like that." Evie yawned again. "I don't think I've seen any pictures of you with blonde hair."

"Evie." Her mother tapped under Evie's chin. "Cover your mouth when you yawn." She went on. "It was during my Teena Marie phase, just for a short time. God, maybe I should go back to blonde. What do you think, Linds?" She looked at her reflection from the kitchen cupboard's glass door.

"Oh, *sí, Señora,*" Lindsay agreed as she brought Evie a small glass of orange juice. "You would look even *más linda.*"

Evie threw Lindsay a look. *God, can you be any more* falsa? *¿Habladora hipócrita?*

But Lindsay just smiled back innocently. Apparently she could be.

* * *

With her mother's enthusiastic nod of approval, Evie felt even more unsure about her new hair color. The last thing you wanted was your own mother lifting your style. What if her mother *did* dye her hair blonde? What was next? Competing in the Mother and Daughter Look-Alike Contest at the county fair?

As Evie went through her closet in search of clothes to match her new look, she started thinking of Raquel again. At Villanueva, Evie had always been known as her little shadow, or, as of late, the freaky Flojo with the blue hair. But today she was introducing an entirely new look. She couldn't help but be a little excited. After all, she wasn't bland blonde, *blanquita* blonde, like the girls at the Pacific View Mall, or just blonde blonde like Dee Dee and the Sangros, she was *Honey Blonde.*

* * *

Alex was the first Flojo to see Evie. She and Dee Dee walked up behind him while he was at his locker and Dee Dee covered his eyes with her hands.

"Can you guess what's behind Door Number One?"

"Hey . . ." Alex slowly turned around.

Dee Dee uncovered his eyes and Alex paused for a moment when he looked at Evie. His face crinkled in disapproval. "What did you do to your hair?"

Not the reaction she had hoped for.

"¿Qué guapa, no?" Dee Dee put one hand on her hip like a game-show model and used the other to display Evie, as if she was a brand-new Chrysler up for grabs.

"I dunno." Alex continued to look Evie over. "But if that was the look you were trying for . . ."

Trying for? As if Evie was attempting to do something but didn't quite accomplish it?

"It *was* the look I was trying for," Evie snapped. "And the one I achieved."

"Don't trip, Eves." Alex frowned. "Dee Dee just asked me a question."

"And I just gave you an answer." Evie was embarrassed, but didn't want to show it.

"What's up with all the changes?" Alex looked at Evie's ears. Sure, she had at the last minute thrown on some hoop earrings, borrowed from her mother, but they weren't *that* big.

"You know, Alex, you can be so dense. What, am I supposed to look the same every day? Every year? Forever?" Evie linked arms with Dee Dee. "Come on Dela. He's obviously not *en la moda.*"

Dee Dee giggled. "Sorry you don't approve, Alejandro."

She tapped the left side of his head. "But call us if you ever wanna do something with that crazy cowlick."

* * *

Evie vowed to herself that Alex's opinion wasn't going to ruin her morning, but, in reality, it did. His comments clung to her as she walked to first period. Why was she was so concerned about what *he* thought? What did he know about fashion or style? She never saw *Cargo* floating around in his truck. Him, in the same ol' rubber flojos he'd worn since last year. His feet must surely stink awful.

"Oh, what do we have here?" Mr. McDaniel-Galván, Evie's Spanish II teacher, smiled widely as she entered class. "I almost didn't recognize you. *Very* nice."

"Oh, yeah," Evie suddenly felt on the spot. Was she now truly a *taco de ojo* and he was hungry? *Not* the kind of attention she was thinking of. Mr. McDaniel-Galván was, like, fifty years old. That's one hundred in teenage years. "I went under the bottle," she joked.

"¿En español?" he asked.

"Uh, *dormí con mi botella."*

A couple of students, two football players Evie knew only by the numbers of their jerseys that they *always* wore, entered the class. They both overheard Evie and laughed.

"Dude," Number Forty-eight informed her. "You said, 'I slept with my bottle.'"

"What, your *baby* bottle?" Number Nine quipped after him.

"Maybe her *beer* bottle," Number Forty-eight added.

"Yeah, her forty!" Number Nine laughed at his own joke.

What, Evie wondered, *are they the jock version of Mondo and Jose?*

"Gentlemen, gentlemen." Mr. McDaniel-Galván directed both Numbers to their desks. "Just take your seats so we can start class." He turned back to Evie. "Actually, you wouldn't have a direct translation. You would say, 'I colored my hair.'"

"Right." Evie nodded. "I colored my hair."

"No," Mr. McDaniel-Galván smiled. *"En español, por favor."*

Evie repeated it slowly in Spanish. *"Me pinté el cabeza."*

"Well," Mr. McDaniel-Galván sighed. "You're *getting* there. You know, for a moment I thought you were your friend."

"My friend?"

"Sí, Dela de LaFuente.*"*

So much for radical individualism, Evie thought as she took her seat.

* * *

After fourth period, Evie was finally free to have time to worry about her hair and Alex's fashion-backward opinion of it. She welcomed lunch time and headed toward the cafeteria to meet up with Dee Dee and the Sangros for lunch. She hadn't seen Raquel all morning, and for her, that was a good thing. Two negative comments from two separate Flojos might be a little too much for her to handle.

But as she walked by the boys' P.E. building, she was a bit startled by a long, slow whistle coming from behind her. She turned around and was surprised to find Jose and Mondo.

It seemed like forever since any of them had exchanged words.

But there they were now, just the three of them, in front of the boys' gym.

"Hey, look at you." Mondo half-smiled as he pulled up his shades for a better look.

"Oh, hey," Evie answered timidly. Was Raquel around? She didn't know if she was ready to face her just yet.

"Nice hair." Mondo's admiration continued. "*Very* Cameron."

"All right . . ." Mondo was never this nice. She waited for a cutting remark, Mondo style. "Go ahead and say it."

"No, I mean it." He got closer and looked her over like he'd never looked her over before. "You look hot."

Hot?

"Oh, thanks," was all Evie could say. She looked around. Raquel wasn't anywhere near.

Jose came up on the other side and stretched his arm out

against the wall, blocking her path. She was caught between the two, Mondo behind her and Jose in the front. As Flojos they'd shared tight spaces together, in the front seat of Mondo's car, the mosh pit of the last Huasipungo show at the fairgrounds, but this was definitely different. The energy felt, well, *too* frisky for friendship.

"So . . . " Jose lowered his head and caressed his labret. He moved closer to Evie. "Have you found out?"

"Found out what?" Evie asked. Jeez, was he trying to *sniff* her?

"If blondes have more fun?"

"Jose, stop it!" She pushed his arm away. "Quit being stupid." She wanted to sound tough, but deep down she felt awkward. What had she told Dee Dee? To just ignore him? "So," Evie said looking down the hall. "Where's Raquel?" What she meant to convey was: Where is your *girlfriend*?

"Dunno." Jose's arm dropped and he shrugged his shoulders casually. "My hip ain't tied to hers."

"No, but your dick is," Mondo quipped.

Evie let out an unexpected chuckle.

"Hey." Jose looked at Evie. "At least I'm not the one dumping my best friend for some Sangro slut."

"Dela's not a slut," Evie snapped. "Is that what you think or is that what Raquel programmed you to think?"

But before he could answer, Raquel was already coming toward all three of them.

"Hey, Jose!" she called out. "I've been *waiting* at the tree. Where have—" Raquel's mouth was wide-open in disbelief.

"You have *got* to be kidding!" She came up to Jose and nudged him in the ribs. "Can you believe this?" She looked over Evie's hair. "What are you? Some pseudo Sangro now?"

"Yeah." Jose half-smiled. "We were just saying that."

Actually, Evie thought, *you were not "just saying" that.*

"Oh *my God,* Evie," Raquel went on. "You have *totally* lost it. Totally."

She actually circled Evie. "Who do you think you are trying to be?

"I'm not trying to be anyone." Evie brushed back the side of her hair with her hand. "I just changed the color. It's no big deal, Raquel."

"What, was this Dee Dee's idea?" Raquel asked.

"No, not at all," Evie answered.

"Yeah, I'm sure it was. She's always had you wrapped around her little finger. Even when we were kids. God, Evie, can't you ever think for yourself? I knew, just knew something like this was gonna happen."

Evie clenched her jaw.

"I definitely approve." Mondo squinted his eyes and continued looking at Evie. "I think she looks hot."

"Hot?" Raquel questioned.

"What, you jealous, Rocky?" Mondo asked. "Maybe you should think about lightening up. In more ways than one."

"Oh, shut up." Raquel pushed her hands into Mondo's chest. "Come on, Jose." She put her arm around his slim waist. "There ain't nothing to see here."

And with her hand tucked in the back pocket of Jose's cords, Raquel led Jose from Evie, and Mondo followed. But as they walked away, Jose looked back over his shoulder and winked at Evie. Was it just more flirtation? Morse code to signal that he was still her friend? Either way, Evie couldn't help but feel a bit triumphant. She finally had a little something over Raquel.

* * *

Evie was still feeling a tightness in her jaw when she reached the lunchroom, but it lifted slightly when she saw all the Sangros smiling and waving her over with such enthusiasm.

"*¡Ay!*" Alejandra twirled Evie around in a salsa-inspired dance move. Twirls did not come easy for Evie in her flip-flops and she stumbled. "Now that your hair's fixed, we just have to do something about your *chanclas*!" Alejandra noticed.

Evie looked down at her flojos and pursed her lips. *Hmmm, not likely.* Blonde hair was one thing, but her beloved flojos? They defined her, reminded her who and what she was. Asking her to give up her flojos would be like asking Dorothy to give up her ruby slippers!

"No." Alejandra's eyes lit up like a lightbulb had just been clicked on inside her head. "I know." She looked at the other Sangros and Dee Dee with a mischievous expression on her face. "We *have* to celebrate. To initiate her, big time. And you know what that means . . . "

"Basilio?" Natalia smiled.

"Basilio," Alejandra affirmed.

Alejandra looked at Evie. "Do *not* make any plans this Friday, *chica. Vamos a divertirnos.* I'll see Basilio today after school and plan everything."

11

Evie's week passed fast, and went well. More than well, actually. Raquel and Alex seemed to be the only students at Villanueva who *didn't* "get" Evie's new look. She was getting compliments left and right, ahead and behind, and all of a sudden she was noticing guys checking her out, when up until now she'd felt pretty much invisible. Maybe it was the hair, maybe it was the hoops, maybe it was a new sense of confidence, but whatever it was, she had to admit, it felt all good.

By Friday night, she had her weekender bag packed and was all ready for, as Alejandra had said, "fun." The other Sangros had been talking about Basilio all week, but wouldn't let Evie in on their surprise plans. Who was he and how was he connected to Evie celebrating a new hair color? Dee Dee knew nothing of him. Or maybe she was just keeping it hush-hush? Was Basilio, Evie feared, some male stripper with a waxed back? Were the Sangros planning a little dorm party and Basilio was gonna pop out of some cardboard cake gyrating to *reggaetón* in a G-string? *Ew.*

❋ ❋ ❋

Dee Dee, of course, was running late that evening and, of course, it bothered Evie. It was now *Evie's* big night and here her best friend didn't even have the decency to be on time.

Evie paced around her bedroom, stopping only to brush and rebrush her hair in front of her closet mirrors. Thank God it had grown since that fateful night with the Ginghar scissors. Her hair was almost as long as Mondo's. Her cell blared Moz and she went over to pull it out from her furry UGG bag.

Yeah, yeah, Dela, I know. You're running late.

But it was Alex.

"Hey, you wanna head out to Sea Street tomorrow?" he asked. "It would just be you and me."

"Oh, *tomorrow?*" Evie looked over at her long board. She had owned it a full four months and still had yet to even take it out of the corner of her room. "I can't."

"We don't have to do DP," Alex suggested. "We can go later in the day. I actually gotta help my dad in the afternoon."

Evie hesitated. Alejandra had said to keep Friday night and most of Saturday afternoon free. She didn't want to bail early and let all the girls down. She was the guest of honor. Besides, she was very intrigued to meet this Basilio. Maybe he was a surfer too?

"Mmm." Evie clicked her tongue. "I really can't, Alex. I'm busy. Sorry."

"So," Alex started, "I thought you wanted to surf."

"I do."

"But every time I ask you, you can never go, or you don't wanna go. What's going on?"

"Nothing." Evie looked at herself in her closet mirrors. "Nothing's going on and I *do* wanna surf. It's just, it's not a priority right now."

"Oh." Alex's enthusiasm dropped a notch. "Not a priority. O-*kay*."

"What is that supposed to mean?" Evie asked.

"Nothing," Alex said. "I'm just agreeing with you. You know, Evie, surfing takes a lot of discipline. It's a lot of work. It's not like you are gonna have one lesson and be the total girl in the curl."

Girl in the what?

Evie could tell he was annoyed. What was he not understanding? She continued to look at herself in her closet mirrors. She *did* look good. "You know what, Alex?"

"What?"

"Can you call me by my proper name? From now on?"

"Your *proper* name?" Evie could sense a smirk forming on Alex's face.

"Yes," Evie said curtly. "Evelina."

Alex got quiet on the other end.

"Alex," she asked, "you still there?"

"Yeah." He let out an exasperated sigh. "I'm still here. O-*kay*, Evelina. I'll talk to you *later*."

And he hung up before Evie could even say good-bye.

Evie looked at her phone. What the hell was that about? He actually hung up on her? She flipped her phone shut and looked at herself again in the closet mirrors. Why was he PMSing all of a sudden? Besides, didn't he know that sand and seawater were a lethal combo for chemically treated hair?

"E-vie!" her mother called from downstairs, announcing that Dee Dee had finally arrived.

Evie didn't want to give Alex's guilt-tripping another thought. She tossed her cell back in her bag, slipped on her Fur Real Sanuks, grabbed her Weekender, and went to meet Dee Dee downstairs.

"*Hola,* Vicki." Dee Dee hugged Evie's mother as she entered the Gomezes' foyer. Dee Dee looked up at Evie who was coming down the stairs. "*¡Ay, lo siento, Evelina!* Rocio kept me on the phone and I couldn't switch over to my cell—"

"Yeah, yeah," Evie stopped her before she could go on.

"How are you, Dee Dee?" Evie's mother kissed Dee Dee's cheek and rubbed her arm. "Evie tells me you're doing just great at school."

"*Mom,*" Evie tilted her head in annoyance. "She wants to be called Dela. I've *told* you that."

"Oh." Her mother cringed, embarrassed. "I'm sorry, Dela."

"It's no big deal, not with you anyway, Vicki." Dee Dee put her arm around Evie. "But, *yes*. Evie's been a big help at school and I've already made a ton of new friends, *otras chicas* from Mexico, too."

"Oh, how wonderful." Evie's mother smiled. "Is that who you're watching videos with tonight?"

"Uh-huh," Dee Dee answered cheerfully. "But it's gonna be an early night, because we all have to study tomorrow. Plus, they live on campus and they have to be back at school by nine P.M."

"Oh, of course." Evie's mother looked completely charmed. Good girls who study and have an early curfew—what mother wouldn't want friends like that for her daughter? "Is Raquel also going?"

"Oh, definitely," Dee Dee said quickly. "Right, Evie?"

"Uh . . . yeah." Evie was taken by surprise.

"And Gracie's gonna order in from California Pizza Kitchen," Dee Dee added.

"Now *that* sounds like a nice night." Vicki Gomez looked tremendously pleased.

As Evie and Dee Dee left the house and got into the Beetle, Evie turned to Dee Dee.

"Why did you tell my mom that Raquel was coming?" Evie asked.

"Oh, that was just to throw her off." Dee Dee lit up a cigarette before starting up her car. "Don't you want her thinking that everything is all good and regular, like the old days?"

"I guess." Evie felt weird. It was one thing for her to lie to her mother, but oddly painful to hear someone else do so, especially Dee Dee. "So, are we going to Alejandra's dorm? Are we gonna hang out there?"

"You'll see." Dee Dee started to pull out of the Gomezes' driveway. "Didn't you hear Ally? Weren't you paying attention? She wants to celebrate, something special."

"Which is?"

"*Cálmate.*" Dee Dee smiled slyly as she drove onto Camino del Rio. "You gotta learn to be patient."

* * *

Dee Dee's Beetle was soon on Ventura Road, the main highway leading into the sleepy town of Ojai, but as they got near Villanueva, Dee Dee drove right by.

"Wait, where are we going?" Evie looked over her shoulder as they passed by their school. With the orange sunset dissolving behind the red tiled roofs, their school looked inviting, almost like a desirable destination. "I thought we were staying at Alejandra's dorm."

"Evie . . ." Dee Dee glanced over at her as she turned off Ventura and drove onto a residential road. "You are as naïve as your mother."

The residential road was lined with eucalyptus trees, and large painted stones to mark the addresses of the single-story ranch-style homes. Evie knew the road. It led right to the Ojai Valley Inn, her mother's favorite place to get, as she said, her "skin and soul rejuvenated." Before Evie knew it, Dee Dee stopped her Beetle in front of the Inn.

"Why are we stopping here?" Evie looked up toward the Inn's main entrance.

"Because," Dee Dee sang, "we . . . are . . . staying . . . here."

"We're staying *here?*"

"Yup." Dee Dee smiled as she got her shoulder bag from the backseat.

The Ojai Valley Inn was one of the ritziest hotels and spas in the whole county, maybe the whole state. Presidents, dignitaries from all over the world had stayed at the Inn.

A Ken doll–looking guy came up to Dee Dee's car. "Good evening, ladies," he greeted on cue. "Welcome to the Ojai Valley Inn." He gave Dee Dee a ticket and took the keys to her Beetle. "Will you be needing any help with your luggage?"

"Oh, no," Dee Dee told him. "We're still waiting for more in our party."

"Dela . . ." Evie felt like an adolescent eyesore with her Weekender bag and Sanuks among all the adult Vuitton and Prada. "This place," she said looking around, "is for high rollers."

"Yeah, it *is* pricey," Dee Dee agreed casually. "'Specially the Presidential Suite."

"The *Presidential Suite?*"

"Yeah, it's over three grand."

"*What?*" Evie balked. "How do you know that?"

"Because that's where we are staying."

"Wait, who's paying for this?"

But Evie soon got her answer.

"*¡Hola, chicas!*" Alejandra came up to both of them. She was with the other Sangros and kissed Dee Dee and Evie on their cheeks. "We just got here, *también*."

"Yeah," Natalia said. "Basilio went to get another golf cart for us."

"Golf cart?" Evie laughed. "What, we gonna do a nine-hole or something?"

But no one paid attention to the supposed guest of honor.

"Oh, there he is!" Alejandra looked over the parked Jaguars and Lexuses and called out. "*¡Hola, Basilio! ¿Qué onda, chulo?*"

¿Chulo?

Basilio was an old man. Make that, a very old man. Small, wrinkled, and missing a row of front teeth as well as a row of acrylic hair from the obvious piece he wore on his head. He pulled up in a beige golf cart, the same color as his uniform. He was followed by another cart, driven by another man, seemingly in his early thirties and with, seemingly, all his own teeth and hair.

"*Bueno, bueno.*" Basilio rubbed his hands together in excited nervousness as he stepped out of the cart.

"You have the room for us?" Alejandra asked.

"*Sí, sí.*" He wiped his forehead and looked over at the

blonde team of valet parkers. "*Pero,* we can't have any problems. Not like last time."

"Now, Basilio." Alejandra gave him a sideways glance and put her arm around him. His perspiring face came up to her breasts. "What have I told you? That was *not* my fault and I told you my father would pay for it and didn't he? Didn't he pay for the entire hot tub and the chandelier?"

"*Sí, sí,* I know. *Pero, mis jefes.*" He looked over again at the main entrance of the Inn. "I can't have any problems."

"Oh, Basilio," Alejandra smoothed the few thin strands of his hair that lay across his furrowed brow and looked right at him. "Am I a troublemaker? Do I cause problems? Should we all just go home now?"

Basilio looked alarmed. "*Ay,* no. No, Alejandra. Here, follow me. I have your room ready."

"El Suite Presidente?" Alejandra asked.

"Sí," he nodded. *"Claro que sí."*

Basilio got into his golf cart and Alejandra and Natalia and Fabiola got in with him.

"Come on," Xiomara said to Dee Dee and Evie as she got on the second cart.

Both carts putted slowly down the narrow strip of asphalt, the private employees' road. They passed Sueños, the main restaurant, one of the Inn's Olympic-sized swimming pools, the tennis courts, and the Inn's renowned Chumash Indian sweat lodge. They finally reached the last building, separate from the rest of the Inn. It was a two-story, hacienda-style bungalow, painted off-white, with green shutters on the outside of every window.

"Oh." Dee Dee opened her mouth in awe. "It is so cute! Oh my God, *¡como Guanajuato!*"

"Yeah," Natalia boasted. "It may look all cute on the *outside,* but inside it's *laid down.*"

Evie felt like she was in some surreal new reality show. *Mexico's Most Naughty*? *Punk'd*? Oooh, she looked around. Was Ashton Kutcher gonna come running out in a trucker cap any minute? She wasn't quite sure what to make of all of this, but she knew one thing for certain: None of this would *ever* have happened if she were still hanging out with the Flojos.

Basilio got off of his golf cart and walked up brick stairs to the suite. The girls followed.

"*Mira.*" Basilio handed Alejandra a set of plastic cards. "Here are the keys. Two extra for your sisters." He looked over at Fabiola and Xiomara.

"Oh, you are a doll," Alejandra cooed. "Too sweet for words. *Oye, mi'jo,* one last thing . . ."

"¿Sí?" Basilio asked.

"This time, can you make *sure* you keep the buckets of champagne coming? Last time we had to wait."

"Oh, *sí. Claro que sí.*"

"And a late checkout," Xiomara added as she took one of the cards and let herself into the suite. "We don't wanna be rushed out of here tomorrow."

As soon as Basilio left, Alejandra immediately took charge of the luxurious multiroom suite. The Presidential Suite was done up in presidential colors, that's if the president was a Native American from a Californian tribe. Handwoven blankets, textiles hung on the walls, and deep-red pottery-accented rooms that were painted in cobalt blue and earthy beige tones. Alejandra pulled the cord of the overhead fan and drew back the heavy plush drapes of the main French doors that led out onto a private terrace encased with blooming dark red bougainvillea.

"Ooh." Evie stepped out to the terrace behind Alejandra. Below them was a spectacular view of rural Ojai Valley and above, a blanket of twinkling stars spread out across the jet-black sky.

"How did you get this amazing hookup?" Evie asked.

But Alejandra didn't answer. She inhaled deeply and stretched her arms out. "I might just sleep out here with all this *naturaleza*. Anyone want to join me?"

"Not me." Fabiola flopped herself on one of the overstuffed white minisofas. "I'm gonna sleep in the meditation loft."

"No, if anything," Natalia started, "Evelina should sleep up there."

"Up where?" Evie walked back into the main suite.

"There." Natalia pointed to an alcove, above the living room. A Native-American ladder, the kind used in kivas, led up to the private sleeping area. A dozen or so candles ready to be lit and pillows the color of California poppies were carefully arranged to convey that carelessly arranged look. It looked wonderfully calm and relaxing.

Fabiola picked up the cordless phone. "I'm going to order an in-room massage." She grabbed the service list off the glass coffee table. A single tree stump balanced the tabletop in place. "Actually, I'm gonna get a Pixie Tangerine body scrub. Does anyone else want one?"

"We're already in October." Natalia went behind a mahogany wood bar and opened up the fully stocked liquor cabinet. She pulled out a bottle of Maker's Mark and opened it as if it was all routine. "They won't have Pixie Tangerine."

"So, what will they have?" Fabiola looked over the in-room service list.

"Melon Pumpkin." Alejandra came in from the terrace. She answered as though having to be the one to know all the resort's information had become tiresome. "Hey." She looked at Evie and Dee Dee. "Do you guys wanna see the master bathroom? It's got a sunken Jacuzzi bathtub and a snail-shell shower that you won't believe."

"Wait, wait." Evie was still feeling overwhelmed. "How did you get all this? With Basilio?"

"Yeah," Dee Dee admitted. "I'm curious as well."

"Oh." Alejandra gave a deceptive grin. "*That.* Let's just say I've got my ways . . ."

"No," Evie pressed. "Really."

"You *really* wanna know?" Alejandra asked.

"*Yes,*" Evie insisted. "I *think* I wanna know. We're not doing anything illegal, are we?"

"Illegal?" Alejandra looked at Evie. "Not *really*. Basilio's been working here for years. He's the head building and maintenance supervisor. He can, at any time, say that a room is being worked on and that it's off limits for a while. No one's gonna check up on him, really."

"But that's not all," Natalia started. "Alejandra has just led poor Basilio to believe that she is the one and only favorite niece of the one and only favorite sister of the one and only *Vicente.*"

"And," Xiomara continued, "if dear Basilio ever, ever, needed anything, anything at all, Alejandra would do everything she possibly could to get it for him."

"Vicente?" Evie had to think for a moment. "As in Fox? The *President* of Mexico?

"What?" Dee Dee covered her mouth and laughed. "You gonna get dual citizenship for him and his whole family?"

"No, *tontas.*" Alejandra laughed. "Vicente *Fernandez,* the president of . . . Rancheras!"

"Ally!" Dee Dee cried. "You told him you were related to Vicente Fernandez? *¿El cantante*? You're horrible!"

"Yeah." Alejandra fell back into a love seat, pleased with herself. "At Vicente's, or should I say *Uncle* Vicente's, next *concierto* at El Estadio Azteca, front row, center seats and backstage passes are Basilio's."

"That's if," Dee Dee reminded Alejandra, "you actually *knew* Vicente Fernandez."

"Hey, what can I say?" Alejandra took an apple from the overfilled fruit bowl and took a large bite. She tossed the remaining apple back in the bowl. "I'll just tell my father I need him to get the tickets and then I'll cry or something and he'll figure out a way. He always does!"

"You are so bad." Evie shook her head.

"It works all the time," Alejandra said matter-of-factly. "Yeah, you know how it is. We are all one big happy *familia mexicana.*"

She got up and opened the suite's doors. She looked down the stairs and across the courtyard. "Where the fuck *is* that slow-ass Basilio?" she complained to no one in particular. "I want the champagne already."

* * *

Fortunately for Evie, when Xiomara hooked her iPod to the suite's stereo system, she didn't have Vicente Fernandez on her program. "Uncle Vicente's" ranchera music made Evie sad. Not the "*Ay, qué triste*, my forlorn heart" kind of sad, but sad knowing that when his music took over the Gomez household it meant that Lindsay was in a sad mood and she cleaned a lot slower. A *lot* slower. Which, of course, upset Evie's mother. Not in the "our slow-ass housekeeper" kind of way, but rather,

"*Ay*, poor Lindsay. She misses her family in Mexico. We should help her." Which meant Evie had to give up her weekend to pitch in and clean their two-story house. *Qué* sad, all right.

After Xiomara and Fabiola got their in-room, three-hundred-dollar authentic Chumash mud body wraps, the night began to wind down. Someone clicked on LaTV and a repeat of *Mex 2 the Max*, with the sound turned off, set visuals to the beats of Xiomara's iPod.

Evie drank champagne on the couch, her body feeling tingly and refreshed from her own pumpkin melon body treatment. Her mother claimed that a visit to the Inn's spa made her feel years younger. Evie wondered, should she be feeling nine or ten years old?

Natalia opened her metallic-gold fanny pack. With its jewel studs and heavy black stitching, it was the ugliest fanny pack (or was that redundant?) that Evie had ever seen. Why would Natalia even own something so gauche? Who would ever want, Evie wondered, such an atrocious accessory in their proximity?

All the girls gathered in a semicircle around Natalia as if they all knew what was to come next.

"All *right*." Fabiola smiled as she eyed Natalia's bag. "You saw Mondo?"

Evie looked over. Had she heard right?

"Your friend, Mondo, has the best *mota*, no?" Alejandra asked Evie as she pulled out rolling papers.

"Mondo?" Evie asked. She had heard right. "You got this from Mondo?"

"Yeah." Xiomara looked at Evie as though she was crazy. "Everybody does."

Evie wondered if Raquel knew that Mondo dealt with the Sangros. Well, she guessed, business is business, and dealers don't discriminate.

Dee Dee looked up at the large-faced clock above the gigantic rock fireplace. "Go ahead, start without me." She got up and went to one of the bedrooms to get her bag. She pulled out her cell phone and stood in the doorway, checking for messages.

"*Dela.*" Alejandra looked after her. "*Qué* rude! You are here, *with us.* Aren't you going to party?"

"Yeah, it's just, you know, I talk to Rocio every Friday." Dee Dee stood away from the group, listening to her messages. "And I don't want to miss his call."

Alejandra started to roll herself a joint. "Dela, you gotta get yourself a sidekick."

"Why?" Dee Dee scrunched her forehead. "I like my phone."

"No, a *sidekick,*" Alejandra said. "*Un sancho.* This 'Dude *en* D.F.' is so *seco* already."

"But I love Rocio," Dee Dee said in a rehearsed tone. She continued to listen to her messages. "Is it my fault that he is so far away?"

"It's nobody's fault," Fabiola agreed. "But come on, be realistic."

"It's not about love, Dela," Natalia agreed. "You don't think he's getting action back there while you're out here?"

"*What?*" Dee was horrified at the thought.

"Pu-leeze," Alejandra rolled her eyes.

Dee Dee looked around the suite, then up at the loft. "Evie, do you mind if I go up to the meditation loft? I think I should call him."

"Ay, *Dios.*" Alejandra rolled her eyes.

"Yeah, sure." Evie took a sip from her champagne flute. "I don't care. Just move my bags and stuff to the side."

"You are *losing* it, *chica,*" Alejandra told Dee Dee as she took a puff off her joint.

Dee Dee ignored her and climbed up the kiva ladder into the loft.

Fabiola took a hit off of Alejandra's joint. "That *chica* needs some help," she told Evie.

"Yeah," Natalia said. "She's letting herself get carried away."

"Rule number one, Evie . . ." Alejandra looked at Evie. Her eyes were already small, squinty, and red from her first hit. "Do not get carried away over some boy."

"Rule number two," Fabiola said. "Get it where you can. Anywhere you can."

"Uh . . ." Evie wasn't sure what "it" meant. "Get what?"

Alejandra tilted her head. "Evie, you know. *It.*"

"Oh, right." Evie took another sip of her champagne. What exactly was *it*?

"You know, Evie"—Natalia leaned over and put her arm around Evie—"I really, really love your hair."

"Me too. A lot."

"No, really. You are a really, really pretty girl." Alejandra's words got muddled and soothing. "*¿Qué linda . . . sí?*" She looked at the other girls.

"Oh, *claro que sí*," they all said in a slo-mo chorus.

"See, *chica*," Alejandra said. "I told you I always thought you were pretty. Prettier than that Raquel." She held up her joint toward Evie, in a salute. "Here's to Evie!"

"*¡Sí!* Evie!" The Sangros repeated enthusiastically.

"*Otra vez*?" Alejandra yelled.

"Evie!"

Evie took another sip of her champagne and suddenly felt incredibly light and happy. There was no other place she would rather be in the world than in the Presidential Suite with her wonderful, wonderful new *ah*-migas—Fabiol*a*, Xiomar*a*, Natali*a*, and of course, Alejand*rra*. She looked around the room. They had hooked everything up, the plans, the arrangements with Basilio, all for her. It was almost like a birthday party and nobody—not her mother, not Raquel, none of the Flojos, that's for sure—had ever planned anything as extravagant as this solely for her. And was this something she had craved?

Claro que sí.

* * *

It was 3 A.M. by the time the lights in the suite were turned off and all the girls had headed to separate rooms to crash on their California king-size beds. Evie grabbed her Weekender and trudged up the kiva ladder to her meditation loft. She was suddenly *so* tired. She saw Dee Dee passed out on the luxury egg-foam sleeping pad. She was still in her clothes and *still* holding on to the phone. She *was* getting carried away.

Evie went through her bag looking for her cami to change into when she noticed the red light on her cell phone was blinking. God, she hoped it wasn't her mother. What a buzz kill if she had to call her back. Evie flipped open her phone and saw it was Alex. He had sent her a text message just a few minutes earlier. What was Alex doing up at 3 A.M.? He faithfully went to sleep early the night before doing DP. She flipped open her phone to read his text.

U up?

She wrote back:

Ys.

A few minutes later, he texted back:

I cant sleep

Srry abot 2nte. U mad?

She responded:

No, nt really.

He texted back quickly:

Can i make it up 2 u?

Evie was confused.

?

Alex wrote again:

i wnt 2 make it up 2 u

She texted back:

No worries. No prob.

She tossed her phone on the sleeping pad and started to change. She was surprised to see the cell's red light blinking again.

Yr not mad at me?

Why was Alex so concerned? She was feeling sleepy and just wanted to go to bed, but before she could text him back, he sent her another message:

Cnt sleep Whr r u?

Where *was* she? What, was he gonna come over? What was up with Alex? She didn't know if she should tell him that she was with the Sangros. Ever since he had asked her what was up with her "changes," she wasn't so sure she wanted to tell him all the different things she had been doing. All the seemingly "un-Evie" things. She typed back.

Jst chillin. Whr r u?

He texted back:

In bed

In bed? This surprised Evie. What was Alex doing, texting her while he was in bed? Like, under the covers *in bed*? And if so, what was he wearing? Was he naked? Evie didn't know what to write back. Alex was her friend, a friend she had gotten to know somewhat over the last year, but it seemed like . . . Was he was flirting with her? Jose and Mondo were always silly with her, but Alex was different. She felt excited, somewhat strangely excited. Besides, it's so hard to tell with text messaging. But she knew one thing: He was in bed and he was thinking of her. Whereas if Mondo had texted this it would have seemed crass or icky but . . . well, with Alex it just seemed . . . *nice*. She was definitely not used to this kind of attention from him.

He texted again:

U still there?

She wanted to write something back. All she could think of was a simple:

Ys

A few seconds later:

Thght u fell aslp

She wrote back:

No.

No? God, couldn't she be a little bit more creative?

Alex:

I dnt like fightin w/ u

Evie:

Me 2.

Alex:

Wsh u wre goin 2mrow

Evie:

Me 2, srry

Evie's chest suddenly felt warm. It tingled. He wished he could *be with her*. He wanted to be with her . . . tomorrow. Wait, was she reading too much into his texts? Had he ever been this way with her before? She tried to think. Alex had always been super nice and sweet to her, but he was that way with everyone. He was that way, big-time, with Dee. Sigh. She felt a bit dizzy. Maybe she was reading too much into his words?

Alex:

Ill cll aftr DP

Evie:

K

Alex:

Sleep sweet . . . Evelina

Sleep sweet? Alex had never, *ever* said (or in this case, *texted*) anything like that to her. And he called her Evelina. Was he just hiding behind the security of text messaging? Behind the safety of numbers, symbols, and letters from his cell phone?

Evie's head felt light and her mouth was dry. Alex? *Alex?* She started to think about him. All the sweet little things he'd done for her, walking with her into the Bard party, finding the shell and (at first) wanting to give it to her. He was always so nice to her parents, and when her grandma Sally came to visit last summer, he tried so hard to impress her with his Spanish. She really liked the way he never let other people's issues get in the way of what he thought was right. That's one of the reasons she was confident enough to let him teach her to surf. Even with the Sea Street lineup of aggro short boarders, who were notorious for icing girls who got in the way of their waves, she knew she'd be okay with Alex around.

Wow, Evie thought to herself, Alex *was* really great! How could she not have seen it before?

She turned to her other side and held her cell phone in her hands, the back screen lit up, creating a red glow in the darkness against the—what did the Inn's pamphlet say?—four or five-hundred-thread-count sheets? She went through their message history, reading and rereading what he had typed to her.

Wsh u wre goin 2morw

i wnt 2 make it up 2 u

In bed

Bed. She wasn't imagining it. She reread his last text.

Sleep sweet . . . Evelina

No text shorthand with that. He was clear and direct. He wanted her to sleep sweet. She snapped her phone shut and held her phone close to her chest. She closed her eyes. She would sleep sweet. Alex *was* into her and maybe, yes, she could be into him, too.

* * *

It was already late in the afternoon, right after Dee Dee had dropped off Evie after their night at the Ojai Inn, when Alex finally called. Her cell blared out Daddy Yankee as she walked across the driveway to her house. Not her first choice of a *reggaetón* ringtone, but Fabiola strongly assured her that his beats would grow on her. "Hey," Evie answered the phone, holding it between her left cheek and shoulder. She was juggling her suede shoulder bag, her Weekender, and all the things she'd brought back with her from the Ojai Valley Inn gift shop: body salts with lavender and vanilla ($58), oiled scented candles with blown glass holder ($95), the wonderful feeling that Alex may possibly be into her? *(Priceless!)*

"Hello?" Alex asked. His voice alone excited her. How did *this* happen? He used to be "just Alex"; now he was *Alex*.

"Hey . . . ," Evie breathed eagerly into the phone. She was still on a high from his texting from the night before. She'd reread the text history between them about a million more times before she'd finally fallen asleep.

"I can't . . . you," Alex spoke choppily. "You keep fading . . . and out."

"What?"

"I . . . you. Fading in . . . out."

Great. After checking and rechecking her phone all morning and afternoon, he finally called and they couldn't hear each other.

"Let me call you from the house line," she told him as she started to unlock her front door. "I'll call you right back."

"What?" he asked.

"I'll call you right back."

"What . . . say?"

Grrrr!

"I'll call back, NOW!"

She went inside her house and ran upstairs to her room. She shut the door behind her.

"Evie, are you home?" It was her mother, calling from her own bedroom.

"Yeah," she called out as she threw her Weekender and all the bags on the carpet. Her phone was missing from its cradle. "I'll be out in a sec."

"Did you have fun?" Her mother was now coming down the hall.

"Uh-huh," Evie answered. She looked around for her cordless.

"Evie." Her mother stood on the other side of the closed door. "Why are you being so evasive? Did you color your hair again?"

"No," Evie called out. "You can come in. I'm just looking for my phone."

Her mother opened the door and came in. She immediately noticed the bag from the Ojai Inn. "What is all this?"

Shit.

"Oh, Dela gave it to me," Evie said trying to sound nonchalant.

"Dela?" Her mother opened the bag and went through the items.

"Yeah," Evie went on. "She went with Graciela and . . . it was just a lot that she didn't want." *Where* was her phone?

"Wow." Her mother held up the jar and read the label. "That was very generous of her. You know this mud is from the Dead Sea, from Israel. It's very expensive."

"Uh-huh. I guess."

"You know," her mother said, "I think it's really great you are making new friends."

"Yeah, me too." Evie continued to search for the cordless.

"Not that I have any problem with Raquel." Her mother opened a tube of organic carrot cream and tried it on her hands. "And you know I just adore Alex."

Yeah, me too, Mom. Now help me find the phone so I can adore him some more! "Do you know where my cordless is?" Evie asked.

"How would I know where your phone is?" She put the tube back in the bag and looked around. "How would you know where anything is in this room? Evie, I didn't have California Closets come here to customize our closets just so you could leave all your clothes on the floor."

"Mom, *please,*" Evie begged. "I have to make a major important call."

"A major important call? Evie, you've been with all your girlfriends all night. Who could you possibly need to call so urgently?"

"Mom . . ." Evie was on the verge of an emotional breakdown. She could not find the landline and Alex was waiting. "Where is my cordless?!"

Evie went into the bathroom and looked around. She yanked up her vintage Señor Lopez from the floor, scaring poor Meho, who was napping under it. He yowled and ran away in terror.

"Ooh." Evie looked after him. "Sorry, Meho!"

"Oh," her mother started as though she just remembered something. "It's Lindsay's birthday tomorrow. Did you know that?"

"Nuh-uh." Evie came out of the bathroom. *Where* was her phone?

"Your dad and I want to take her to dinner tonight," her mother went on. "You need to come."

"Okay." Evie rummaged through the piles of clothes strewn about her bedroom floor. "I'll be there." She lifted her Hawaiian fabric pillows and Baja Road Trip blanket. Still no phone.

Her mother finally chipped in and lifted up some spiral notebooks. And yes, the cordless phone was under one of them.

"Of course." Her mother held the receiver out to Evie. "It would be here, under your notebooks. You never touch *them*."

"Okay, Mom." Evie grabbed the phone eagerly. "I have to make a call."

"Okay, okay, Evie." Her mother held her hands up, feigning surrender. "Remember, no plans tonight. Lindsay's husband and sister are coming also."

Evie held the phone to her side and walked her mother out. As soon as she was out of her bedroom, she shut the door behind her.

Evie grabbed the pillows off the floor and slipped off her flojos. *Finally!* She propped the pillows against her headboard and leaned back against them. She wanted everything to be perfect when she returned Alex's call. It was going to be their first conversation since their sexy texty from the night before, since Alex had confessed his true feelings for her. Or, more appropriately, hs tru feelins 4 hr.

She dialed his number. But now his line was busy. *Busy?* On a cell? Maybe Alex was calling her?

When she clicked off, she saw he had just left her a message. She immediately called him back, but got his voice mail. And cells were supposed to *assist* with communication? Normally, not reaching Alex wouldn't be such a big deal. Evie would just catch up with him at school on Monday, but now she just *had* to hear his voice. She had to know what all that texting meant.

She listened to his message.

"Hey, Eves, I thought . . . call . . . right back. Anyway . . . leave with . . . dad. So . . . I guess . . . I try . . . later."

Later? Evie cringed. She replayed the message. "I try . . . later?" It was so hard to make out was he was saying. What was up with his phone? Did he mean later as in later *that* night? But she had to go to dinner with her family . . . she would miss his call! Maybe he meant later, as in *later* over the weekend? Or maybe he meant much later? As in Monday at school?

She tossed her cell phone on her bed and turned to her side. She looked up at her P. Rod poster. Until getting the texts from Alex, he had been the only boy on her mind, in her life. He was distant and safe. But now Evie felt dizzy with agony. She desperately wanted to talk with Alex, but she didn't want to call him *again*. She refused to appear so needy. It was just like the Sangros had said the night before: Do *not* get carried away over some boy.

Alex, unfortunately, didn't call back the whole rest of the afternoon. And then, double unfortunately, Evie had to leave with her family to celebrate Lindsay's birthday. As she and her parents drove to the Elephant Bar to meet Lindsay; her husband, Jack; and her sister Eileen, Evie sat in the backseat checking and rechecking her phone. What, Evie wondered, had people done before cell phones? Waited at home?

Evie had a hard time being in a celebratory mood at the Elephant Bar, even though Lindsay was in great spirits, especially for someone turning sixty-three years old.

"Una vieja!" Lindsay pretended to cry on Jack's shoulder.

"Mi'ja." Jack looked at Evie. "Lindsay tells me your *amiguita*, Dee Dee, is back. How nice for you. I bet you missed her."

"Oh, yeah," was all Evie could say.

"I remember when you all were little girls—you, Dee Dee,

and Raquel. You were the best of friends. You had the biggest crush on Alfredo. Remember that?"

"Yeah."

"But now you must have so many boyfriends."

"Well, not really." Evie looked around. Seeing the other couples with their hands intertwined, exchanging romantic glances, made Evie's chest ache. She looked at her phone. Alex *still* hadn't called. She let her mind wander for a second, wondering what would happen if they did get together. Would they have one of those cute combined names like celebrity couples always got? What would they be? Alevie? Evex? Hmmm, maybe not. Sounded too much like a decongestant, or worse, a hemorrhoid ointment.

"Evie." Her mother firmly tapped Evie's shin under the table. "Put your phone away. You are being rude."

Rude? And kicking someone in public wasn't?

Nonetheless, Evie reluctantly put her phone down, but didn't put it away. She simply put it on vibrate and discreetly placed it between her legs. Sangro rule number two: Get it where you can. Anywhere you can.

* * *

The next afternoon, Sunday, Evie and the Sangros went over to Dee Dee's to lay out by the pool. Saturday's weather had been disappointingly overcast and they were all anxious to make up for lost tanning time. The end of each chaise longue (six in total) was pointed directly toward the sun, as if such strategic positioning would help them obtain a tan faster.

"What did you do last night?" Dee Dee asked Evie. The straps of her white bikini top were untied and dangling at her sides. Evie glanced over and saw that her left breast was still pure. Thank God. She still hadn't got that cheesy *DF* tattoo she had claimed she was going to get.

"It was Lindsay's birthday," Evie told her. She kept her eyes closed under her sunglasses. "We all went to the Elephant Bar."

She couldn't stop thinking about Alex. He still hadn't called her back. Had he changed his mind about calling? Or was he waiting? Was *he* trying not to appear too eager? Or was he busy doing something else and not even thinking about her? Maybe "later" meant "later," as in *after* the weekend? She was going crazy interpreting his cryptic messages. Why couldn't he just be more direct? "I will call you at nine fifteen tonight." And then he would have done so and that would have been that.

"Who's Lindsay?" Xiomara asked. She was on the opposite side of Evie. She didn't have her bikini straps untied. She was completely topless. A hearty dab of white sunblock topped each breast, making them look like two mini Disneyland Matterhorns or, in a Sangro's case, two mini Popocatepetls.

"She's our housekeeper." Evie picked up her cell and checked to see if it had somehow magically turned itself off. Nope, still on.

"You went out with your *maid*?" Alejandra leaned up and looked over Xiomara and Natalia's oiled bodies to face Evie. "On a Saturday night?"

"Yeah, why not?"

Alejandra lifted her sunglasses and looked at Evie.

"I wouldn't be caught dead with my *criada* in public," she said. "Maybe if she had to pick me up, like from shopping or something."

"Or if you needed her to pick you up from the health clinic, to sign papers." Fabiola smirked. *"Again."*

"Lindsay's actually not a maid," Evie asserted. "She doesn't even live with us. Besides, you don't even have a maid, Alejandra. You live in the dorms."

"Yeah, I do," Alejandra checked the tan line from her bikini bottom before turning over to her side. "Back home, in Mexico. But they always screw up my mother's clothes and then she is always firing them and we have to get new ones. When I go home for vacation, I never know which two new *Indios* I'm gonna have to meet."

"*Ally*." Dee Dee looked over at Alejandra. "You don't have to be so harsh."

"Well, it's true." Alejandra let out an exaggerated exhale. "Am I lying, Fabiola?"

"No," Fabiola agreed. "Your mom is a total *perra* when it comes to her clothes."

"That's because she has nice ones." Alejandra leaned over

and grabbed her diet orange soda. "Not like the standard stuff you find here in malls. In Mexico City"—she looked over at Evie—"we have boutiques with customized tailored clothing. Oh!" Her eyes suddenly lit up. "You should see what my mother's sending me for *Día de los Muertos.*"

"You mean for the dance?" Evie had almost forgotten about it.

"Yeah." Alejandra took a sip from her soda. "And this year, it'd better be good. I don't want my costume flown in from Mexico for nothing."

"Your costume's from Mexico?" Dee Dee asked. Evie could sense a competitive tone in her voice. "Who are you going as?"

"María Félix," Alejandra sang with an air of superiority. "I *love* 1940s film stars, but *only* Mexican ones."

"Ooh, *qué* sexy!" Natalia raved. "You are gonna look *caliente.* Only *you* could pull María Félix off."

"Yeah, only you," Dee Dee echoed the sentiment, sounding a little reluctant.

Despite the larger-than-life announcement on Villanueva's main marquee, Evie had forgotten about the dance. It was now just a week away, the first Saturday of November.

"But wait," Evie said suddenly. "Isn't the dance the same night as Fabiola's birthday party?"

"Nuh-uh," said Xiomara. "Her party's the night before, on Friday."

"Yeah, and don't be all *coda* and not bring a present."

Fabiola held her right elbow up and hit it with her left hand a couple of times. The girls all laughed, except Natalia.

"Hey." Natalia frowned. "My family's from Monterrey and we are *not* cheap!"

Evie leaned up from her chaise and checked her cell.

"What's with you?" Dee Dee shaded her eyes as she looked over at Evie. "You've been checking your phone all day."

"Maybe she's waiting for Lindsay to call her," Xiomara ribbed.

"Yeah," Natalia said dryly. "They're gonna hit the night clubs later tonight."

"Hey," Alejandra said, "at least she'll be able to buy you liquor. Make her good for *something*."

"Yeah, I'll have her get us more Patrón!" Evie found herself giggling. But, she couldn't help but feel a twinge of shame as they giggled with her. She cared a lot about Lindsay. She was like family. But as soon as she saw that she had no new messages on her cell, her spirits just fell even more.

* * *

After the afternoon sun slowly drifted below the Pacific Ocean, or more appropriately, the stucco walls of Rio Estates, shade enveloped the de LaFuentes' backyard. The impromptu tanning party at Dee Dee's came to an end and after comparing tan lines, the Sangros gathered up their things and headed back to their dorms.

"Ay." Dee Dee clicked her tongue at Alejandra. "You got too dark, Ally. María Félix was *más güera*!"

"It doesn't really matter," Alejandra said calmly as she pulled the car keys to her Beemer from her bag. "My costume is so amazing, no one is even going to bother with my tan."

"O-*kay*." Dee Dee wanted to make sure Alejandra knew she wasn't so convinced.

After all the Sangros had gone, Evie mentioned to Dee Dee that she didn't plan on going to the dance.

"*What?*" Dee Dee looked at her. "Why?"

"It's just not my thing." Evie started picking up the glasses, soda cans, and chip bowls from around the pool.

"Oh, just leave those," Dee Dee told her. "Marcela will come out and clean up. "But why don't you wanna go to the dance?"

"We never go to school dances."

"Who's 'we'?" Dee Dee asked.

"Okay, *I* never go to the school stuff," Evie said. "It's sorta dorky."

"Oh, and sitting around, being all *floja*, doing nothing, is so cool?" She gathered her magazines off the chaise.

"Hey," Evie said. "*I'm* not the one who planned a whole afternoon of sunbathing around my pool."

"Evie, you *have* to go to the dance. I already have our outfits!" Dee Dee ignored her last comment.

"*Our* outfits?" Evie raised her eyebrows.

"Yeah," Dee Dee continued. "Ally's not the only one with such *fabulous* connections. Gracie has all this great stuff from

Mexico, all these fancy embroidered clothes, crinolines, hats, some jewelry. She used to be an actress in the Mexican soaps."

"Really?" Evie wondered if Lindsay would know of her. "Which one?"

"Oh, just about all the *telenovelas,*" Dee Dee bragged. "But you know how the stories just run for a limited time, and she just had minor roles. She was always the *amante* and I guess she was good, because she was given a *lot* of the leftover costumes, and that doesn't always happen for actresses with bit parts."

Graciela, a seductress? *Imagínate.* Wait until Evie told her mother.

"Anyway," Dee Dee continued as she opened the sliding glass door to her house, "you, Alejandro, and I *have* to go to the dance together. I have it all planned."

"Alex?" Evie asked. "When did you talk to Alex?" Her stomach suddenly felt jumpy. When did he talk to Dee Dee? And why hadn't he called her?

"I haven't talked to him . . . yet," Dee Dee admitted. "But he'll do it."

Evie couldn't help but feel unnerved by Dee Dee's statement. *Yeah, like you got him dancing in the palm of your hand.*

"I got it all figured out," Dee Dee went on. "You'll be Frida Kahlo, Alex can be Diego Rivera, and I'll be Cristina, Frida's sister. *Qué* cute, no?"

"What?" Evie balked. "Uh, *no.* Dela, I'm not gonna be Frida Kahlo."

She caught her reflection in the sliding glass doors and tousled her blonde bangs.

"Evie, *yes*." Dee Dee walked into the kitchen. "You *have* to, to make it work."

"Dela . . ." Evie followed her. "Frida is so played out. Everyone goes as Frida."

"How do you know?" Dee Dee asked. "You said you never go to school stuff."

"I mean, she's played out everywhere. Even my *mother* is over Frida."

"Yeah." Dee Dee put her *Teen People* on the counter. "But I bet nobody here knows how to do her right. You should see the stuff that Gracie has. You won't believe it. We'll be different than anyone at the dance. Even Alejandra."

"No, *you*'ll be different. Nobody ever dresses as Cristina. What did she even look like?"

"Oh," Dee Dee said knowingly, pulling her hair out of her ponytail. "She was very beautiful, quite the Coyoacán *chica*."

Great. So Dee Dee was gonna be the sexy one and Evie was gonna be stuck with an ugly unibrow and manly moustache. In front of Alex? No *way*.

"Uh, no thanks," Evie said. "I mean, thanks for offering the costume and everything."

"Evie . . ." Dee Dee opened the fridge and looked through it. She kept her back to Evie. "You *have* to go as Frida. Nobody will know I'm Cristina unless there's a Frida and a Diego."

"Dela, nobody is gonna care," Evie said. "It's not that kind of dance, or school, for that matter."

Dee Dee suddenly got quiet. She got a soda from the refrigerator and popped it open. She looked away from Evie and said nothing.

"Dela, why don't you dress as Frida and I'll go as Cristina?" There, a compromise.

"Because," Dee Dee said softly. "I already had the outfit for Cristina tailored to fit me. The dance is a week away and I thought for sure you would want to go with me. Remember how much fun we had, dressing up for the Marina Park Beauty Pageant? Remember when we were kids?"

"Yeah." Evie sighed. She hated to let Dee Dee down. "Okay, I'll think about it. We'll figure something out."

"Well, I hope you do. I still have to tell Alejandro." She started to smile. "So, you want something to drink?"

"Yeah, okay." Evie looked in the fridge and helped herself to a Kiwi Strawberry Snapple.

"What's the Snapple Fact?" Dee Dee asked as Evie twisted off the cap.

Evie looked and read it out loud. "Snapple Fact #168, One brow wrinkle is the result of 200,000 frowns."

"That can't be true," Dee Dee said. "How would they know something like that?"

"Let's not try and find out." Evie threw her a look, making

sure not to frown herself. "So, quit pressuring me. I don't want to be pushed into Botox before my time."

But really, Evie wondered, why was Dee Dee so eager to always have Alex in the picture? He had been practically her personal escort at school, her potential private swim instructor and now her date for the *Día de los Muertos* dance? Why even *have* Evie along? She drank her Snapple. Then she remembered: Didn't Diego have an affair with Frida's sister, Cristina? She was sure of it. Yes. And *that's* a Snapple Fact.

12

ShaggyMA (8:07 PM): Plans tonight?
RioChica (8:08 PM): Party, again.
ShaggyMA (8:08 PM): You are the butterfly!

It was Friday night, the evening of Fabiola's birthday party. The whole week at school had been a blur for Evie. When she'd finally gotten to speak with Alex, it was already Monday before lunch.

"Hey, sorry I couldn't call you back," he said when he came by her locker. "I went out to Bakersfield with my dad." Bakersfield? Wasn't that the point of having a cell phone? So you could call anyone, from anywhere?

Alex seemed nervous, like he had to explain more. "My cell line was shaky. I don't know what's up with my phone lately. I gotta get it checked out."

"Yeah, I guess you should do that." Evie shut her locker. "So, thanks for the text messages the other night," she started. Why was *she* the one to bring it up? "They were sweet."

"Sweet?" Alex smiled uncomfortably. His neck turned a light pink. "Sweet in what way?"

"I mean . . ." Evie stumbled over her words. "Just nice."

Why did she feel so awkward? He was still "just Alex," right? And why was he just looking at her, waiting? Say something, already!

"So," Alex started slowly, "what are you doing tonight? You wanna hang out?"

"Hang out?" Evie asked. What exactly did that mean? "Hang out"? Hanging out pre–sexy texty meant to simply "hang out," but now, *post*–sexy texty, did hanging out mean a date?

"Yeah, I can hang out," Evie said. Then she suddenly remembered. "Oh, wait. It's Fabiola's birthday. I can't." She gripped her backpack tightly. "Uh, do you wanna come with? It's gonna be at *La Pantera Negra*. I sorta have to go."

"Nah," Alex said. "I mean, no offense, she's nice and everything, but those girls, I don't know, they ain't my tribe. You know what I mean?"

"Yeah, I guess." *Tribe?* And what tribe did the Flojos belong to? They-Who-Do-Nada Nation?

"Besides," Alex said, "I'm gonna do Dawn Patrol tomorrow. I gotta get to bed early."

Why didn't he ask her to go? Maybe he was already losing interest in her?

* * *

Later that evening, Alex text messaged her:

Hve fun 2nite

Evie:

Thx

Whre r u?

She waited and waited for him to text something back, but he didn't. She finally closed her phone. That was it? No "Sleep sweet"? No "Wsh I cld C U 2mrow"? What had happened between her and Alex?

Evie had to get Alex out of her mind. She decided the best thing she could do was just relax and concentrate on Fabiola's birthday party. She went over to Dee Dee's to get ready.

"Clip or no clips?" she asked Dee Dee later that night as they elbowed each other for mirror space in Dee Dee's bathroom.

"Either." Dee Dee didn't even look over at her.

Evie held up two different barrettes. "Velvet or rhinestone?"

"Neither."

"You're a lot of help," Evie complained sarcastically. She tossed the barrettes back in Dee Dee's plastic makeup bin. "I thought shorter hair was easier."

"Beauty is never easy." Dee Dee sighed as she looked over her profile and sucked in her stomach. She had removed her navel ring for the evening and clasped a thin gold belly chain around her waist. She had also put on her blue contacts. Something, Evie noticed, that Dee Dee did only for special occasions.

As soon as Evie figured out what to do with her hair (more Garnier surf paste, no clips), she had a new problem to tackle. She sat on top of the toilet seat and looked down at the silver two-inch sandals that Dee Dee strongly suggested she wear. They were already pinching painfully into the sides of her feet.

"I still don't know about these," Evie said, referring to the borrowed slinky-slinks. "Don't you think they're a bit too much?"

"Of course they are!" Dee Dee agreed as she sprayed more Curious in the air and walked through it. "Remember when we were kids? You always talked about wanting to wear your sister's heels. I don't understand what the problem is now."

"The problem is I think they *are* my sister's heels." Evie crossed one foot over her thigh and inspected the semi-spike heel. "You don't think they're a little dated?"

"*Dated?*" Dee Dee was surprised. "Evie, they're retro. You of all people should know that. I got them in L.A. Besides, and don't take this wrong, but have you ever thought of dressing up a bit more? I mean, you look so pretty with your new hair and, I don't know, I'd think you'd want to spice it up a bit."

"Spice it up? What am I? A buffalo wing?"

Dee Dee threw her an exasperated look. "Never mind. Wear whatever you feel comfortable in. I don't care anymore." She held a cord up to the front of her neck and turned her back toward Evie. "Here, can you help me with this?"

Evie stood up and clasped the black silk cord around Dee Dee's neck.

Dee Dee then turned around to show the pendant off to Evie. "Cute, huh?"

But when Evie looked, she saw that it was no mere pendant. It was a small shell. A small iridescent abalone shell, just like the one Alex had found at Bard Beach. Evie's heart dropped. How could he have given her shell to Dee Dee? What *was* going on between them?

"What's wrong?" Dee Dee held the pendant out and looked down at it. "You don't like it?"

"Oh, no." Evie looked away. She wasn't about to admit jealously and she definitely couldn't go into feelings she hadn't even sorted out yet. "It's just these sandals." She brought her foot up. "They really hurt and I don't wanna get blisters. I think I'm gonna change back into my flojos."

"Evie, *no.*" Dee Dee looked down at Evie's feet. "They look so sexy on you. Here." She opened up the bathroom cabinet and pulled out some Band-Aids. "I'll bring supplies, just in case."

As Evie wobbled what seemed like a long journey from

Dee Dee's bedroom to her car in the driveway, she still couldn't take her mind off the necklace. When Alex had found the shell at Bard Beach, he had promised—*promised!*—to "polish it up real good" for Evie and, at the time, she thought it was a sweet gesture. She didn't even wear necklaces, but now, more than anything, she wanted to be the one wearing the shell. How, *how* could Alex have given the shell to Dee Dee? Sure, late-night text messages were nice and all, but he gave Dee Dee a *necklace*. And surely that must mean something? This was going to be a long night.

As they approached Rio Estates' downtown area in Dee Dee's car, Evie was still surprised to learn that Fabiola was actually serious about celebrating her sixteenth birthday at *La Pantera Negra*, a Mexican restaurant and lounge on the main boulevard. It was in the heart of the "historic" downtown district, so named, her father joked, because the city didn't want to pay for an architectural or beautification upgrade. *La Pantera* boasted a bar with a kidney-shaped counter and a mirrored splash-back. Red leather tuck-and-roll booths encased tables topped with ancient Mexican coins and protective glass. On just about every wall hung black velvet paintings of sleek panthers perching on ledges, poised and ready to pounce. It had been years since Evie had even set foot in *La Pantera* and, according to her father and mother, it wasn't the place it used to be. It was now just a dive where *cholos veteranos* (gasp!) hung out, and the cheese was no longer the white crumbling kind, *fresca,* from Mexico, but rather the standard orange kind from Costco (double gasp!).

When she and Dee Dee finally arrived at *La Pantera*, it was already close to ten o'clock P.M. and as Evie got out of the Beetle, she braced herself for a long, painful journey from the car to the front entrance of the restaurant. Is this what Dee Dee used to get Alex's attention? Incredibly painful shoes? "God, when's the last time you were here?" Dee Dee asked, as they walked up to *La Pantera*.

"Not since I was a kid." Evie wasn't in the mood to chitchat with Dee Dee. As soon as they got into the restaurant, she planned to bail on her.

"When I was younger," Dee Dee started as she opened the door and let Evie go in ahead of her, "I thought *La Pantera Negra* was the most glamorous place in the world. I even fantasized about someday having my wedding reception there. *¿Qué chiste*, huh?"

Evie said nothing. She just wanted the night to be over as soon as possible. As she followed Dee Dee to the back area, she pulled out her cell phone. No new message from Alex.

* * *

The lounge of *La Pantera* was already packed with people but Evie and Dee Dee immediately found Fabiola at the head of a long banquet table. She was surrounded by all the Sangros, some other friends Evie didn't recognize, and a mountain of wrapped gifts. Everyone was dressed to the *nueves*: silky camisoles and short skirts on the girls, sport coats and polo shirts for the guys. The air contained a mix of flowery perfume and woodsy cologne. Maybe it was a good thing that Evie had worn the slinky-slinks.

"Feliz cumpleaños," Evie said and kissed Fabiola on the cheek.

"Thank you, *chica*!" Fabiola seemed high from all the attention. She wore a pearl-studded tiara, a smashed purple bow was taped to the side of her head, and her face was covered in red and pink lipstick kissy marks. "You know I'm having my real birthday party in Mexico. A big bash at my parent's ranch, near Lake Chapala!"

"Oh, really?" Evie smiled.

"Yeah, we're all flying back for a three-day weekend. You should come!"

"When?" Evie asked. But Fabiola was pulled in another direction before she could answer.

Dee Dee turned to Evie. "So, do you want anything to drink?"

Evie's feet and heart were aching. What, was she gonna drown her misery in a Diet Coke? "Uh . . ." She looked at the drink menu above the bar. "What do they have?"

"Oh, we can get anything!" Dee Dee started swaying to blaring hip-hop. "You know how *La Pantera* is with their drinking policy."

Without even waiting for Evie to say something, Dee Dee

headed toward the bar and she soon disappeared into the thick of the party. Evie suddenly found herself feeling uncomfortably alone. She craned her neck to look for Dee Dee, but soon lost sight of her. Hey, wasn't *she* the one who was going to skip out on *her*?

As the minutes clicked by, more people who Evie didn't recognize arrived. Everyone was dressed up fancy and seemed to be in a party mood. With all their additional body heat, it soon felt as if the entire oxygen supply from *La Pantera* were being sucked out. Soon, everyone was fanning themselves with the plastic dinner menus and wiping their foreheads with the delicate cream-colored cocktail napkins.

Evie began to feel even more out of place. None of the guests made attempts to meet her, and all the Sangros—Fabiola, Natalia, Xiomara—appeared to be engaged in exclusive conversations. Alejandra was now nowhere to be seen.

Evie finally saw Dee Dee again, laughing and looking like she was having a grand old time, wedged tight between two unknown revelers in a small red leather booth. Evie was about to make her way toward her when she saw the abalone shell, dangling precariously from the thin cord around her neck. She swallowed hard. She would definitely rather be alone than be with Dee Dee, that's for sure. What was that saying that Lindsay had told her? "*Vale más estar sola que mal acompañada*"? It's better to be alone than with bad company? Yeah, something like that.

Evie continued to walk around the dimly lit lounge, trying not to look *so* aimless.

"Hey, Evie!" It was Fabiola calling out to her.

"Yeah?" Evie asked eagerly.

"Have some *pastel*!" Fabiola handed Evie a small plate with a slice of chocolate cake on it. However she didn't, Evie noticed, ask her to join in eating the cake with her. "And please," Fabiola said looking at her, "try not to look *tan seriosa*. This *is* a celebration, *chica*!"

Evie took her slice of Fabiola's birthday cake and walked away, trying hard to look less *seriosa*. She figured, as long as she looked like she was enjoying the birthday cake, she *was* part of the celebration, whether or not anyone talked to her. However, when she was finally scraping the side of her dessert plate with her fork, she knew it was time to find a new focus for the evening. Fortunately, that's when she saw it—the old jukebox in the far back corner of the lounge. It looked like the same grand, gaudy jukebox she remembered as a kid. A bit smaller, of course, but that's what happens when you grow up—things shrink on you.

Evie went over to the jukebox and flipped through choices that ranged from Los Tigres del Norte to Green Day. The old juke had been updated with CDs rather than the vinyl 45s that once slid out onto a turntable. She finally found something she wanted to hear. She put in two coins and pressed down on two separate buttons, G and 4.

"What did you pick?"

Evie looked up and found a guy looking over her shoulder. He looked down at the selections with her and she quickly glanced over at him. She didn't want to blatantly check him out. He was tall with short dark hair, dark eyes, thick eyebrows, and had a small mole on the left side of his chin. Okay, maybe it was obvious she was looking him over.

"G4."

"Ah yes." He smiled. "G4. I just downloaded them."

"No." She laughed. "I mean Audioslave."

He smiled wider. "What's your name?"

"Ev— Evelina."

"Do you want anything to drink?"

"Me? Oh . . ." She then noticed that he was wearing a black *guayabera* and a pair of Ben Davis work pants. "Oh." She laughed to herself. "I'm sorry. I totally thought you were a guest."

"What?" The boy seemed confused.

Evie decided to take a chance on *La Pantera*'s drinking policy. "Yeah, can I get, um, some champagne?"

"What do you mean, you thought I was a guest?"

"Wait, what do *you* mean?" she asked.

"I don't work here," he said.

"Oh!" Evie covered her mouth. "I'm sorry, I just thought—"

"The way that I'm dressed." The boy sounded insulted. "That I look like I work in the kitchen or something?"

"No, it's just . . ." Evie felt stupid.

"What?" he said sarcastically. "I'm too *rasquache* for your *Chilanga* taste?"

"Chilanga?" Evie frowned. "I'm not from Mexico City."

"You could have fooled me. I guess you're like all my cousin Fabiola's friends."

"You're Fabiola's cousin?"

"Yeah, I'm from D.F. too, *La Condesa*, but I don't go around flaunting it like all these fools." He looked around.

"No," Evie started. "I mean, yeah, I totally know what you mean. My parents, they also have money but—"

"What's that supposed to mean?"

"No, nothing."

He looked around. "Yeah, well, I need to get going anyway. See you around, Evelina . . ."

"No, wait . . ."

But it was too late. He'd already gone back into the crowd. Her eyes followed him and saw him hug Fabiola tightly before heading for the front exit.

Evie felt horrible. This guy was misjudging her for misjudging him! She didn't care how he dressed. The only person at the whole party who seemed to be *a lot* like her and she actually made him run for the exit. God, could this Sangro party get any worse? She was alone again.

Evie made her way back through the crowd as the slinky-slinks pinched the top of her feet even more. She had thought that she and Dee Dee wore the same size, but it didn't *feel* that way. Doesn't a size seven Mexican translate to a size seven American? Maybe that's what happens when you wear flojos all the time. The feet, they expand *mucho*.

Even through the dim lighting of the lounge she could see a large blister beginning to form on her right foot. She remembered the Band-Aids that Dee Dee had brought, but now Dee Dee was nowhere to be seen. Evie decided to head to the restroom where she could at least get some toilet paper to cushion the throbbing. But on her way, she passed by *La Pantera*'s retro photo booth. She was surprised it was still there, in seemingly working condition. When they were kids, she and Raquel used to beg their fathers for quarters so they could get their picture taken. Raquel would always make funny faces inside the booth, trying to get Evie to laugh right before the flash went off.

The pain on her right foot was becoming unbearable, so Evie bent down to loosen her sandal strap and when she did, she gasped. There, on the other side of the photo booth's curtain, were two pairs of flojos. A pair of faded suede Sanuks and a pair of brand-new red Roxys. She *knew* those flojos. At least, the Sanuks. They belonged to Jose. Evie could barely believe it. What was *he* doing at *La Pantera*? She looked closer and, yup, the feet were definitely Jose's. Who else had a beaver's tail tattooed on the outside of his ankle? And Raquel's feet? Evie couldn't help but notice how uncharacteristically pale they looked.

Evie immediately felt relieved. Jose and Raquel were her friends, really. Sure, they hadn't been speaking, but they were outnumbered this evening and probably feeling it. After all, why else would they be holed up in a photo booth, waiting to make a clear escape from the Sangro convention?

Without giving it another thought, Evie pulled the curtain open, and all but toppled right into Jose. Damn those slinky-slinks!

"Whoa, whoa, Blondie." Jose looked up in surprise. He leaned over from the booth's stool and helped Evie up. "Someone's had a little too much to drink?"

Evie helped herself up, "No, no, I just—" She felt her face grow warm with embarrassment. She looked up, thinking that maybe she and Raquel could share a laugh about it, her falling over in her ridiculous shoes. But to her horror, she discovered that the girl enveloped around Jose was not Raquel. It was Alejandra de los Santos.

"Evie!" Alejandra exclaimed. "*¡Ay!* You scared me! Hey, take a photo with us!" She scooted over on Jose's lap to make more room.

"Yeah," Jose patted his free knee, indicating Evie should sit on it. "I'm down for a ménage à trois."

Both of them looked disheveled; Alejandra's always straightened hair was tousled and the top buttons of her blouse were undone. Jose's Trunk Ltd T-shirt was pulled up and out of his cords.

"Evie!" Alejandra continued to gush. "Come on, let's take a photo together!"

Evie looked behind her at the crowd. Was everyone totally oblivious to the fact that Jose and Alejandra were practically having sex in the photo booth? Didn't any of the other Sangros see that Jose, who they all knew was Raquel's boyfriend, was with Alejandra? Is this how guys were? How the Sangros were? She looked over at the booth where Dee Dee was sitting, still laughing with two strangers she had yet to introduce Evie to. Did she even notice that Evie was gone? It seemed as though everyone went after what they each wanted. Maybe it was time she did, too.

Sangro rule number one: Don't get carried away over some boy and rule number two: Get it where you can. Anywhere you can. That was good enough for her.

Evie stepped back into the booth.

"Yeah." Jose smiled and patted his left knee again. "Sit down and tell Santy what you want for Christmas."

Evie positioned herself on his thigh as best she could and Alejandra took over the right side of his lap. It was a tight fit for all three of them crammed in the small, narrow booth.

Alejandra lifted her feet up to show off her flojos. "Look, look what Josito bought me! *Muy chistoso, ¿no?* And it's not even *my* birthday!"

"Yeah, cool." Evie looked down at Alejandra's feet.

"Let's take the picture!" Alejandra pulled out her wallet from her handbag.

"Yeah." Jose looked over at Evie. "Let's capture the moment, right, Blondie?"

"Right." Evie smiled back at Jose. If Alex wasn't gonna own up to his text messaging or give her the attention she deserved, well, why not have some harmless cutesy time with Jose? She tapped the labret on his chin. "So, does this ever hurt?"

"Depends on how much pain your inner thighs can take."

Evie giggled and squeezed his arm. "You are *so* bad!"

Jose winked at her. He *was* cute! But, Evie reminded herself, he *was* Raquel's.

"Okay." Alejandra was not paying attention to them. She positioned a quarter near the machine's slot. "I'm gonna put the money in and then it's gonna be fast, so get ready."

Jose had his arm around Evie. She could feel his hand inch under her arm and closer to the outer wire of her bra. She moved, but just a little.

"What's wrong?" he asked.

"Nothing."

The timer for the first photo started flashing.

"Okay," Alejandra squealed as she tilted her head down and brushed her hair forward. "Smile, sexy like!"

The camera flash went off quickly, before Evie could even think of a pose.

"Here comes the next one!" Alejandra announced.

"Let's do something goofy," Evie quickly suggested.

"Yeah, let's." Alejandra giggled and pulled out her cheeks with her fingers.

Evie crossed her eyes and stuck out her tongue.

"My . . ." Jose looked over at Evie. "What a long tongue you have, Grandma."

Evie giggled. The camera flash went off.

Alejandra pounded Jose's shoulder and pouted. "Jose! You didn't make a goofy face!"

"Okay, okay." Jose looked straight at the camera. "Now the last one I want you ladies to throw Papa a kiss, right here on each cheek." He tilted his head up.

Alejandra put her arms around Jose and puckered up. She was getting ready for the timer, but when the camera flash went off, Jose turned his entire head toward Evie and pressed his face into hers. He slid his tongue deep into her mouth and at the same time, moved his hand higher, around her chest, and rubbed his hand slowly across her breast.

Evie felt a dangerous bolt of electricity shoot across her body.

"Jose!" She jerked away.

"Oh, Evie." He leaned back into Alejandra and just laughed. "Don't be such a prude."

"I'm not a prude." Evie wiped her mouth. "You're an asshole!"

"Hey," Alejandra pouted. "What's going on?!" She obviously hadn't seen exactly what Jose had just done.

Evie started to get up from the booth's seat.

"Where you going?" Jose hung on to her hand.

"Out of here." Evie crossed her arms, covering her chest.

"What's wrong, Evelina?" Alejandra asked. "Camera shy?"

"Yeah." Evie glared at her. "*Exactly.*" She looked behind her, at the party. "I gotta go to the bathroom."

Alejandra put her skinny arms around Jose again. "Okay, come back, yeah?"

Evie didn't answer. She stepped out and Alejandra wasted no time closing the booth's curtain.

"Hey, Evie." Jose poked his head out from the curtain.

Evie looked back. "Yeah?"

"You be a good girl." He looked at her firmly. "Okay?"

"What do you mean?"

"You know what I mean."

And unfortunately, she did. She wasn't to say anything to Raquel.

Evie left the grinding, slobbery couple to themselves and made her way to the back exit of *La Pantera.* She needed fresh air and a lot of it. She couldn't believe what had just happened. She could taste the cigarette smoke from Jose's mouth inside hers. And Jose with Alejandra de los Santos? How long had *that* been going on? Did Dee Dee know about them? Did Raquel know, or even suspect? No, there was no way Raquel would put up with such crap. *No way.*

She felt so disgusted. How could she let Jose get up all over her? God, how could she do that to Raquel? To herself? She deserved much better for her first big-time kiss. She looked at her phone. Why hadn't Alex returned her text message?

Evie paced the back parking lot. It was already close to

midnight and most of the shops and taco shop on the main drag were shutting down, making the whole downtown area feel like a ghost town. Evie felt totally, completely alone, as if every slight movement she made was magnified, demonstrating that she had no one with her, in the parking lot, in her life. She crossed her arms tightly across her chest. She wasn't used to hanging around the downtown area alone. She wanted to be home, in her bed, cuddling with Meho—immediately. But how would she get back? Take a bus? Yeah, right. The transfer at Plaza Park alone would take at least five hours.

Her mother always told her that if there was ever an emergency, any type of emergency, she could always call home and she would come and pick her up, no questions asked. Did this count as an emergency? Probably not.

Evie flipped open her phone and dialed 411.

"Can you connect me with a taxi service?" she asked the operator.

Living in a three-auto household and having friends with cars, Evie'd never had the opportunity to use a taxi in Rio Estates. The only time she'd used a cab was when the whole family visited Sabrina at Stanford and they all made shopping trips into San Francisco. Her mother, overwhelmed by the one-way vertical streets, would always spring for a taxi.

"I'm sorry." The operator didn't sound so sorry. "We can't recommend a business. You have to give us a name."

"Okay, um," Evie thought out loud. "How about Yellow . . . Yellow Checkered Cab Service?" That sounded like something a taxi service might be called. And there had to be at least one listed in all of Ventura County, right?

"Do you have a street address?" the operator asked impatiently.

"Uh, do you have anything downtown?"

"I'm sorry, but I need an address."

Evie clicked off. She looked at her cell. She was losing time. Should she just call her mother? She walked back into *La Pantera* and peered into the back lounge area. Guests were still dancing and waiters were still taking orders. The party was far from ending. She checked the time on her cell phone. It was nearly midnight. She had thirty minutes to get home.

She went back outside and realized that if she wanted to get home right away there was only one person she could rely on: Alex. Despite the fact that he hadn't texted her back and he'd given her necklace to Dee Dee and probably didn't like her as anything more than a friend, he was still good old trustworthy Alex.

She dialed his number with her speed dial.

"Hullo?" His voice sounded groggy when he answered. She had clearly woken him up.

"Alex, it's me, Evelina." Evie felt embarrassed. "I hate to bother you. But do you think you can come get me? I'm stuck downtown."

"Evie." his voice already sounded apologetic. "I've already crashed. I'm doing dawn tomorrow."

"Please?" Evie begged. "I don't have a ride and I, I just . . ."

"You just what?" he asked.

"Just please, Alex . . ."

"Evie," Alex said sounding more awake. "Are you okay?"

"No," Evie's voice started to crack.

"Okay, Evie," Alex said quickly. "I'll be there."

❋ ❋ ❋

Evie waited in the front of *La Pantera* for Alex and as she walked back and forth on the sidewalk she felt even more embarrassed that she had called him. Who did she think she was, expecting him to come and get her in the middle of the night? That's the sort of thing a girl could ask of her boyfriend maybe. But *not* something Evie should have been asking of Alex. Maybe Dee Dee could have asked him, since he did give her the necklace and everything. The necklace . . . ugh! Oh why, why, why did he give it to Dee Dee?

When Alex finally pulled up, Evie got in the cab of his truck. It was warm and he had *Dios Malos*, one of his favorite bands, playing on his iTrip. She couldn't bear to look at him. It's almost as though she was afraid he could read her thoughts if she looked into his eyes. She felt horribly ashamed about what had just happened between her and Jose.

She flipped open her cell and looked at the time. It was 12:13 A.M.

She tried to focus on something else. "Alex, I only have seventeen minutes to get home."

Alex looked over at her. "Are you kidding me? Don't I even get a thank-you?"

"Oh, right. Of course." Couldn't she do anything right? "Thanks, Alex. I mean it. I'll make this up to you." She leaned over and started to unbuckle the slinky-slinks.

"Don't worry about it," he told her.

"No, really," Evie insisted, feeling like a huge idiot. "Let me take you out or something, this weekend. Like, the Coastal Creamery or something."

Alex frowned. "What would I get at the Coastal Creamery? You know I'm lactose intolerant."

"Oh, yeah. That's right." Evie looked out the window. *¡Mensa!*

Alex yawned as soon as they were at a red light at the intersection. "So, what's this all about?"

Evie tilted her head into her hand. All of a sudden she felt reluctant to mention how the whole night had gone, especially the part about Jose. God, what if Jose told him? "It's just been a bad night."

"That's *all*?" Alex was exasperated. "First you cancel on me—twice, you don't answer my texts, and then you drag me out of bed 'cause you're having a bad night?"

"No, it's just . . ." Evie trailed off. "Wait, what texts?"

"I sent you two text messages tonight. You never replied."

"What? Alex, I didn't get any messages. She pulled out her phone from her bag and checked her text history. "No," she told him. "Nothing."

"Well, I sent them."

"What did they say?

"Nothing." Alex looked straight ahead, at the road. "It doesn't matter now."

"Alex . . ." Evie looked out his truck's window. "I'm having a really tough time here. It's like I just don't know who my friends are anymore."

Alex was quiet for a long time before he spoke up. "Maybe they don't know who you are."

"What is that supposed to mean?"

"I dunno, Evie. You tell me."

"I have *no* idea what you are talking about."

"Okay, well, first you try to be a badass," Alex started. "With your blue hair and everything. Then you hook up with Dee Dee and Alejandra and that crew and then you try to be like them."

"I'm not trying to be like them!"

"Oh, really?" He looked at her sandals and then at her hair. "You could have fooled me."

"Alex"—she pulled on the side of her blonde hair—"*this* was *my* decision."

"It would be cool if it really was, but I don't think it was. Like I've said before, I don't care what you do with your hair, but I don't get it. You're smart and one of the coolest girls I know and I don't know why you are letting everyone lead you around."

Evie sat back in her seat and crossed her arms. Why was Alex lecturing her? Who gave him the authority to issue reality checks? Look what he did with the abalone shell he had promised to give her. Yeah, nice friend. She looked out the window and could feel her eyes begin to well up. Do. Not. Cry.

"I mean, when's the last time you even hung out at Sea Street?" Alex continued. "Have you even tried out the new board I helped you pick out? You were going on and on about how you wanted to surf and I took all this time to help you pick out—"

"Oh, sorry if I wasted your time, *Alex*."

"No, it's not that. I'm just saying that I spent the time helping you because I was actually looking forward to doing something with someone, with you." He shook his head. "Maybe you need to take a good long hard look at yourself in the mirror."

"*I* need to take a good look at myself? What about you, Alex?"

"Me? Evie, just remember who is driving you home. Just remember who *you* woke up in the middle of the night and who *you* called to get up and come out and drive *you* home. I really like you Evie, but sometimes you can be so self-absorbed."

"Self-absorbed? You know what, Alex?" She unsnapped her seat belt. "Don't do me any favors." She motioned to an *El Pollo Loco* up ahead on the boulevard. "Just drop me off here."

"Oh, Evie, come on. I'm not gonna leave you here. Don't be silly."

"No, I mean it." Evie was near her breaking point. "I don't need a frigging lift from you. You call yourself a friend? Giving things you promise to me to someone else!"

"What?" Alex looked confused. "What are you talking about."

"Alex! Let me out . . . *now!*" Evie yelled.

"Evie . . ." Alex was perplexed. "Come on . . ."

"Alex!" She yelled louder. "Let me out!"

"Okay, okay." He finally slowed down and pulled into the parking lot. "Have it your way."

He parked his truck and looked around the lot. The interior lights were on in *El Pollo Loco,* but the eating area looked vacant. "Are you gonna be okay?"

"Like you really care." She grabbed the sandals and slammed the car door.

Alex let his truck idle a bit as he waited for Evie to change her mind and get back into his car, but she didn't. She stormed, barefoot, to the other side of building to get out of his sight.

But when Evie got to the side entrance, she discovered that *El Pollo Loco* was closed. Only its twenty-four-hour drive-through service was open, but by the time she realized this, Alex had already driven away. *Crap*. She sat grimly on the concrete curb near the poorly lit, unattended order window.

"'Scuse me," a voice crackled over the loudspeaker. "But this is for car drive-through only."

Evie whipped around and glared at the attendant. "*I know, thank you!*"

She looked down at her feet and saw that she had at least three throbbing blisters, large, pink, and full of liquid. How could this night have gone so wrong? Why did it seem that, lately, every night went badly?

She flipped open her phone. The time was 12:23 A.M. She would never make it home in time for her curfew. She punched in her home phone number.

"Mom," she said as soon as the other end picked up. "Can you come get me?"

13

The next morning, Evie couldn't shake off her funk from the night before. She brushed her teeth and gargled with mouthwash as soon as she got home, all to get the residue of Jose out of her mouth. Her eyes were swollen from an entire night of crying and she wondered if her parents, whose room was just down the hall, had heard her. She was exhausted.

It was all a blur after she'd gotten out of Alex's truck. Her mother had picked her up at *El Pollo Loco* and, thankfully, stuck to her "no questions asked" promise. She didn't even point out that it was almost one A.M. by the time she picked up Evie. Evie hoped the "No questions asked" rule applied to the morning after, too.

Evie's cell vibrated.

Alex?

But she saw it was Dee Dee. Evie looked at her cell. None

of this—her getting attacked by Jose, her yelling at Alex—would have happened if Dee Dee hadn't bailed on her last night. And Evie wouldn't have even wanted to be bailed on by Dee Dee if Dee Dee hadn't accepted the shell necklace from Alex. It looked like all the blame fell back on Dee Dee. Raquel was right. Dee Dee was definitely not the sweet girl they used to know and trust.

She let her cell go unanswered, but seconds later it started vibrating again. And again. And again. She knew once Dee Dee was on redial mode, she would not give up. Evie finally flipped her phone open.

"Hey, *chica.*" Dee Dee was munching on something crispy. Pita Chips? *Chicharrones*? Dee Dee had been crazy about pork rinds as a kid. "*¿Qué pasó?* You just took off last night without saying good-bye. I was so worried."

So worried? How could she even eat when she was supposedly "so worried"? It annoyed Evie even more.

"I told Natalia I was leaving," Evie lied. "I had to get home for my curfew and I didn't wanna bug you. She didn't tell you?"

"Nuh-uh."

"Well, to be honest," Evie started, "I didn't even know where you were. You sorta just took off as soon as we got to the party."

"What?" Dee Dee asked between chomping. "No, I (*chomp, crunch*!) was there. I was just talking to some friends of Fabiola's from San Diego. Evie, I'm sorry. You're (*chomp, crunch*!) not mad, are you?"

"No, not really." She was actually far more upset about what happened between her and Jose.

"Hey, so what's up with Alejandra?"

"What do you mean?" Dee Dee asked.

"Doesn't she have a boyfriend?" Evie said.

"Alejandra?" Dee Dee repeated. "She has a lot of boyfriends. Why?"

"Nothing . . ."

"What? Is there something I'm missing?"

"No," Evie said. "I was just wondering."

"Okay. The chomping continued as Dee Dee switched gears. So anyway, . . . I'm calling about tonight."

"Tonight?"

"Yes, *tonight*. The *Día de los Muertos* dance."

Evie groaned. "Dela, I'm dead."

"Good, then you'll fit right in at the dance." Dee Dee giggled.

"No, I mean, I'm way tired. I think I'm gonna call in granny and stay home."

"*What?*" Dee Dee finally stopped her annoying munching. "Evie, you promised. I have the costumes and everything. Graciela even made adjustments and took in the Frida skirt just to fit you. Alejandro flaked on me and now you?"

"Alex isn't going?" Evie wondered exactly when Alex had called Dee Dee.

"No," Dee Dee said. "So you have to come!"

"Oh." Evie put her fist to her forehead. "Lemme think about it." But that was another lie. She just wanted to get off the phone. There was no way she was going to a dance. She had too many issues to deal with, and besides, her feet and eyes were swollen to the size of her mother's exercise ball.

But Dee Dee didn't give up. "Why don't I come over now and we can—"

"Dela," Evie interrupted, "my phone is about to die." This was, fortunately, true. Evie could see the low-battery warning flash.

"Then call me from the landline," Dee Dee suggested.

"I can't. My dad's on." Lie number two. "With business."

"Argh! You are make things so difficult." Dee Dee went back to chomping. "Okay, call me back as *soon* as your phone is on. We are *not* done (*chomp, crunch*!) discussing this."

When Evie hung up, she felt like her head was going to explode. Images kept popping into her head: Dee Dee's disappointment, Alex's confusion . . . and worse, Jose's long, slimy tongue . . . right in her mouth. Ugh! She turned to her side and petted Meho, but even his affectionate purring didn't make her feel better. She couldn't believe she let herself get so out of control in front of Alex. What was worse? Yelling at Alex or making out with Jose? Well, they didn't technically make out, but she *did* have his tongue in her mouth. Evie curled into a ball. How did that even happen? Why did she even go into the photo booth? Why was she even *at the party*? How would she even begin to tell Raquel that she was in a photo booth with both Alejandra and Jose?

Evie definitely owed it to Raquel to tell her about what happened between her and Jose. She leaned over and grabbed her cordless. She started to punch Raquel's number. It seemed strange. Had it been that long since she had called Raquel? Unlike her cell, her cordless didn't have Raquel's number on speed dial and Evie actually had to pause and remember the digits. Finally, after what seemed like an eternity of rings, Raquel answered.

"What?" It was clear from her tone Raquel had caller ID for both lines and knew it was Evie.

"Hey." Evie instantly regretted dialing her number. "It's me."

"Yeah, I know," Raquel said. "What do you want?"

Evie took a deep breath. "So, I went out last night."

"Did you call to share that with me?"

"No, I'm trying to say that I went out last night and I . . ." Evie bit her lower lip. She didn't want to continue, but she knew she had to. "I saw Jose."

Raquel was silent.

"Raquel . . ." Evie's left leg was twitching like crazy. "I don't wanna be the bearer of bad news, but you gotta listen. Jose was with Alejandra."

"Alejandra who?" Raquel's voice sounded less harsh, quieter.

"De los Santos. They were at *La Pantera Negra,* in the photo booth."

Raquel let out a long drawn-out sigh. "God, Evie, is this what it has come to? You making up stories just to get back at me?"

"Back at you? Hold up, you're the one who's been mean to me."

"*Me?* Evie, I have loyalty to my friends. Dee Dee was a bitch to me from day one. And what do you do? Nothing. You do nothing the next day at your mother's brunch, and then you show up Monday at school with her? What the hell is that?"

"Raquel," Evie started, "yeah, I agree. Dela was a c-bag that first night, but really, she's been our friend since we were kids and everything just started off wrong. I mean, listen to me."

"You know what? I don't have to listen to you and you know what? *I* was with Jose last night."

"What?" Evie asked. "When?"

"It doesn't even matter."

"But that doesn't make sense," Evie said. "I *saw* him, last night. I talked to him and he was all grabby, even to me. I was just thinking we were having fun but then he got all gross and . . . Raquel, he is *so* not cool."

"He was grabbing at *you?*" Raquel laughed sarcastically. "Exactly what do you have that he could grab at? You know what, Evie? I got another call."

"Wait, Raquel."

"'*Bye,* Evie."

And with that, Raquel hung up.

Evie was stunned. She was too shocked to even get upset. Raquel didn't believe her. She thought she was lying! Since when had Evie *ever* lied to her? How could she think that? Raquel was acting as if Evie were an entirely different person. She looked over at herself in the closet mirrors. Was Alex right? *Did* she need to take a long, hard look at herself?

The phone rang again, startling Evie. She quickly picked it up, but it wasn't Raquel phoning back, as she had hoped.

"Evelina?" the voice on the other end asked.

"Oh. Hi." Evie was taken off guard. It was her sister, Sabrina.

"'*Oh. Hi.*'" Sabrina mimicked Evie's disappointed tone. "Sorry to let you down."

"No, I just thought you were someone else."

Sabrina sighed. "Yeah, this morning, I wish I was someone else." She sighed again. This time heavier. "Did Mom tell you I called?"

"Uh, yeah." Evie suddenly felt bad. Her sister sounded uncharacteristically down. "I've just been busy. Did you know that Dela, Dee Dee, is back? Did Mom mention that?"

"Yeah, she did. That must be nice for you. So, is she around?"

"Who?"

"*Mom,*" Sabrina said.

"Oh, sorry. Um, I don't know. I just woke up. Let me check." Evie held the phone to her side and called out. Sure enough her mother was outside on the deck. She waited until her mother picked up the cordless and just as Evie was hanging up, she could hear her mother soothe through the receiver. "*Ay*, what's the problem, *mi'ja*?" her mother cooed softly. "What's wrong, precious?"

After she hung up the upstairs line, Evie could still hear, through her opened bedroom window, the compassion in her mother's voice from the deck outside. Her mother and Sabrina talked for a long time. Evie wondered what was wrong. Why hadn't her sister just told her? Finally, after it sounded like her mother was finally off the phone, Evie went outside to join her on the deck.

"How's Sabrina?" Evie slid onto a canvas chair. The fabric was warm and felt nice on the back of her legs.

"Oh, she's not doing too good." Her mother was gluing plastic yellow daises to a terra-cotta planter that she had painted orange. It was her latest interest, buying inexpensive pots from Green Thumb; painting them in bold, vivid colors; and then lining the rim with plastic doodads from Michael's arts and crafts. If she knew of the grand planters Graciela had in her home, her mother would die from shame.

"What happened?" Evie hoped her sister wasn't sick or anything.

"She just had a breakup. Remember Robert?

"Nuh-uh." Her sister went on about so many guys that Evie had lost count.

"She had been dating him for the last year," her mother said.

The last *year*? How could Evie's sister have been hanging out with someone for a whole year and Evie not even know? God, was Alex right? Was she that self-absorbed?

"Anyway," her mother continued, "he broke up with her and Sabrina's pretty upset about it. She's coming home next weekend."

"She's coming home?" This was really unlike her sister, who claimed to be so involved with so many projects and school activities that she could never leave the Bay Area.

"Yes." Her mother looked at her. "But how are you doing this morning, Evelina? Feeling any better?"

"I'm okay." Evie picked at her light-pink toe polish. She wasn't ready to have her mother's attention all on her. "But Sabrina's all pretty and popular," she said matter-of-factly. "She'll be over him soon enough. And what's the use? Boyfriends cheat on you anyway."

Her mother frowned, "Evie, how can you be so callous? She just lost a really good friend."

"I thought you said he was her boyfriend."

"A boyfriend is a friend."

"No, a friend is a friend," she asserted. "I'm not gonna be swapping spit with my friends."

"Evie, there's more to a romantic relationship than just 'swapping spit.'"

Eeew. The last thing she wanted was to hear her mother try to talk "cool."

"Okay," Evie said abruptly. "Is that today's paper?" She looked at the newspaper her mother had spread out on the patio table. "I wanna look up movie times."

Her mother looked at her for a moment. "No, it's yesterday's."

Evie knew it was rude to cut her mother off like that. Why couldn't she just talk to her mother like Sabrina could? Or the way Dee Dee did? Was she so bad at talking to people?

"So," Evie tried slowly, "were you and Dad friends before you started dating?"

Please, just the facts. No details.

"Oh, yeah," her mother replied. Evie watched her measure out the plastic daisies, making sure each one was a similar distance from the others around the rim of the planter. "We were very good friends."

"Well," Evie started, "it seems like all my so-called good friends are mad at me or vice versa."

"Why?" her mother asked. "What happened?"

Before she knew it, Evie was telling her mother all that had been going on for the past month. Her own version, of course. She left out all the references of liquor; *mota*; the Ojai Valley Inn; and naked, tattooed Sangros.

"And then, last night," Evie continued, not taking a breath,

"I was with Alex. I mean, at first I was with Dela. Remember, we were going to the birthday party? But then Dela really did something uncool, and then I saw Jose at the birthday party with another girl, and he's supposed to be all loyal to Raquel and everything, and then he tries to be cute with me and then I got all mad at Alex and . . . I dunno. You know what I mean?"

"I think so." Evie's mother looked like her head was spinning. TMI? "So why did you get upset with Alex?"

"He made a promise to me and he broke it."

"Did he have a good reason for breaking it?"

"I dunno," Evie said.

"He didn't explain?" Her mother seemed confused.

"I never asked him, but he never said anything. He sorta doesn't know that I know that he broke his promise. I'm not talking to him."

"Evie," her mother began, "that's the first thing about being a good friend. Communication. Only a coward hides behind a veil of silence. You have to give someone a chance to explain. Besides, sometimes we put our friends on pedestals and we expect too much from them. We have to remember that they're just people. We have to allow them space to make mistakes. We have to allow ourselves to make mistakes too."

"Yeah, I guess." Evie felt sorta foolish. It sounded so obvious when her mother said it. *Had* she been too harsh on some of her friends? On herself?

"But I know you'll figure this out. You're smart that way. That's something you're good at, questioning people and their actions."

"Good at?" Evie never thought she was so "good at" anything. At least, nothing her parents recognized.

"Yes," her mother said. "You're a bit more of a fighter. I wish I was."

"What do you mean?"

"Oh, I've just had so many arguments with your *tías*, my sisters," her mother said as she dipped her paintbrush in crimson paint. "They would have all lasted so much longer if one of us hadn't had the courage to take the first step. Like just last weekend I had an argument with your aunt Connie."

"And you apologized?" Evie asked. "You took the first step?"

"Uh, not yet." Her mother looked sheepish and went back to gluing the plastic daisies on the planter. "But who do you think I'm making this for?"

* * *

Evie was surprised by the talk she had had with her mother. It was the first talk they'd had in a very long time that wasn't about cleaning her room or about curfew or her hair. It was the first talk that felt like it was about something *real*.

She started thinking about what her mother had said about

friendship and relationships. Her mind instantly jumped to Alex and a knot formed in her stomach. She did not want to lose Alex. She had to call him. What had she done lately, besides push him away, over and over again? And why? For what?

She grabbed her cell, but then stopped. Oh God, what would she say? So many times they talked on the phone, in his truck, during lunch near Juniper's Tree, but none of those talks had been as important as this one was about to be. She wanted to make sure she said the absolute right thing.

She took a deep breath and dialed. But her call went straight to voice mail.

"Hey, you've reached Alex. You know what to do at the sound of the beep."

Evie's confidence level dropped. She hoped he really was at Sea Street and not just ignoring her call. Should she just hang up or leave a message? She hung up.

Coward.

She called him again.

His line was busy, most likely his voice mail processing her hang up. *Argh!* She waited a few seconds and redialed.

"Uh, hi Alex, it's me," she said as soon as she heard the beep. "Uh, I guess I didn't know what to do at the sound of the beep, hee-hee." *Stupid!* "Anyway, that was me who just called a second ago." *Stupid, again! Of course, he would know it was her. She had only programmed her number in his cell herself.*

"Um, I'm sorry about last night. Really, that I woke you up and everything. It was so nice of you to pick me up."

Nice? Guys don't like to be called "nice." What should she have said? That it was so muscular and strong of you to pick me up? "Well, anyway, I'm just calling because I'm sorry about last night." *Duh! She already said that!* "And I'm hoping you'll call me back and I—" *Beep.*

She was cut off! Too much and too long. Should she call again?

No, she didn't wanna come off as a stalker. She'd just have to wait until he called her back.

Sigh. She went over to her bedroom bookshelf and got her yearbook from last year. After looking up Alex's photos she concluded that he *was* cute. Not that she ever thought he was ugly. Then she flipped to the back cover and found what he'd written:

To the coolest girl I know,
Looking forward to getting to know you better this summer!

He thought she was cool! How had she overlooked that? And he had even said that again last night.

God, Evie thought, Alex *would* make for a really great boyfriend, but now he wasn't even talking to her.

The cordless rang back. *Yes!* She picked it up right away.

But it was Dee Dee.

"Hey," Dee Dee asked. "Is your dad finished on the phone?"

"Yeah." Evie felt defeated. "He's all done." It was no use hiding, or even getting a temporary break, from her. Dee Dee was on a roll.

"Good. Okay, now about tonight . . ."

And before Evie knew it, she had agreed to go to the Day of the Dead Dance. Maybe her mother was right and she was putting people on pedestals and expecting too much. She had to give people room to make mistakes. And staying mad at Dee Dee wasn't worth it. Besides, she was running out of friends. If anything, it would be better just to get out of the house rather than sulk around. She could ask Dee Dee about the shell necklace because that's what you had to do with friends—talk things out. That's what true friendship was all about—communication. That, and a hand-painted terra-cotta planter.

14

Later that night, Evie walked into the Villanueva gym with Dee Dee and was immediately blown away by all the elaborate decorations for the dance. It was a sensory overload of multi-colored *papeles picados,* sugar skulls, burning incense, and bright orange *cempazulti* (correct Evie pronunciation: marigolds) scattered around the floor.

"Wow, I am impressed." Dee Dee looked the gym over. "Look," she said and nudged Evie. "They even have an altar. A bit *rasquache,* but still."

The makeshift altar was actually a pyramid of cafeteria tables, two on the bottom and one on top and draped in dark velour fabric, sitting directly under the gym's scoreboard. The altar was covered in dozens of votive candles, black-and-white photos, colored photo cubes, as well as piles of things the dearly departed used to enjoy: bowls of dry food and plates of cooked food—everything from SpaghettiOs to Greek *dolmas.* There was even an old fishing pole laid out across everything.

Evie had brought a few things to place on the altar. A miniature Dalmatian figurine in honor of her great-grandpa Rudy, who was once a fire captain in Rio Estates, and for her great-grandma Conchita, a piece of *pan dulce* from her father's bakery. *Not* the fat-free kind, of course. Great-grandma Conchita wouldn't be merely rolling over in her grave at such a thing, she'd be doing double-twisted rotating backflips.

Evie wondered if Dee Dee had brought anything to offer for her mother. Since she'd been back to Rio Estates, Dee Dee had barely mentioned the subject of her mother's death. Maybe, Evie figured, it was just something Dee Dee didn't want to talk about. She knew *she* sure wouldn't want to, so she decided not to push it with Dee Dee.

Evie looked around the gym and sighed to herself. She knew Alex was going to be a no-show, but she was still hoping to hear from him. Hadn't he gotten her message? She pulled her cell out of the little black velvet purse Dee Dee had loaned her and checked her cell phone. *Is this how Dee Dee felt?* She wondered. *Waiting and waiting for Rocio to call? Is this what it is like to have a boyfriend?* She put the cell back in her purse and snapped it shut. *Do not check again!*

Dee Dee was right. The clothes Graciela had brought back from all the soap operas in Mexico were incredible. Even with a lightly penciled moustache and unibrow, Evie felt quite glamorous. Her full skirt (from *Una Vida, Tres Hombres)* had a hand-embroidered flower motif stitched with sequins. She wore a frilly off-the-shoulder blouse (courtesy of *La Mala Lengua*), lots of vintage glass beads (direct from the set of *La Cueva Sucia de Doña Luisa*) around her neck, and a pair of small, gold hoop earrings (on permanent loan from *Amigos, Amantes y Abogados*). Who even knows if Frida Kahlo actually dressed that way? Maybe she would have, if she had had her own *telenovela* on Univision.

Dee Dee's costume was somewhat similar to Evie's, minus the unibrow and penciled-in moustache. And while Evie's hair was pinned under a thick, dark wig with two braids woven on top, Dee Dee's long, blonde hair was loose and flowing. *Sexy.* Of course, her whole costume was tight in some parts and showy in others. Would Frida's sister actually have worn red fishnets, a push-up bra, and so much red lipstick? To Evie, Dee Dee looked more cancan girl than "Coyoacán *chica*."

Dee Dee surveyed the gym. "I wonder where Alejandra is and that great costume of hers."

"Yeah," Evie said. Where *was* she? In a dark photo booth with Jose?

"Well," Dee Dee said, after realizing that Alejandra was not there, "let's go get some *pan muerto*."

Evie agreed. Anything was better than standing around, wondering where Alejandra was or waiting for Alex's call. She followed Dee Dee toward the refreshment table.

"You know," Evie started, looking over the breads, "all the *pan* came from my dad's bakery."

"Oh, yeah?" Dee Dee nodded. "Hey, check out your dad!"

"What?" Evie followed her eyes. *Oh* my *God.* Was that really her father dressed as a pirate and arranging dead bread with Ernie and Bobby from the bakery? She discreetly moved toward him.

"Dad!" Evie whispered sternly to her father. "What are *you* doing here? Dressed like that?"

"What am I doing here? What are you talking about? I always bring the *pan muerto* to the dance. What are *you* doing here? You never come to the dances."

"Dad, *please.* When are you leaving?"

"Yargh!" Her father adjusted his eye patch and drawled in a pirate voice. "Don't you be a worry, Miss Evie. Me mates and I are just abandoning ship!"

"Dad!" Evie was horrified.

"Evie . . ." He was used to her melodrama. "*Cálmate.* Joe called in sick and we had to get all this bread here. Plus, I thought it might be fun to get into the spirit."

"Dad, *please.*" Evie looked around the gym in a panic. "Does anyone know you're my dad?

"Hi, Mr. Gomez!" Dee Dee came up from behind. Two other classmates of Evie's, Steve Cuevas and Sammy Zoabi, looked over at Evie's father, then at Evie.

"Well, they do now." He raised his eyebrows as if to say,

"Oops!" He looked at Dee Dee. "Hey there, Dee Dee. Oh, you sure look cute. Who are you supposed to be?"

"Dad," Evie pleaded. "It's *not* important. *Please.*"

"Okay, okay. Jeez," he said. "I remember the times you *wanted* me to stay at school with you. Remember that, Dee Dee? When you two started kindergarten at RioReal and Evie was crying and crying because she was so scared? Remember she didn't want me to leave?"

"Oh, yeah." Dee Dee puckered her lips and made an exaggerated sad face. She looked over at Evie. "*Poor* Evie!"

"Dad, stop it!" Evie checked to see if any of her classmates were hearing such gory details. "Please, just leave!"

"Okay, okay." Her father gathered his aluminum trays and finally said good-bye to the girls. Evie finally exhaled.

"You're too harsh on your dad," Dee Dee said thoughtfully. "I think it's cute the way he wants to help at the dance. I wish my father was more involved with stuff I was into."

"No, you don't," Evie insisted. "Trust me. Besides, it's not so much about being involved with me. *Día de los Muertos* is one of his busiest times of year. He supplies all the dead bread for just about all the celebrations in the area."

Dee Dee reached out and took a piece of the bread. She put a bit in her mouth and chewed and swallowed. Then she smacked her tongue on her front teeth. "Well, let's see if they have some *champurrado* or something." She gave Evie a wide grin. "No offense, but this bread's *dead.*"

"I'll make *sure* I tell my dad that," Evie said sarcastically.

Dee Dee took Evie's arm and they both crossed the gym to look for *champurrado* "or something." That's exactly what they found, *something*.

"Nasty." Dee Dee made a face when she took a sip from her Styrofoam cup. "What is this?"

"The senior class version of *champurrado*," Evie quipped dryly. It was a watery gruel of corn and chocolate.

Just then, Fabiola and her date, Arnie, came up to the table. She was dressed as Marilyn Monroe and he was James Dean.

"Oh, you two look *so* cute!" Fabiola cried.

Arnie looked over Dee Dee and Evie. "What are you, two? A couple of Mexican lesbians?"

"*What?*" Evie said.

"No, *tonto*!" Dee Dee replied, indignant. "Evie's Frida and I'm her sister, Cristina." Dee Dee tilted her head sideways and threw out her hip in a sexy pose. "Can't you tell?"

"Not really," Arnie said. "But hey, didn't Frida hook up with her sister?"

"*No.*" Fabiola slapped his arm. "Quit being stupid."

"But I saw the movie," Arnie protested.

"Arnie, *no*." Fabiola's eyes looked upward. "Cristina slept with Frida's *husband*, Diego Rivera. You know who *he* is, right?"

"We had a Diego, but he flaked on us." Dee Dee said with a frown. She looked around the gym casually. "So, have you guys seen Alejandra? She's supposed to be María Félix or something like that."

As Dee Dee talked with Fabiola and Arnie, Evie looked over and was surprised to see Mondo. He walked by, not even recognizing her. The last time she had spoken to him was that day he and Jose practically cornered her by the boys' P.E. building.

"Hey, Mondo," Evie called out.

He turned around. "Oh, hey, Evie." He looked at her and frowned. "What happened to your hair?"

"Oh!" She had forgotten she was wearing a wig. "It's a wig." He was wearing a standard Trunk Ltd T and baggy cords. "Who are you supposed to be?"

"Who am I supposed to be?" Mondo rolled his eyes. "I'm *supposed to be* making a delivery, but Jose dragged me by here and now he just took off. I gotta get to the west side."

"Jose?" Evie looked around. She suddenly felt frightened. What was *he* doing at the dance? He and Raquel *never* came to school functions. Was Raquel with him?

"Yeah." Mondo looked around, annoyed. "He's around somewhere."

"So," Evie asked cautiously, "have you talked to Alex?"

"Nah." Mondo crumpled his punch cup and tossed it on the floor. The school dance was so definitely not his scene.

"Well," Evie said, "I hope you find him."

"Who?"

"Jose."

"Oh, right." Mondo looked past Evie and his eyes lit up. "Ah, there he is. Later, Evie." He brushed by her.

Evie turned around and looked in the direction that Mondo was heading. Then she saw Jose. He was in the hallway, near the back of the gym's bleachers. Of course, he wasn't in costume, but Alejandra de los Santos, aka Mexican film star María Félix, definitely was. She had on a 1940s-style gown, a dark green strapless silk number that defined every curve. Her 1940s vintage platforms made her even taller, and her hair was colored dark with perfectly salon-styled waves. Jose had his hands clenched around her hips and his head was pressed into the side of her head.

Evie watched Mondo talk to Jose for a moment and then leave, without Jose, who went back to sucking the life out of Alejandra's face.

"How long has that been going on?" Evie nudged Dee Dee and looked toward Jose and Alejandra. Fabiola and Arnie had danced away into the crowd.

Dee Dee looked over. "What, them talking?"

Jose had just pulled away and it now looked like they were just merely having a conversation.

"No, them being together."

"What are you talking about?" Dee Dee bobbed her head to DJ Buick's mix and picked at her dead bread. "Alejandra has a boyfriend, actually *two* of them, in Mexico. You know that. They're just talking."

"Dela," Evie said. "Are you blind? No, look, watch them."

"Evie, I'm not gonna watch them all night, hoping to *catch* them doing something. But look at her dress." Dee Dee sniffed. "It's not all that *especial.* I don't see what the big deal was. Gracie's things are a lot better. Oops." She wiped the crumbs off her blouse.

"*¡Ay! ¡Qué chiste!*" Natalia came up behind Dee Dee and squeezed the sides of her waist. "You make a *great* Cristina! Don't be stealing any husbands tonight!"

"Only if they look like frogs," Dee Dee mused in reference to Diego Rivera's so-called amphibian-like features.

"Are you going to Xiomara's dorm after the dance?" Natalia asked.

"Oh, *sí. Claro,* right Evie?" Dee Dee asked.

But Evie didn't answer. All she could do was look at Jose and Alejandra. She was so angry, she couldn't even see straight. Raquel thought she was a liar, Dee Dee thought she was imagining things, and Jose was getting away with his lying ass intact.

* * *

Despite all the mental and emotional distractions, Evie actually managed to have a decent time at the dance.

People thought her costume was really cute and cool. But, *ay,* poor Dee Dee. All night she had to explain who she was supposed to be. And then she'd go drag Evie over and still no one quite got it.

Finally, before Evie knew it, DJ Buick announced the last songs for the evening. And that was fine with Evie. She sat on a chair and rubbed her feet.

Allen Luc, a friend from math class who Evie had been dancing with for the last couple songs, came up to her. "You not gonna skip the last song, are you?"

"My feet are killing me," Evie told him.

"Wow." He lifted his glasses and looked down, squinting. Even though they'd been dancing together, somehow he hadn't noticed her feet. "Whoa. I've never seen you in shoes before. Weird."

Dee Dee came up to both of them. "So, Evie, you wanna get going to Xiomara's dorm? You should come too, Allen. She's having an after-party."

"How?" Evie asked. Villanueva had a strict policy against get-togethers in student housing. No guests after nine P.M., and absolutely no guests of the opposite sex.

"It's on the DL," Dee Dee said knowingly. She tucked some hair behind her left ear. "Oh, no." She touched her left ear lobe. "I lost an earring. Gracie will kill me. I gotta go look for it."

"Are you serious?" Evie asked. "Aren't they the ones from *My Mother-in-Law, My Lover*?"

"What kind of store is that?" Allen asked, confused.

"Let me go with you," Evie offered. "I'll help you look."

"No, it's okay," Dee Dee said. "I think it might be in the bathroom on the counter." She gave Evie her car keys. "Here, wait in the car if you want. Then we can walk over to Xiomara's dorm."

Evie took the keys and headed out to Dee Dee's car. Some of the other students were already out there turning the parking lot into one big tailgate party. But, this being Villanueva, most of the tailgates belonged to rides worth upwards of sixty grand.

"Evie?"

She looked up. It was Raquel.

"Raquel?" Evie couldn't believe it. What was Raquel doing at the dance? She was walking up from the side of her mother's Beemer convertible in faded jeans and a gray sweatshirt. Her eyes were puffy and bloodshot and she looked somberly out of place in a parking lot full of laughter and colorful costumes.

Evie had no time to think. "What's wrong? Are you okay?"

"No," Raquel admitted. "I'm *not* okay."

She reached into the inside of her fleece jacket and she pulled out a strip of paper, the pictures from the photo booth at Fabiola's birthday party.

Evie's stomach dropped.

"You were right," Raquel said looking at the photos.

"Raquel . . ."

"He is such an asshole, Evie."

Evie looked at the photo strip. There was Jose sandwiched between her and Alejandra de los Santos. Even in the photo you could see the awkwardness in Evie's eyes. The third and final photo, Jose's face was jammed up against Evie, whose face was contorted in disgust.

"I found it in his wallet," Raquel said.

"His wallet?"

"Yeah, what an idiot." Raquel took a drag from her cigarette. "He knows we have total access to each other's flow and he leaves *this* in his wallet? I'm sure he gets a kick out of showing it off to his friends."

His friends? Oh no, Evie suddenly worried. Had he shown Alex? Oh God, she hoped not. Maybe he already had shown Alex and maybe that's why he hadn't called her.

"When Jose told me he couldn't hang out tonight," Raquel continued, "I knew something was going on. Mondo had a pick-up from his cousin out on the west side. His cousin from Humboldt State. You know what I mean?"

"Uh-huh." Everybody knew that Humboldt was known for its hearty harvest of *"verde buena."*

"And we were all gonna hang out tonight. Me, Mondo, and Jose, and then Jose just suddenly turned *that* down."

"Yeah." Evie sighed. "I see what you mean."

"He's just been doing that a lot lately. Flaking on me last minute and then when you called me . . . " She didn't finish. She looked over Evie's shoulder. Her face dropped.

Evie turned around and saw Jose and Alejandra coming out of the gym. Jose had his arm around Alejandra's bare shoulders and her body was turned into Jose's as they walked slowly across the parking lot and toward the dorms. Her fingers played with his black hair.

"Hey," Raquel called out. "Hey, Jose!"

Jose looked up. He immediately yanked his arm off of Alejandra.

"So, what's going on?" she asked calmly.

What's going on?

"Whoa, whoa baby." Jose went toward Raquel. "It's not what you think."

"What would I be thinking?"

"Uh, I dunno. I just swung by, with Mondo. Have you seen him?"

"Nuh-uh."

This was so unlike Raquel, to be so relaxed in the middle of a situation like this.

Raquel looked at Alejandra and then at Jose. "Aren't you supposed to be in costume?" she asked as though nothing at all was wrong.

Jose looked confused and a little scared.

"Yeah." He laughed uncomfortably. "I forgot."

"No, you got it right." She looked him up and down. "What are you supposed to be, some trust-fund kid? In your eighty-dollar vintage rock T?"

"Huh?"

"Or are you dressed as a pussyfooting liar who can't even be direct with his girlfriend so he can sneak out to a school dance so he could get a couple of cheap feels from a Sang-ho?"

"*Excuse* me?" Alejandra finally said.

"No, no. Wait." Raquel paced in front of Jose and squeezed the side of her forehead. "Or maybe you're dressed as a moocher who has to rely on his best friend to drive him around, like his mommy or something, because he didn't pass his driving test for the third time?"

"You told me you had a car, but that you couldn't drive it because of your grades," Alejandra said to Jose.

"Oh, and speaking of grades," Raquel continued, "let me give you a grade in the lover department, Jose."

"Raquel . . ." Jose's face was bright red.

Oh, this was gonna be good.

"No, no." Raquel put her palm out to quiet him. "Let me finish and then you can go back to your date. Let's see, an *E* for effort, an *S* for sloppy, and *T* as in *too* soon. *Always* too soon. You better be careful, Alejandra. The way he gets overly excited, he might just dirty that little pretty dress of yours without any warning."

"*What?*" Alejandra looked horrified.

Raquel tapped the side of Jose's chin.

"See you around, Jose. And you know what? Don't worry about the money you owe me. You can use it"—she tugged on his belt buckle—"for that little medical problem of yours."

Raquel threw her cigarette down and put it out with her dark pink platformed flojo.

Bravo! Well done!

As Raquel walked away into the darkness, she left Evie, Alejandra, and Jose pretty much speechless until Jose looked over at Evie.

"You little bitch," he started in on her. "You had to go and open your hole, didn't you?"

"*Me?*" Evie protested. "I didn't say anything. I didn't have to."

"Yeah, right." Jose narrowed his eyes and came right into Evie. She leaned back, as far as she could, into the door of a parked car. Wasn't there anyone around to help her? She glanced around. All the other students were in their own world and Alejandra was doing jack besides standing there, fuming over Raquel's words.

Jose moved closer to Evie. She could feel the anger flaring from his eyes and nostrils. Soon his belt buckle was actually pressing against her.

"What. The. Fuck. *Evie?*"

"What?" She faced him back, directly. She tried to sound tough. But inside she was dying.

"You know, somebody's gotta teach you a lesson."

Evie closed her eyes and braced herself. *Be strong.*

Just then, her ringtone of Daddy Yankee rang out, cutting through the tension.

Jose backed up, a bit thrown off.

The Daddy Yankee rang again.

"It's my dad," Evie lied. "He and my uncle Louie are picking me up."

"Your dad?"

"Yeah," Evie said. "And my uncle Louie."

At the same time, Dee Dee came out of the gym. She saw Jose's tight grip on Evie's blouse and immediately knew something was not right.

"Jose!" she called out firmly. She sprinted over with amazing speed for someone in three-inch heels. "What's going on?"

"Nothing." He loosened his grip on Evie and finally backed off. "Nothing. She ain't worth it."

"Worth *what?*" Dee Dee demanded to know. "What the hell's going on?"

Jose looked over at Alejandra. "Come on."

But Alejandra was standing off to the side, holding her phone to her ear. "Uh, sorry Josito," she said, covering the mouthpiece of her phone with her hand. "But I'm on a long-distance call. I'll find you later."

"What the—?" He waved his hand aside. "Man, I do not need this hen party." He rubbed his hair with both his hands and turned to leave. "Good riddance to all you bitches."

"What happened?" Dee Dee asked after he left.

"Jose's pissed 'cause Raquel found out about him and Alejandra," Evie told her. "She was just here."

"Raquel?" Dee Dee looked around. "Was here?"

"Yeah." Evie got her breath. "Just a minute ago. She just took off."

Dee Dee looked over at Alejandra who just got off her call. "Alejandra, is that true? How could you be after someone else's boyfriend? Don't you get enough attention?"

"Dela, I do not *chase* men," Alejandra sniffed and she patted her hair in place. "I don't *need* to."

"How could you not do anything to help Evie?"

"Oh, Dela, you're overreacting. He wasn't going to do anything to Evie. He was just mad."

"He could have fooled me." Evie finally exhaled. Her body was still shaking.

Alejandra rolled her eyes. "Come on, this boring dance is over." She took hold of Dee Dee's arm. "Let's go to Xiomara's dorm."

"Not me." Dee Dee pulled away.

"What?" Alejandra laughed uncomfortably. "You gonna go looking for *La Llorona*?"

"I'd rather be with a weeping woman than a cheating one."

Alejandra put her hands on her hips. "Well, do what you want, Dela."

"Thank you," Dee Dee said. "I will."

"You are so fake, anyway. You think because you lived in D.F. for a few years that you're my *paisa*? *Mira, mi'ja*, you got a *long* way to go." She turned to leave.

Dee Dee didn't say or do anything. She didn't even look fazed by Alejandra's abrupt departure and Evie couldn't believe what she had just witnessed.

"You can go, really," Evie suggested.

"Nah." Dee Dee watched Alejandra seethe and disappear into the parking lot. "So not feeling it." She sighed heavily. "Haven't been for a while."

* * *

Evie and Dee Dee stood together. "I guess you were right about her and Jose," Dee Dee told Evie after Alejandra was finally out of sight. "I thought they were just talking. That's what it looked like to me."

"In a dark corner, behind the bleachers?" Evie asked.

"I dunno. I mean, how would anyone know, right?"

"I might not have, but I saw them last night."

"Last night?" Dee Dee asked. *"¿Dónde?"*

"At Fabiola's party," Evie said. "In the old photo booth."

"At *La Pantera*? Are you serious? Why didn't you say something last night?"

"I was just too upset. And actually . . . " Evie thought it was probably just best to bring it up and get it over with. "Can I ask you something?"

"What?" Dee Dee asked.

"Your shell necklace, the one you wore last night," Evie started. "Who gave it to you?"

"My necklace?" Dee asked. "Nobody. I got it in Veracruz."

Evie felt relief flood her body. "In Veracruz? Are you serious?"

"Yeah," Dee Dee said. "Why would I lie?"

"It's just that it looks exactly like the abalone shell Alex had found for me at Bard Beach. We were at a party there a while ago."

"At Bard Beach?" Dee Dee raised her eyebrows. "You were at Bard Beach?"

"Yeah, at the abalone farm."

"Well, no, Alex didn't give me any necklace. I got mine in Veracruz. They sell them all over the streets. But, I'll have you know," Dee Dee said, feigning snobbery, "it's *not* abalone. It's mother-of-pearl and I chose the necklace over the mother-of-pearl paperweight with the wiggly eyes glued on."

Evie laughed.

"But what's the big deal with the necklace?"

"Oh . . . nothing."

"Nothing?" Dee Dee was not convinced, but didn't press. "So . . ." She looked around the parking lot. "Where do you think Raquel went?"

Evie saw Kitty Diaz's car still parked in the lot. "I think I know where she is. I should go get her."

"I'm guessing you want me to go with you?" Dee Dee said.

"Actually," Evie said, "yeah."

Dee Dee took a deep breath. "Okay."

They started to cross the parking lot and headed toward the

quad area. It was the same parking lot where Raquel had made Dee Dee huff away just over a month earlier and now here they were again. But this time Dee Dee was skipping a party, a *Sangro* party, just to go find Raquel.

"By the way, that was pretty ballsy of you," Evie told Dee Dee. "Confronting Jose and all."

"Ballsy of me?" Dee Dee said. "What about you? Going to parties out on Bard Beach? Now *that* takes *huevos*!"

Evie suddenly remembered her cell phone. Someone had called and she knew it wasn't really her father. She pulled her phone out of her purse and saw she had one new voice mail. She clicked on call history, and yes! It was Alex. Finally! But she wouldn't call him back just yet. Because she and Dee Dee, well, they had more important matters to attend to.

* * *

Sure enough, Raquel was at Juniper's Tree.

She was sitting on the exposed thick roots of the old oak, her arms cradling her legs at the knees and her face buried between them. Evie could see Raquel's body trembling. Her chest heaved up and down in anguish, yet she remained silent. She had never seen her like this. Even Dee Dee, who remained a good distance away, seemed horribly uncomfortable. She said nothing as she nervously pulled on the end of her hair.

"Hey, Raquel," Evie said softly as she hesitantly moved toward her. "Are you okay?"

Stupid question.

"No, Evie," Raquel sobbed. "I'm *not* okay. You keep asking me that. He made me look like a fucking fool in front of everyone!"

"A fool?" Evie said. "Raquel, you are *so* not the fool."

"Yes, I *am*," Raquel cried.

"For what?" Evie asked. "Trusting him? Trusting Jose? He's the fool; he's the idiot."

"But I'm the one who looked like an idiot in front of everyone!"

"*Everyone?* Who? Alejandra? Who is *she* even?" Evie looked over at Dee Dee. "Right, Dee Dee?"

Raquel immediately looked up. She was taken aback to see Dee Dee standing behind Evie. "What is *she* doing here?" Raquel scowled at Evie. "Shouldn't she be with her best friend, Alejand-*rrr*a?"

"Raquel," Evie started, "Dee Dee wanted to come. She *insisted*." A slight twist of the truth, but still . . . "Right, Dee Dee?"

"Uh, right." Dee Dee continued to play with her hair. "Um, and as far as Alejandra, just so you know, and you probably don't even care, but I didn't know anything about her being with Jose. Really, Raquel."

"Yeah, right." Raquel wiped her nose with her sleeve jacket and glared at Dee Dee.

"No," Dee Dee insisted. "Really. Why would I lie about that?"

"Raquel," Evie said. "She's telling the truth. She just told off Alejandra so she could be here with you."

Raquel wasn't convinced. "Yeah, like *you* really would have told off Alejand-*rra*."

"Raquel, she *did*," Evie said. "And Jose too . . . sorta."

"It's not such a big deal," Dee Dee confessed. "I guess I've been burning out on Ally for a while now."

Raquel put her head back between her knees. "I'm *such* an idiot!"

"But you're rid of him, Raquel," Evie said. "Rid of that asshole."

"He's *not* an asshole, Evie."

"Yes," Evie said firmly. "He was. *Is*."

"Okay." Raquel looked up at Evie. "But he was *my* asshole. Is that what you wanna hear? Does that make you feel better?" She buried her head back between her knees.

Quiet.

"But Raquel," Evie said looking back at Dee. "Do you really *need* two assholes?"

More quiet.

Why am I always saying the wrong things?

But then Raquel's body started to tremble again. Lightly at first, then harder. Evie could then hear muffled laughter coming from under Raquel's bowed head and she felt an immediate sense of relief. Raquel's body continued to tremble but suddenly she started to cry again. "Evie, don't!" she sobbed. "*Don't* try to make me laugh in my misery. I *really* loved him!"

"Oh, Raquel." Evie finally knelt down near her. "I know, I mean, I thought he was pretty cool, too. Sometimes. But you know, a real friend wouldn't have done this to you."

"But he wasn't my friend." Raquel kept her face buried between her knees. "He was my boyfriend."

"Yeah," Evie went on. "But he wasn't even *a friend*. You gotta get respect and trust from a friend, right?"

Raquel looked up. Black mascara had collected at the sides of her puffy and pink-rimmed eyes. Her cheeks were smeared with tears and her upper lip had a thin coat of translucent mucus. "What the hell are you talking about?"

"I'm just saying he was, *is*, not a good person."

"It's gonna suck now," Dee Dee added. "But it's really for the better. Really."

Raquel looked up at Evie, as if Dee Dee didn't exist. "Why is *she* still even here?"

"*Raquel.*" Evie was getting exasperated. "Dee Dee came because she was worried about you."

"Yeah, right," Raquel shot back. "So now I'm a charity case?"

"Look, Raquel," Evie said standing up and putting her hands on her hips. "Neither one of us has to be here. We *want* to be here. And if you're gonna put on your tough little show, like the grand one you just did for Jose, okay, then go ahead. But I think we deserve better than that. And if you just want to be left alone . . . then we can go ahead and leave you alone. I am so tired of trying to figure you out and trying to make things right by you!"

"No, *you* look." Raquel narrowed her eyes toward Evie. "I didn't ask you to come follow me. And I sure as hell didn't ask Dee Dee to come along. Why does she even care? Dee Dee has always gotten everything she wants, and now what? She wants to see me get dumped, lose my boyfriend? What the fuck does *she* know about losing someone?"

The second after Raquel said that, Evie could see the look on her face—it was an expression of horror, shame, and regret that she would actually say something like that about Dee Dee.

"Uh . . . " Raquel's mouth was as wide as her eyes. She looked at Evie for help. "I mean . . . "

Dee Dee crossed her arms and looked directly into Raquel's eyes. "Jeez, Rocky, I wish it was *me* who had just lost a *boyfriend*. Man, how lucky can you get? I mean, I *only* lost my mother."

"Wait, wait, wait!" Evie could feel everything was getting out of hand.

"Dee Dee," Raquel suddenly pleaded. "No, I'm sorry. Really. I'm just, I'm just so . . . " And she started crying again. "Oh my God, I'm such an idiot!"

Evie looked up at Dee Dee and shrugged. She was at a loss for what to do.

Dee Dee crossed her arms and looked away. It was obvious she was pissed.

"You know," she told Evie, "I'm gonna get going. She's useless."

"Wait, Dela, please." Evie lowered her voice and looked at Raquel. "Please, don't go. She's so upset. I mean, come on, she never gets like this. She's crying. When have you ever known her to cry?"

Dee Dee looked at Evie as though she was actually taking in what Evie was saying. She pursed her lips and looked around the grassy quad area. She finally uncrossed her arms and stepped toward Raquel. She took a breath.

"Look, Raquel," she started, "I don't mean to play down your pain, but *híjole chica*, if I could, and, oh my God, I can't believe I'm saying this, but if I could trade in my boyfriend, Rocio, just to have my mother back . . . I'd do it in a second. I mean, I'm not saying I want him to die or anything, but if he were to leave me . . . I don't know. There is no comparison." She looked up at Evie and bit her lower lip. "When my mother died, I had to think about who I still had left. I had my father. I mean, even with Jose being out of the picture, you still have us. Me and Evie. We're still your friends. We will always be your friends."

Raquel continued to keep her head between her knees.

"Raquel," Dee Dee continued, "you are just about the toughest girl I know. You've always been, and you *will* get over

Jose." Her voice softened. "You know, Rocky, this is only the second time, in my whole life, that I've ever seen you cry."

"Huh?" Raquel looked up at Dee Dee.

Evie also didn't know what Dee Dee meant by that comment either.

"Uh-huh," Dee Dee started. "The first time I saw you cry . . . "

"Yeah?"

" . . . was four years ago at my mother's funeral."

"It was?" Raquel's face creased in surprise. "At your mom's funeral?"

"Yeah." Dee Dee's voice got higher and she looked away into the distance. "I remember, at Santa Clara Cemetery. I was sitting with my family and I tried *so* hard not to cry. So hard. I really wanted to be strong for my dad, you know? But then I looked over and saw you, sitting next to your mom and dad, and you were crying. I mean, *really, really* letting it out. I had never seen you like that, so much emotion like that. I don't know, I almost lost it."

Evie remembered Margaret de LaFuente's funeral. The crowded mass at Santa Clara Church, followed by the long car procession to the Santa Clara Cemetery. She herself cried, as much as her mother and sister did, but she now remembered how much Raquel had just wailed. *How* could she have forgotten that?

"I didn't want to worry my dad," Dee Dee continued. "You really don't know how he can be. When my mother died, it wasn't just like half of him died, it's like all of him died. They had the best relationship. I mean, I guess it's like Evie said; they were great friends. They really loved each other."

"Dee Dee," Raquel started slowly, "I don't know if I ever told you this, but I really, really liked your mother. I mean, she was so cool. Really ahead of her time, you know? Like, I never felt judged. She was just so nice to me, always asking how I felt about things, not just that standard 'How is school going?' drill."

"Yeah." Dee Dee half-smiled. "I know. But really, I don't like talking about it. I'd rather not think about my mother. It makes me too sad. I just wanna think happy thoughts."

"But you can think happy thoughts about your mother," Evie said. "It doesn't have to be one or the other."

"I guess . . . " Dee Dee pursed her lips and looked up at the branches of Juniper's Tree.

"You can guess all you want," Evie insisted. "But I *know*. . . . In Mexico, all the times you celebrated *Día de los Muertos,* how did you honor your mother?"

"Well, I didn't, really," Dee Dee confessed. "I really didn't want to think about her not being around. I mean, I guess I just went through the motions. My father and I and all my classmates and friends, we went to all the ceremonies and stuff, I mean, they're so beautiful and artistic and it *is* tradition."

"So you never honored your mom?" Evie asked. "When you were at the ceremonies? At all?"

"Hmmm . . . " Dee Dee thought out loud. Her face turned flat and her voice got even higher. Evie remembered, from when Dee Dee had to give a speech in the sixth grade, that that's how she looked and sounded when she got nervous. "Sometimes I have no choice. Like when it's her birthday, or when it's Mother's Day, or when's it's my birthday. That's the worst. How can I have a birthday and *not* think of my mother? I mean, she's the first one you see the day you are born, right? And then every birthday after that, she's just about the first one to tell you happy birthday."

Evie didn't know what to say. She had never had to deal with such a situation, such a gigantic loss.

Raquel wiped her tears and announced abruptly. "I think we need to honor your mother, somehow. I know I want to."

"Yeah," Dee Dee said. "I know . . . I guess when I'm ready."

"But how are you gonna know when you are ready?" Evie asked.

"Um," Dee Dee said. "I guess I don't really know . . . "

"Let's go for a drive." Raquel sat up, suddenly. "I got an idea. But you totally have to trust me."

Evie wasn't so sure about the "trust" part, especially coming from Raquel. But what could she say, after she had just given Raquel her little speech about friends and trust and respect? It was just a relief not to see either Dee Dee or Raquel so upset anymore.

"It'll be cool." Raquel got up quickly and brushed the damp dirt off her jeans. "We can all go in my mother's car."

* * *

Raquel pulled her mother's Mercedes up to the main gates of Santa Clara Cemetery. She put the car into "park."

This was Raquel's idea of honoring Dee Dee's mother? Evie thought. Going to a bone yard in the middle of the night? *Hola*? Hadn't anyone seen *Night of the Living Dead?*

Evie looked behind her, down H Street, the street they had just pulled up on. It was completely deserted. There would be no one around to hear them scream for help—that is, if they had to.

The main entrance to Santa Clara Cemetery—high white wrought-iron gates—was locked. Visiting hours had ended hours ago and the entire grounds were vacant and pitch-black.

Raquel turned to face Dee Dee, who was sitting in the passenger seat. "When was the last time you were here?"

"Me?" Dee Dee looked through the gate. "Uh, I don't know. I guess, probably before I moved. I mean, before my dad and I did."

"I remember when we were at the funeral, all of us," Raquel said. "And you were sitting with your father."

"Yeah . . . "

"And right after the funeral, after Father Benitez talked, you immediately just left. I mean, you just bailed for the limo."

"Yeah . . . I remember."

"I remember that, too," Evie said. "'Cause usually you stay seated, right? And then you wait for people to come by and offer their condolences. But you just got back into the limo. We didn't even get to talk to you."

"Did you ever get to really say good-bye to your mom?" Raquel asked. "Or even have some time with her?"

"Not really," Dee Dee said. "I mean, not officially."

"I think you need to do that," Raquel said. "Don't you Evie?"

"Yeah." Evie sat in the backseat and started to scratch the side of her neck. "Totally."

"But we couldn't go in if we wanted to," Dee Dee said looking at the entrance. "It's closed."

Whew. "So, why don't we just come back in the morning?"

"You guys." Raquel unbuckled her seat belt and got out of the car. "Kitty Diaz always keeps emergency supplies."

"Emergency supplies?" Evie's eyes followed Raquel as she headed for the back of the car. "For what?"

"Well, in this case"—Raquel popped open the trunk—"supplies to scale the wall."

"Scale the wall?" Evie got out of the car and Dee Dee followed. "What are we now, taggers?"

Raquel didn't answer as she pulled out the large, heavy-duty flashlight and a bright orange beach towel from the trunk. She switched on the flashlight and directed the beam toward the cemetery's main gates. "Okay, so she doesn't have anything, but we won't have to jump the wall." She squinted her eyes and looked it over. "We can just jump the gate. No problem."

"*No problem?*" Evie balked. "Raquel, are you crazy? We can't go busting in on a graveyard! This isn't like crashing some kegger." She peered through the wrought iron. "They gotta have extra security tonight, for Halloween. You know, for pranks and stuff."

"But it ain't Halloween," Raquel reminded Evie.

"Right." Dee Dee looked at Evie. "It's *Día de los Muertos.*"

Raquel put the flashlight on the ground, bent her legs, and clasped her hands together. "Come on, Dee Dee, I'll give you a lift."

"Are you sure?" Dee Dee looked at the wrought-iron gate.

"Yeah, yeah," Raquel said. "I totally got you."

Dee Dee started to lift her ruffled sequined skirt and put one foot into the cup of Raquel's folded hands.

"Dela, what are you doing?" Evie asked as she looked around. "Besides, you're gonna tear your costume and didn't you say Graciela would freak? Isn't it from *Amigos y Amantes*?"

Dee Dee ignored her and, with Raquel's help, hoisted herself onto the gate.

"Ay." Dee Dee wobbled on the wrought iron. "It's a little higher than I thought."

"Don't look down," Raquel said. "Just take your time and place your feet in all the little curlicues."

Dee Dee carefully made her way down the other side and took her last step, a quick leap to the ground.

"Here," Raquel said and passed the beach towel to Dee Dee and then looked at Evie. "Come on, Frida *Bandida*. You're next."

"I can get over myself, thank you," Evie said proudly. She took off her wig and placed it on the hood of the car, then she lifted her skirt and hoisted herself up. It was a bit of a struggle to place each foot in the crook of each curlicue of the wrought iron's intricate design, but she made it over and so did Raquel. They met Dee Dee on the other side.

Evie rubbed the sides of her arms and looked around the cemetery grounds. She was *so* not cool with any of this. Couldn't they just honor Dee Dee's mother with family photos over a nice, well-lit kitchen table? Maybe with some nice *Abuelita* hot chocolate?

"God." Dee Dee looked around. "In Mexico the cemeteries are filled with people, I mean just *flooded* with families on *Día de los Muertos*, everyone picnicking and talking and laughing."

"That's what I've heard," Evie said. "They really embrace the memory, rather than just try to forget it . . . like people do sometimes. I guess to not feel the pain."

She glanced over at the children's section and saw that just about every site was decorated with mini plastic jack-o'-lanterns and paper-wrapped candies. Whenever a slight breeze passed through, all the decorative pinwheels spun and battery-operated musical greeting cards went off, creating a melody of chimed tunes. Evie felt her chest get heavy when she read one of the headstones: *Nuestro niño por vida—Our Baby Forever.*

"So, where is your mom?" Raquel asked hesitantly.

"I think over there, by the start of that row of trees," Dee Dee pointed with her chin. "Right across from the mausoleum."

Evie and Raquel followed Dee Dee on the paved road that circled the inner part of the grounds. Evie remembered being in the cemetery the day of Margaret de LaFuente's funeral.

The same narrow road was then lined with cars, dozens upon dozens of cars, and there were a few black limos, and of course, a hearse. It had been springtime when she died and the funeral was held in the late morning, but it was already hot—that dry California hot. Everyone had their Kleenex out to wipe away either tears or perspiration, or both.

Dee Dee stopped and looked around on the gravestones. "Yeah, I remember the trees, around here."

"Here?" Raquel asked. "But I totally remember everyone being more over there." She pointed a few yards ahead of them. "Near that faucet. 'Cause I remember my father getting water for the flowers."

"But I really remember trees," Dee Dee said.

"Yeah," Evie said. "Me too.

"What color is it?" Raquel asked.

"What?" Dee Dee frowned. "The tree?"

"*No.*" Raquel smirked. "The headstone."

"Uh, rock color?" Dee Dee guessed.

"Well, *that* says a lot," Raquel said sarcastically.

"*Raquel.*" Evie threw her a look.

"Maybe we should just split up," Raquel suggested.

"Split up?" Evie's eyes widened.

"We'll find it quicker," Raquel reasoned.

"Yeah," Dee Dee agreed. "Let's split up."

"You know what?" Evie started. "This is all just getting a little too goth for me. Why don't we just come back in the morning? Like first thing? I'm sure we can find someone who works here to help us. Don't they keep a record of stuff like this?"

Neither Dee Dee nor Raquel answered her.

"I'm gonna go look closer to the mausoleum," Raquel told Dee Dee as she started to walk in that direction. "Why don't you stay here, around the faucet?" She handed the light to Dee Dee. "Here, you can use the flashlight."

"What about me?" Evie asked. "Maybe I should stay with Dee Dee?"

"No, why don't you look by the trees?" Dee Dee suggested. "Because I really remember being closer to at least one tree."

Great, the trees, Evie thought. Where anyone or anything could be hiding, perhaps with claws extended, ready to pounce on her.

After Dee Dee and Raquel went their own way, Evie immediately felt frightened. There was no moonlight to speak of and Rio Estates was devoid of bright city lights. It was difficult to actually read any of the headstones, but Evie kept her head down, squinting and searching for Margaret de LaFuente's grave site.

Suddenly Dee Dee cried out.

"Oh, my God!"

Oh, my God was right. Evie's heart started pounding hard in her chest. Someone or something had attacked Dee Dee. Evie knew this was coming. She jerked up and saw Raquel running toward Dee Dee. Without even thinking, she ran to her as well.

"I found it!" Dee Dee exclaimed. "Right here. Look." She

knelt down in front of a crimson quartz headstone. The inscription, dark with a white outline, was hard to make out and the whole face of the marker was weatherworn, caked with dirt and oxidation.

"You can't even read what we had inscribed." Dee Dee's voice started to crack. She yanked at the crabgrass that had grown over the edges of the stone. "I can't believe how bad it looks. I *can't* believe it."

Dee Dee pulled weeds out from around the edges and Evie and Raquel helped her. When all the crabgrass was gone, they sat back and looked at the marker.

"Why does it say Margarita?" Evie asked. "Is that your mom's real name?"

"Uh-huh," Dee Dee sighed.

Evie read it over and smiled. "Wow, that's really nice. I had never read the inscription. This is the first time."

"Yeah," Dee Dee said. "It takes a while for it to get done, I mean, after you order it and everything, and we had already left for Mexico. This is the first time I'm seeing it, too."

"What? Are you serious?" Raquel read the engraving. "The first time?"

Evie asked, "How did you come up with this inscription?"

"Remember how my mom and I used to watch old movies every Sunday?" Dee Dee reminded them.

"Oh, yeah," Evie said. "You always watched those old black-and-white ones from the 40s."

"Yeah," Dee Dee said. She picked at the impacted dirt on

the stone marker. "My mom just loved the Rita Hayworth movies. Mostly because they shared the same name, proper name, and both she and Rita Hayworth had Mexican mothers and they both had that reddish hair. So, when we had to pick out the inscription, I wondered what was on Rita Hayworth's headstone."

"And this is what's on hers, on Rita Hayworth's headstone?"

"Yeah, nice, right? It was easy enough to find out. It just seemed perfect."

"It *is* perfect." Evie felt the back of her throat dry up. "It is *so* nice, Dela."

"Yeah," Dee Dee said wistfully. "I think it is. I wish we could read it better."

"We can fix that," Raquel said. "There's all sorts of stuff in my mom's car. I'm sure I can find some rags and some clippers and stuff. I can get them and we can clean it all up."

"Really?" Dee Dee smiled hopefully. "Are you serious?"

"Totally, no problem." Raquel got up. "I'll go get them." She laid out the beach towel. "Here, just kick back. The grass is sorta wet."

As Raquel was about to leave, she looked at Margaret de LaFuente's headstone one more time. "You know," she said, "this inscription, it could almost be for us."

Evie and Dee Dee looked it over.

"Think about it." Raquel read the inscription out loud, "'To Yesterday's Companionship and Tomorrow's Reunion.'"

"Yeah . . . " Evie felt a tingling across her body. "That *is* just like us!"

"Yeah." Dee Dee wiped her eyes and started to smile wider. "I didn't think about that."

"Well, I'm gonna go look for some stuff to clean it," Raquel said.

While Raquel walked back to her mother's car, Dee Dee started to pull out the plot's canister. After a bit of a struggle, it finally came out of the earth and she got up to fill it with water at the faucet. The wind picked up and all the helium balloons and decorative pinwheels stirred about. Evie looked at Dee Dee and Raquel. It may be *Día de los Muertos*, she thought, but it was definitely a night of new life for the three friends.

15

RioChica (9:38 PM): I'm doing Dawn Patrol tomorrow!
ShaggyMA (9:39 PM): I just looked at Surfline. Should be a nice south swell in your neck of the state. Have fun!
RioChica (9:39 PM): Thank you. I will. TTYL!

It seemed like ages since Evie had been to the beach at Sea Street. Actually, it had only been a few months, but in California, a few months away from the beach? That's a lifetime.

Evie had taken Alex's advice and brought a full winter wetsuit, her brand-new Heat 3Q Zip by O'Neill. Her father had balked at the price tag, but gave in when he saw how eager Evie was to try something new. Well, not something new, just *something*.

And now there she was, bright and early on a Sunday morning, standing on the beach and waiting for her first surf lesson. She'd managed to convince Raquel and Dee Dee to drive her over, and now her stomach was knotted in anticipation. The ocean was choppy and full of whitecaps. The waves were supposedly beginner waves, baby three footers as Alex had called them earlier that morning on the phone after listening to the surf report, but to her they looked threatening, intimidating, fierce. But it wasn't just the ocean that tested Evie's nerves. She was nervous about something, or rather someone, else.

Alex.

After that night at the cemetery Dee Dee had claimed that Alex was totally into Evie.

"It's so obvious," Dee Dee had said. "That night after the welcome-back party, we went to The Coffee Bean & Tea Leaf and he kept going on and on about how you were so angry with him and he didn't know what to do. He was so upset. To be honest," she admitted, "it got sorta annoying after a while."

And Raquel had agreed. "I have better proof than that," she'd said with a slow smile. "Jose told me that Alex has *always* had a crush on you."

"What?" Evie couldn't believe it. "*Always?* And you never told me?"

"Why would I? You never seemed interested. Besides, I swore to Jose that I would never tell you. But, please." Raquel looked at her fingernails. "I have no loyalty to him now, that's for sure."

Evie stood on the beach at Sea Street, holding all this valuable information and jumpiness inside.

"Hey, Raquel, can you help me with this?" Evie called over as she struggled to get the rest of the suit pulled up past her waist. It fit like a girdle, making her feel like an awkward walrus, but Alex had assured her that she'd appreciate the blubber warmth once she was out in the ocean. Yeah, it was south Cali, but it was still November.

Raquel got up from her striped canvas beach chair, where she was sitting next to Dee Dee. Both girls were bundled up, head to toe, in layers of wool, cashmere, and thermal clothing. "You need to take this raggedy Mexican blanket off first," Raquel said yanking at Evie's thick pullover.

"It ain't no blanket." Evie smirked knowingly. "It's a Señor Lopez, *vintage*."

"What?" Dee Dee looked over. "J.Lo's father has a clothing line too?"

"Well, whatever you wanna call it, " Raquel stated matter-of-factly, "you gotta take it off to put on the rest of your suit."

"But I'm freezing!" Evie chattered her teeth to emphasize her discomfort. She reluctantly pulled off her Señor López and when she did she revealed a metallic-gold bikini top.

"What is *this*?" Dee Dee pulled up her sunglasses and eyed Evie.

Okay, so maybe she picked up a little something from the Sangros. Is that *so* wrong?

"Oh." Evie got sheepish. "I sorta borrowed it from Xiomara and I sorta haven't returned it."

Raquel pulled at the side of her top. "And it's just sorta a little baggy."

"Is it *that* bad?" Evie puffed out her chest and looked down.

"Nah," Raquel said. "Don't worry about it. Besides, doesn't cold water cause shrinkage?"

"I hope only with fabric," Evie said. "I can't afford any more shrinkage."

"So," Raquel inquired looking at Evie's bikini top, "is it healing okay? Are you sure it's okay to go into the ocean?"

Evie pulled the left side of her bikini top over and looked down. Two very small, cursive letters, RE, were linked on the upper left side of her breast.

"*¡Qué chido!*" Dee Dee smiled. "That girl did a good job, on all of us." She patted the left side of her own chest lightly.

"On me, too," Raquel said. "But my RE is more stretched out, 'cause I got a larger canvas!" she bragged.

Evie threw Raquel a look, then, as quickly as possible, she pulled up the rest of her wetsuit and Raquel zipped it up.

"I don't know *why* you have to do this." Raquel jiggled up and down, trying to keep warm. She rubbed the sides of her arms. "It's so friggin' early in the morning and the sun is barely out."

"Yeah." Evie looked out toward the Pacific. "I don't *have* to do this."

"*Good!*" Raquel zipped her black hoodie all the way up to her chin. "Let's go home. I got a nice, warm goose down comforter with my name on it."

"No," Evie insisted. "I mean, I *want* to do this. All the times we went to the beach as kids and I rarely went in past my waist. I would always watch the surfers and think they were just the coolest. They were so brave and it's just—"

"Hey," Dee Dee interrupted and looked over toward the parking lot above them. "Alejandro is here. Speaking of courage, now's your time, *chica*."

Evie looked up and saw Alex coming down the rocks with his board. Her stomach was doing flip-flops.

* * *

"So you *did* come." He smiled as he met the three of them on the cold sand, but his eyes were really only on Evie. "I'm impressed. You've walked your walk."

"Uh, yeah." Evie smirked. "We've been here for, like, an hour. I called you when we were leaving, but your phone is still jacked up."

"Yeah," Alex said. "*Got* to get it fixed. Sorry 'bout all the miscommunication. Hey, your hair . . . "

"Oh, yeah." Evie tried to be nonchalant. Who knew how he would react this time?

"It looks good." He tilted his head and smiled slowly. "It reminds me of . . . "

"*What?*" Evie asked quickly.

"Nothing."

"No," she insisted. "*Don't* do that!"

"I was gonna say," Alex started, "it reminds me of when I first met you. Like, last year."

"Is that a good thing?" Evie asked.

"Yeah." Alex smiled, his eyes directly looking into hers. "A *very* good thing."

Okay, Evie thought, *time for best friends to bail.*

And just as best friends do, they read her mind and went back to their chairs.

* * *

"Come on." Alex led Evie closer to the water. "Did you already do your stretches?"

"Uh, yeah," Evie lied.

"And you worked on your pop-ups?"

"*¡Sí, maestro!*" Another lie. It was just *too* cold to be warming up on the ice-cold sand.

"Hey." Alex opened his wetsuit's key pocket on the sleeve. "I got a little something for you. For your first Dawn Patrol."

"Huh?"

He pulled out a rubber cord. Bits of abalone shell dangled from it.

Evie couldn't believe it. "Is this the shell, from that night at Bard?" she asked.

"Yeah," Alex held up the necklace. "Cool, right?"

Her heart was beating fast and the back of her throat felt tight.

"I was such an idiot and dropped it." Alex seemed embarrassed. "That's why it's in all these little pieces. I didn't know what to do with it and I had promised to give it to you."

He kept his promise.

"So you like?"

"Yeah," Evie said looking at it. *Please offer to put it on me.*

"Lemme put it on for you . . ."

Evie lifted up her hair and Alex went behind her. He put his arms around her shoulders. Could she feel any more lightheaded? Could he notice the nervous goosebumps sprouting on her arms and back? He tied the cord around Evie's neck and the pieces of broken shell immediately dug into her skin. *Ow. Not* the most comfortable piece of jewelry she'd ever owned. But still . . .

She turned around. "How does it look?"

"Nice." He smiled and his neck turned bright pink. "Is it comfortable?"

"Oh, yeah, totally. I love it."

He looked over at Dee Dee and Raquel from the distance. "So, uh, how's Rocky doing?"

"She was sad, then mad, and now . . . " Evie trailed off. "At least she knows the truth."

"Yeah, that goes for both of us," Alex said. "Jose never said anything to me. I had no idea. I'm sure Mondo probably knew. So *not* cool. But you gotta know, all guys aren't like that, especially me."

"Okay."

"Now I know why you were all upset that night I picked you up at *La Pantera*. Mondo told me that Jose was trying to get all up on you."

"Yeah," Evie replied. "That was pretty bad." She winced at the memory and took a deep breath. It seemed like a good time to be honest about the whole evening, so she decided to just go for it. "But that wasn't all of it. I mean, that was a big part, but I was also really upset and you're gonna think this is stupid, but I thought you had given the shell necklace to Dela."

"Dela?" Alex looked perplexed. "Why would I give it to Dela?"

"I dunno." Evie felt foolish. "I mean, for a while there it seemed as though you were into her."

"*Into* Dela?" Alex frowned. "Uh, no. I mean, I wanted to be extra nice to her, because I knew what a good friend she was to you. I mean, I like her and all, but I don't know, she's just not my type. "To be honest," Alex continued, "I wasn't into your blue hair or that blonde look, either. I mean, I think you look good just as yourself. You don't need anything extra."

Evie didn't know what to say. She felt like her face was going to crack from excitement.

"So, you ready?" Alex asked her.

Evie looked out at the ocean. There was already a line-up of short boarders and she immediately felt intimidated.

She tried to sound confident. "Yeah, I'm ready."

She followed Alex to the water and when the white foam hit her feet it felt like ice. Damn, she should have bought the matching booties! Her board had started to slip from under her left arm and she struggled to keep a strong hold on it. It was heavier than she remembered. Maybe that's because when she had picked it up from Max, Alex held on to one end while they carried it out to his truck? Evie flopped her board on the water and tied her leash to her ankle. She thought of all the things Alex had told her once she got her board out into the ocean: Paddle hard, cup your hands, long strong strokes, and keep your legs together.

Alex got onto his board and started to paddle out. Evie followed his cue. She was only a few feet behind him, but suddenly she fell far behind him. Then, *very* far. She paddled to keep up but her back and upper arms were already beginning to ache. Alex was right. Surfing *was* hard work and she hadn't even gotten past the first break. Her board kept teetering from side to side and she tried to keep her balance, but it seemed virtually impossible. Alex had said to expect that, being a novice on a new board, but this was ridiculous. She could not keep her board or herself balanced. She looked ahead and wondered how much farther she had to paddle. More white water rushed right toward her.

Alex looked over his shoulder and saw Evie struggling. He slowed down and, after what seemed like forever, Evie finally caught up to him.

"How are you doing?" he called out.

"Great!" She tried to smile. "Good!" Her pride wouldn't let her admit the pain she felt across her back and the fact that she felt like her lungs were bursting.

"Hey, let me help you." Alex stretched out his right foot and firmly placed the top of it on the nose of her board. He then paddled harder, pulling her and her board behind him. Evie was about to protest, but the plain truth was, she was so tired.

"Alex," she finally called out. "I don't think I can do it! I'm not that strong!"

"Yes, you can!" he yelled over his shoulder.

Evie looked ahead. "The waves, they look too big."

"They really aren't," he called back to her. "If you're worried, we can go back in. But I promise, I won't let anything happen to you. Remember, I used to be a lifeguard!"

Evie couldn't help but laugh to herself.

Alex looked over his shoulder and watched her. He opened his mouth with an excited smile. "See! You're getting it!"

She felt like an idiot. She paddled harder. Left, right, left. Gushes of white water slammed into her, the salt from the ocean stung her eyes. She kept paddling and soon it did feel like she was falling into a rhythm. The strokes were getting a little bit easier, but the pain across her back was still there.

"How are you doing, Blue Crush?" Alex called out.

"*Hello?*" Evie yelled back. "I am *not* blue!"

"Oh, yeah." Alex smiled over his shoulder. "That's right!"

And she was right. Evie wasn't blue. She was happy, very happy. And she wasn't blonde, she was brown. Born Brown, is what it said on the package when she recolored her hair with Dee Dee and Raquel. And crush? Okay, yes. She *was* crushing on Alex and it was *so* nice because it was obvious he was crushing on her in return.

Evie pressed her chest onto her board and cautiously

turned her head to look back toward the beach. Her board rocked a bit. *No, no, no . . . steady.*

She saw Dee Dee and Raquel. They were jumping up and down. At first she thought they were doing some kind of jumping jacks to keep warm. But then she noticed they were only waving their arms, frantically.

"Go, Evie!" they yelled at the top of their lungs. "Go, Gomez!"

Go, Gomez? Had Evie heard right?

"Go, Gomez!" she heard Dee Dee and Raquel yell again.

Yes, she did hear right! *She* was putting the "Go" into Gomez! She was carrying on the family name! Dee Dee and Raquel cheered her on and she couldn't help but paddle harder. She didn't want to let down her best friends and, more important, she couldn't let herself down. She paddled long, even strokes on the side of her board, cupping her hands with the Pacific Ocean. She was going to do it. She was going to make it. And that Sunday morning at approximately 6:30 A.M., Evie Gomez suddenly felt alive, focused, and had only one thing on her mind and that was the absolute, all-consuming, unending desire to leave the lagging, lazy *z* of her last name behind her . . . for good.

a ten-year-old sedan with no Sirius, DVD player, or heated seats. Okay, so it was far from a g-ride, but beggars can't be choosers, right?

"I don't think so. . . ." Lindsay shook her head slowly. The latest installment of *La Cueva Sucia,* her favorite soap opera, was just starting and she was *not* going to miss it.

"Lindsay," Evie said, following her down the two steps that led into the den. As anyone knows, a firm "I don't think so" is as good as a semisoft "maybe," which is basically a yes. "We live on a cul de sac. It's not like cars go speeding by all the time. It'll be totally safe. And the more I practice," she continued, "the better I'll be for my test. Then you won't be having to cart me around anymore. Don't you want a break from being a chauffeur?"

She cocked her head forward and to the right, a gesture copied from her best friend, Dee Dee de LaFuente. Whenever Dee Dee let the right side of her head tip to the side, she got her way. Sure, Dee Dee had angelic, long blond hair, delicate features, and those hypnotizing blue contact lenses, but couldn't a brunette with medium-length hair and brown eyes get the same effect?

"Well," Lindsay looked at Evie. "I guess . . . maybe . . . it would be okay."

Yes!

"Get the extra keys," she told Evie as she pushed Meho,

READY FOR MORE? Here's a peek at the next Honey Blonde Chica novel, *¡SCANDALOSA!*

"I don't know, Evelina. . . ." Lindsay, the Gomez's housekeeper, shook her head as she stepped down into the den. "Your mother said you have to be with a driver. A *licensed* driver."

Evie was just five weeks away from taking her California state driving test but she had yet to master the challenge of three-point turns, confront the perils of parallel parking, and how the hell, she wondered, could she check her blind spot if it was *blind*? In short, Evie was desperate. And far from ready.

But whenever she practiced driving with her parents they spent the entire time just telling her what she was doing wrong. They could be *so* controlling and wasn't the whole idea of being behind the wheel to savor the taste of freedom?

"I *know,*" Evie exhaled impatiently. "But that's only if I'm gonna be driving on the street and everything, and I'm not. I'm gonna stay on the driveway, just in front of the house."

But this afternoon, her parents were out shopping. It was the perfect time for her to rule the wheel.

But in order to do so, she needed a wheel to rule, which meant she had to ask—okay, *beg*—Lindsay to borrow her car,

Evie's gray tabby, aside and made room for herself on the den's smooth leather sofa. "And stay in front of the house. Do *not* leave Camino del Rio."

"I promise!" Evie sprinted as fast as her metallic gold Havaiana flojos could carry her toward the kitchen. When she saw the keys hanging from the key rack, she didn't know which ones were the spare keys Lindsay had been talking about, but no worries. She snatched both rings off the kitchen's metal key holder, grabbed her iPod (over 1,100 downloads) and her wallet (containing a freshly issued driver's permit), and skipped out of the house.

But once Evie got out to the driveway, her honest-to-goodness plan of taking Lindsay's sedan immediately fell to the wayside. There, parked to the left of Lindsay's car, was Evie's mother's brand-new Mercedes. Actually, not *brand*-new, but definitely new to her mother, Vicki Gomez. The Mercedes was a good thirty years old, a classic by anyone's standards. Detailing by West Coast Customs kept its original leather interior soft and its chrome glistening. The Benz had also been redone with a high-gloss burgundy paint job. But the *cali de la cali*? A fuel conversion by LoveCraft's BioFuel in Los Angeles. Yes, the Mercedes had been converted to run on vegetable oil. Petroleum gas was was *so* passé, and fuel conversions were *the* thing done to cars in SoCal. The Benz, of course, was the talk of Rio Estates, and Vicki Gomez just loved, *loved*, the attention.

Evie looked at the gleaming Mercedes and then at

Lindsay's nondescript four-door sedan, which suddenly seemed dull and lifeless. Was there really a question of which ride she should choose for her practice spin?

Evie opened the driver's-side door of her mother's Mercedes and got in. She inhaled the aroma of the vintage white leather. She took out her cell from the front pocket of her gray and red Señor Lopez pullover and immediately called her boyfriend, Alex. How cool would it be to swing by his house and, for once, offer to drive *him* somewhere? Evie speed-dialed his number but, alas, she got the dreaded voice mail.

Duuude . . . Make it brief. Not a bio.

Evie remembered that Alex had gone to Sea Street with Mondo that morning and felt slightly disappointed. It was almost 1 p.m., and he *still* wasn't back from the beach? At the end of last semester the Flojos, which had consisted of herself, Alex, Mondo, Raquel, and Raquel's former boy, Jose, had pretty much disbanded. But Alex still surfed at Sea Street, and Mondo still tagged along with him. While they all still wore flojos (flip-flops), Evie didn't so much have the same Flojo (lazy) mind-set as she had the semester before. Now she went surfing and was learning how to drive. This semester, she was less Gome*zzzzz* and more Go-*más*.

When Alex's outgoing message finished, Evie decided to leave neither a brief message nor her autobiography, thank you. She hung up and speed-dialed her ADA, Raquel Diaz. The literal Spanish translation for ADA was *Amiga del Alma*, a "friend of the soul," a soul sister, really. ADAs were tighter than mere BFFs and as everyone who was anyone knew, a *sister* was much more *íntimo* than a simple *friend*.

After a few rings, Evie was met with Raquel's infamous Bullwinkle yawn on the other end. "What up?" Raquel answered sleepily.

"Not you, obviously." Evie switched from her mother's favorite old-school station, Hot 92 Jamz, to Díos (Malos). Nothing like brown-boy emo bumping the speakers to calm one's novice nerves. The melodic undertones quickly relaxed Evie. "Hey, I'm coming to pick you up," she announced to Raquel. "Let's cruise the shores."

Raquel lived next door to Evie, a mere eight hundred yards away, and she really didn't need to be picked up to go anywhere. But still, just saying "I'm coming to pick you up" made Evie feel mature, adultlike. Unlike Raquel and their other ADA, Dee Dee de LaFuente, Evie didn't have her own car and had to shotgun it everywhere. From parties in Spanish Hills to surfing at Sea Street, the high school production of "Driving Miss Evie" was outgrowing its rehearsal space. She needed to showcase her driving talent to a wider audience.

"You ain't picking me up to go anywhere," Raquel's voice was throaty and harsh. "I ain't even awake."

"Well, get up," Evie ordered. "I got my mother's car."

"What do you mean, you got your mother's car?" Raquel asked. "Ol' Vicki Gomez must be out of the country, 'cause there's no way you'd risk taking her precious veggie-grease mobile out if she was even near the 805."

"Not quite out of the country," Evie mused. "But the next-best thing: She's at the factory outlets with my dad. They'll be gone all day."

"And la Lindsay?" Raquel inquired.

"Oh, she's far away in *novela-vela land.*" Evie adjusted the seat so it was closer to the gas pedal and positioned the rearview mirror so she could see all things slow and less important behind her. She turned the key in the ignition. "Come on, the day's almost over."

The day was actually far from being over. It was barely one o'clock in the afternoon, but to a party *puta* like Raquel, the day was just starting.

"And," Evie explained. "You know I need a licensed driver to really go anywhere."

"Nuh-uh," Raquel said quickly. "*No* way. Do you know the leading cause of teen death? Teaching a newbie to drive. You best find yourself another tutor, Eves. I'm outs."

"Raq, come on," Evie pleaded. "It'll be fun."

"And who says I ain't already having fun?" Raquel let out a low, muffled laugh. Evie heard another voice in the background—a male voice. She suddenly felt the effects of third-party damage.

"Who's that?" she asked.

"I can tell you who it ain't." Raquel laughed softly again. "It's ain't Jose, that's for sure."

Ever since Raquel had caught Jose sneaking around with Alejandra de los Santos last semester, her buddy list of bad boys was being utilized to the max. It didn't help Raquel's ego that Alejandra de los Santos headed up the Sangros, a foursome of *fresas ricas* from Mexico City whose big designer boots and even bigger attitudes clashed with the Flojos' designer flip-flops and laid-back outlook. Of course, Raquel felt completely humiliated and betrayed when she discovered that her boy had cross-pollinated with one of *them*. Evie and Dee Dee had actually been foolish enough to have become sorta friends with Alejandra last semester. But that was when they were just fresh-off-the-boat freshmen and didn't know better. Not only was Alejandra a *puta*, plain and simple, but she also wore the scarlet letter *P* proudly on her chest.

"Where are you?" Evie asked Raquel. She had no idea who the owner of the background voice was, and she didn't bother asking. If she knew Raquel, the voice and the male attached to it wouldn't last more than a couple of weeks.

"I can tell you where I'm not," Raquel continued to play coy. "I ain't home, that's for sure."

"O-*kay*, Raquel." Evie struggled to shift from reverse to first gear. "I'll let you go do whatever, with whomever. Just call me later."

"Yeah, yeah," Raquel said before hanging up.

Evie looked at the clock on the dashboard of her mother's Mercedes. *La Cueva Sucia* was a one-hour program, which meant she had only forty-eight minutes to roll. She quickly punched Dee Dee's number.

"Hi, Evie!" Dee Dee practically chirped on the other end.

Evie smiled to herself. Dee Dee was the ying to Raquel's yang. Little Miss Sunny Delight to Raquel's Little Miss Understood, Dark, and . . . Delightless. Dee Dee would definitely be up for a drive.

"You're in a good mood," Evie said.

"Oh, I just got off the phone with Rocio," Dee Dee's voice got dreamy. "Oh, Evie, I love him *so* much."

Rocio was Dee Dee's long-lost boyfriend she had to leave behind in Mexico City when she and her family returned to California. Dee Dee had moved to Mexico with her father four years earlier, soon after her mother died. Their new home was on Camino Cortez, just a few blocks away from Evie's and Raquel's houses.

"Hey, so I've got the Mercedes," Evie bragged as she slowly entered Camino del Rio and cautiously looked down the street in both directions. "I thought I could come over and pick you up."

"Right *now*?" Dee Dee asked. "I can't. I have a meeting with Eileen Cervantes."

"Eileen? Who's that?"

"She's connected with Las Hermanas," Dee Dee explained. "And I'm meeting with her at four p.m."

"At four?" Evie rechecked the time on the dashboard. "Dee Dee, it's barely one o'clock."

"I know. I'm totally running late. I'm so nervous. I've already smoked three Caribbean Chills this morning."

"No," Evie started. "I mean, why are you getting ready now?"

"Evie, *it's for Las Hermanas,*" Dee Dee said as if Evie was crazy for asking. "I have to make the right impression. Eileen is the first cousin of the former director's wife and she's going to give me some hints. This is the final year before I can be nominated so I can be a Hermana by junior year."

"Oh," Evie said sarcastically. "I didn't realize what a *great* contact you had."

"Evie, don't make fun. This is important. Las Hermanas has been my dream since forever."

It was true. Ever since Dee Dee was a little girl, she had always talked about being a La Hermana debutante. Her mother was one, her grandmother was one, so, of course, Dee Dee not only wanted to be one, she *had* to be one. Las Hermanas was the oldest and most respected debutante society in the county. It was started by the wives of the early Southern Californian landowners, many of them Hispanic and all of them wealthy. Dee Dee's father didn't have such regal connections with early Ventura County, but Dee Dee's mother, the late Margaret de LaFuente, sure did. Her family had owned multiple ranches in the area long ago, when the area was still a part of Mexico. You couldn't get more regally connected than that.

Between Dee Dee's calculated attempts to obtain the key to the city, Raquel jonesing for a key to the nearest minibar, and she, herself, most desirous of the keys to any available automobile, Evie sometimes wondered how all three girls could each be so unique and remain ADAs. But then again, no matter what kind of keys they each longed for, the three of them had a history. Evie, Dee Dee, and Raquel had been little girls together, in flip-flops, their hair in braids with *respado* juice dripping down their chins. Now, Dee Dee would never be caught dead in flip-flops ("sloppy, give no shape to the calf," she'd claimed) and none of the three girls would be caught dead in braids. But they did like a good raspberry and banana snow cone now and then.

"You really don't need anyone to help you drive," Dee Dee told Evie. "You're really good already. Really."

"If I'm such a good driver . . ." Evie was not buying Dee Dee's flattery. She struggled with the gears. "Then why don't you ever let me drive Jumile?"

Jumile was Dee Dee's VW Beetle and she was very protective of him. She never let Evie drive him, not even once.

Sailors christened boats, socialites attached pretentious tags on pet Chihuahuas, but in SoCal, it was in proper order to conjure up a cutesy name for one's car. To own a nameless vehicle? *Unthinkable.*

Dee Dee had gotten the name "Jumile" from the particular tree beetles found in the hills of Taxco, Mexico. Every year, the first Monday after *El Día de los Muertos,* the locals would hike into the hills of Taxco and gather up the little green beetles, otherwise known as *jumiles.* Later the locals would roast and grind up the beetles, celebrating the new seasonal harvest with bug salsa. *"'Sta loco, no?"* Dee Dee had said, after she'd bragged about the fact that she had been adventurous enough to partake in the beetle eats as if to prove that under her Michael Kelley–styled hair and MAC made-up face, she could be *loca,* too.

Raquel's parents had just bought her a Beetle a month ago for Christmas, and it was Dee Dee's plan that Evie get a VW Beetle just like theirs. The three girls were a team, a dynamic trio, and not having similar modes of transportation would be like the Three Musketeers not having, well, identical mustaches—just plain wrong.

The bud vase in Jumile held incense sticks, and on the back window was a large decal of Dee Dee's favorite band/soap opera's crest, RBD. Raquel's Beetle was black and named B. J., as in "Beetle Juice," not the *other thing.* B. J.'s bud vase held cigarette butts and gum wrappers. Stuck across the top of B. J.'s front window was "So-Cal" in white, Old English script. Both Dee Dee and Raquel, of course, had vanity license plates: JUMILE for Dee Dee and BTLE JCE for Raquel.

Evie wanted her Beetle to be cherry-bomb red with a sunroof, Bose speakers, fresh-cut hibiscus flowers in the bud vase, and the quintessential decal that identified Evie to the hilt—a pair of white, outlined flip-flops stuck smack in the center of her back window. She had already purchased the decal months ago at the Anacapa Surf Shop, and now all she needed was a brand-new car to attach it to. Simple enough, no?

She was going to name her new car Cherry Bomb, and it was her fantasy to drive away from her sixteenth birthday party in CHRY BMB.

In about a month and a half, on February 29 to be exact, Evie was going to turn sixteen, and this particular birthday was uniquely special for two reasons. One was that there was actually going to *be* a February 29 on the year's calendar. Being a leap-year baby, Evie had no choice but to celebrate her birthday either on the twenty-eighth of February or the first of March. Not to be all *sentida* about it, but it sorta sucked to not have your birthday party on your actual birthdate. The second reason that this birthday was going to be extra cool was because Evie's mother was going to throw her a sixteeñera, more Sweet Sixteen, way less *quinceañera*, which meant only one thing—a Mexican-style luau. Evie was planning to have her sixteeñera thrown at Duke's in Malibu. Duke's was a supercool restaurant that overlooked the Pacific Ocean and was named after the OG Hawaiian surfer himself, Duke Kahanamoku. All of Evie's favorite *Laguna Beach* and *O.C.*

stars lunched and "canoodled" at Duke's, so it only made sense that Evie would celebrate her sixteeñera in all of Duke's Polynesian glory. Her reputation as a surfer-flojo-wearing chica depended on it.

As Dee Dee claimed, Evie's sixteeñera party was the talk of Villanueva Prep, and how could it not be? After all, Evie's father had already secured DJ Chancla to spin nothing but classic surf and power pop. There would be Polynesian dancers and a full buffet featuring *lechón*, but Hawaiian style with the pig's head intact and everything. Evie's mother had planned to make gift bags filled with Mr. Zog's Sex Wax, original Flojo brand flip-flops, and a fifty-dollar gift certificate for the Ventura Surf Shop, as well as customized sun visors with the words "Evening with Evie" stitched in hot pink on the front. But the main attraction at Evie's Sweet Sixteeñera? Raquel's connection. Raquel knew this guy, Dario Regalado, who had a cousin, Petey. When Petey wasn't getting all goo-goo eyed whenever he was in the presence of Raquel, he was bartending at Duke's. When he heard about Raquel's ADA having her Sweet Sixteeñera at his workplace, he instantly raised his hand and offered to fire up the Lava Flows and daquiris for all of Evie's guests. He told Raquel that all she had to do was supply the booze, which was no problem because, of course, Raquel had *another* hookup at the Liquor Warehouse. Friggin' Raquel . . . was she the bestest friend or *what*? There were to be no frat-boy plastic red cups full of watered-down keg beer at *her* party. Evie's ad-bevs were going to be classy, lethal, and free. Could a party be *más* cool?

"Well," Evie started. "I guess I'll just take a drive by myself."

"Why don't you take Alejandro or Raquel?" Dee Dee asked.

"Alex is out at Sea Street," Evie said.

"Surfing again?"

"Uh, huh," Evie turned up Díos (Malos). "I'm gonna hook up with him tomorrow. We might take the boards to Santa Barbara."

"Mmm-hmm. No offense," Dee Dee started slowly as though she was applying mascara. "But don't . . . you . . . ever . . . get tired that . . . all . . . you do with Alex is . . . surf?"

"What do you mean?" Evie asked as she shifted down to bring her mother's Mercedes (GO MEZ) to a stop. It stalled. *Sheeyat.* Evie started the Mercedes up again.

"Don't get me . . . wrong. I think . . . it's cool that . . . you . . . two have something major in . . . common, but . . ." Dee Dee finally put her vocal chord on the right RPM. "It's just, I mean, in Mexico, boys take girls out—on dates. You get to dress up and have a nice dinner, go dancing."

"Dee Dee," Evie rolled her eyes to the side. "I'm fine with the stuff we do. Alex is my bud and Sea Street is *our* place."

True, Sea Street had pretty much been deemed Evie and Alex's place, at least by Evie. Last semester, Evie just kicked it on the promenade wall with Raquel, Jose, and Mondo while watching Alex surf. Now that she was Alex's official girlfriend

"Mande?" Dee Dee did not find Evie's jab funny. She was very protective of Mexico City, her beloved former home of four years.

"Nothing," Evie tried to backpedal. She knew better than to diss the almighty *Districto Federal.* Besides, she was now approaching Calle Aqua Caliente and had to focus. The transmission of her mother's Mercedes revved hard as she fumbled into second gear. *Damn.* Could it be that her father had accidentally filled the fuel tank with vinegar instead of vegetable oil? Evie's efforts made her sound like an amateur barista-in-training, grinding espresso beans to a pulp. She reached the intersection just as a silver sports car pulled up, but she could not remember who had the right to go first.

"Hey, *maestro,*" Evie started. "I'm at a four-way stop and I forgot, who has the right of way?"

"The car on the right," Dee Dee said matter-of-factly.

"Uh," Evie looked over at the sports car. "She's not moving."

"Then just go, I guess," Dee Dee said.

A horn behind Evie honked. She looked in her rearview mirror—she'd been completely unaware that there was even a car behind her. She shifted from neutral to first gear and stepped lightly on the gas, but for some reason, her mother's Mercedes screeched backward. *Sheeyat!* She felt a solid thud from the back. Evie had mistakenly put the Mercedes into reverse and smacked . . . right . . . into . . . the . . . car . . . behind her.

and she officially surfed (not very good, but *still*), it was safe to say that Sea Street *was* their place.

"Your *bud*?" Dee Dee asked. "Oh, I thought he was your *boyfriend*."

Evie just knew that Dee Dee's blond, tinted eyebrows (Michael Kelley salon, sixteen dollars a pair) had risen in surprise.

"He is," Evie felt she had to defend his title. "But he's also my buddy, my friend. And that's very important in a relationship."

"*Claro*, of course it's important," Dee Dee agreed. "I was just asking, that's all. So, what about Raquel? Did you call her to go driving?"

"I already did, but she's totally out of it."

"Out of it or hung over?" Dee Dee asked.

Evie was reluctant to get into the minuscule dish she had on Raquel. All three girls loved each other unconditionally, of course, and granted, all of them indulged in ad-bevs, but Dee Dee tended to judge Raquel's recreational behavior. Not that Evie could blame Dee Dee—ever since her breakup with Jose, Raquel's party patterns had been off the chart.

"She was just tired," Evie lied. "I woke her up."

"Woke her up?" Dee Dee exclaimed. "It's after one o'clock! *Ay. That* girl!"

"Yeah, well . . ." Evie wasn't in the mood to talk smack. "So listen, just stay on the line with me," she suggested. "You can be, like, my virtual licensed driver. I guess a Mexico City license is better than nothing."